Miami Justice

by

Patricia Harris

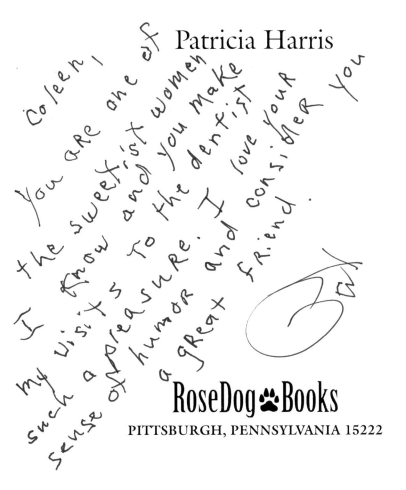

Coleen,
You are one of the sweetist women I know and you make my visits to the dentist such a pleasure. I love your humor and consider you a great friend.

RoseDog❧Books

PITTSBURGH, PENNSYLVANIA 15222

ISBN: 978-1-4349-9908-5
Printed in the United States of America

First Printing

For more information or to order additional books, please contact:
RoseDog Books
701 Smithfield Street
Pittsburgh, Pennsylvania 15222
U.S.A.
1-800-834-1803
www.rosedogbookstore.com

Table of Contents

Chapter 1

American flight 2132 tilted downward in its approach to Miami International Airport. Alexis Saunders glanced up from her papers as the stewardess directed the passengers to put seats in an upright position and trays back in place for a landing in fifteen minutes. Concentration broken, she let the drone of the voice in the next seat sink in. The dowdy stranger with thick-lens glasses, thin lips and huge ears rattled on at the beginning of the flight about principles and statistics of crash landings, his job and his lack of family. Alexis had purposely tuned the stranger out after the first twenty minutes which had been 2 1/2 hours earlier. While feeling sorry for the man's terror of flying, she had still been greatly irritated by his constant stammering chatter.

The stranger had stammered upon takeoff a nervous "I hate flying,.. I...I know that we have a less chance of some-thing...uh...happening on the takeoff than the...the...landing. Do you...um do this...of...often?"

Alexis glanced briefly at the man but muttered in a soothing voice, "It'll be alright, you'll see and yes, I have to fly fairly often in my job."

The man tensed as the plane took off, fingernails blanching as he clutched at the armrests. "I don't think...I...I can't breathe!"

Alexis leaned forward, taking a good look at the man's face and reached upward for the flight attendant button. Press. The deed was done, she thought to herself. It's out of my hands as soon as the flight attendant gets here. Please get here fast. Glancing again at the man, Alexis realized his face was ruddy but lips were white as could be!

"You're going to be okay...just breathe. Breathe! Oh God! Please breathe!" she encouraged urgently. Still failing to inhale, his eyes began to glaze. Alexis, turning toward the man, grabbed his shirt front and shook him with all her might. "Come on! Take a deep breath! Breathe!"

"What's going on here?" the attendant exclaimed, her approach unnoticed by Alexis.

"He's not breathing! For God's sake, do something!" retorted Alexis.

Finally noticing the condition of the man's red face and taunt look, she bent down and took the stranger's hands and began talking confidently to him in a murmur, "Okay sweetie, let's take some short breaths. Come on, take some breaths."

Over and over the stewardess chanted while rubbing up and down the stranger's arms, then his shoulders and on to his neck. All at once the stranger took a gasping breath, then several other small ones. The color in his face, Alexis noted, began to recede and his fingers began to relax.

The attendant rose from her position and offered, "How about some water or some other beverage now?"

"Some water, please," he responded with shaky breath.

"I'll be right back, and by the way, my name is Sue," she replied and scurried away, not bothering to ask Alexis if she needed a stiff drink for her ordeal, Alexis thought wryly.

As Alexis waited for the flight attendant's return, Alexis thought she'd better keep the man's mind occupied, "She'll be right back, you know. And your color is very good. My name is Alexis...what's yours?"

With a somewhat glazed look the man replied, "Chuck, that is Charles, um...I'm so...so sorry that...um...this happened. I really freak ou...out at times and...stressed...I'm stressed…don't…um…um…usually fly. Had to get out…had to…New York."

"Here's your water, sir," once again Sue appeared without either of them noticing. She waited several moments while 'Chuck' drank some of the cool drink. "Do you think you'll be alright now if I leave you to take care of some other passengers?"

"Yeah…a…okay," he replied.

Alexis waited until she left. "Why don't you close your eyes and rest for awhile?"

"Oh no," Chuck responded. "I…um…I'd rather talk!"

That was the beginning of endless chatter for the next ninety minutes or so as the flight soared through the air. Alexis tried to be attentive to this poor soul but the jabbering was of non-consequential topics…which she rarely liked to deal with. Her illustrious actor/producer father had often labeled her the "no nonsense kid" and this had stuck throughout her childhood and into adulthood. Her brother, Cal, and sister, Jasmine, had teased her about never being any fun, never playing pranks on them or their parents or friends. Yet she never deviated from her devotion to her younger siblings as she studiously completed high school in two years, Yale in two and a half years and Harvard law school in two. Nine years later, after a stunning run as a criminal attorney for five years at the prestigious law firm of McMillan and Pretorious, she had become disillusioned with defending high profile clients, many of whom she felt were guilty. With this in mind Alexis had left the law firm even though she was being offered partner and coaxed the district attorney for Miami into giving her a job. Her talents as a criminal defense attorney were not wasted as her boss, D.A. Ben Griffin soon discovered. She was compiling a very nice profile of wins in the courtroom and Griffin was very impressed with her aggressiveness and one-track mind.

Breaking her thoughts, Alexis unbuckled her seat belt and excused herself to Chuck. She hurried to the back of first class and stowed herself in the restroom for awhile, trying to figure out a way to keep the other passenger from bothering her so she could get some work done. Minutes ticked by. Finally leaving the restroom, Alexis stepped toward her first class seat, only to find Chuck looking for her.

"I was...I was just about ready to...um...get...call Sue to see if you were okay," he whined.

"I'm just great but I have some work I must dig into before we touch down," Alexis replied while she crossed over his lap and dug out her large leather briefcase. Pulling down the table and opening the case, she dug out a large manila folder and spread out various interviews and case information.

A few minutes later, Chuck began his incessant talking, "Wow that stuff ...um... looks...to be real...special...important...I mean I'm an ...um...accountant. Ya know...um...a CPA. What do ya do...huh? I bet you are real ...ya know...important to who..."

"I'm an assistant district attorney in Miami," Alexis interrupted. She figured she had better tell all at once and maybe he would stop talking.

"No kidding...well my dead brother's son...uh...he used to work for Federal Express in...um...New York..." Chuck's voice droned on "an' he...um...a...he took papers to ...a...an office of the DA's...there."

"Um, that's nice," in a monotone voice Alexis began looking over her briefs and making notations. She would just have to buckle down and concentrate. This wouldn't be the first time she had to deal with a chatterbox. Her roommate in college had a never-ending stream of conversation going nightly as Alexis had to study for classes. She just learned to tune her out with a few phrases and expletives. `Um...that sounds right....uh huh!...yes...uh huh...hum...`

After an hour of this one-sided conversation, Alexis closed down the lid of her briefcase, stood up and excused herself again. Once more in the bathroom, she took her time and thought of the upcoming Lager murder trial. She would also be presenting evidence to the grand jury in the case against Thompson for perjury, bribery and theft in office as well. This case against Eric Thompson had involved going to New York for various depositions from former partners and girlfriend and had taken her out of the office for three days. She had several other cases on her docket but these first two cases had her priority. Let's face it. She was swamped with work.

No time for anything personal and that's the way I like it, Alexis mused. However, I do have to figure out what to do about Len. I don't have a clue as to how to cut loose from Len Pretorious…she had dated her ex boss's nephew several times but found him wanting. There was no use in further dating because he just wouldn't be swayed from the idea of them as a couple. Well, she was good with words. She'd figure out something.

God, Alexis thought as knocking sounded firmly on the door. I must have been in here for ages. She quickly slid back the bolt and stood face to face with Sue.

"Mr. Brown was worried and asked me to check on you." The flight attendant looked almost too prim and reprimanding as she pursed her lips.

"I'm sorry," Alexis muttered abruptly and scurried back to first class. She slid hurriedly back into her seat and listened once more to Chuck and his stammering. Opening her briefcase she began once again to try to invoke a message to a higher being to please shut Chuck up as she began once again taking notes and injecting her own words into the side columns of her papers. All-the-while, muttering brief 'um…ah ha…yes' to Chuck.

Thank God the pilot just issued the landing warning, Alexis thought about fifteen minutes later. Soon she would be rid of the idle prattle from the man.

Just as the landing gears began to shudder down, Chuck grabbed Alexis' arm.

Alarmed at the sudden movement, but not wanting to have to stay past the departing time with a 'freaked-out guy`, Alexis began rubbing the hand and arm that grabbed her as she cooed and soothed the man with words the attendant had used. Minutes ticked by. The wheels touched down with a swish and the plane jerked as the brakes and flaps were applied. The hand clutching her relaxed as the pilot came on the p.a. system and announced the landing. A sigh of relief was heard but Alexis didn't know if it was herself or Chuck.

Gathering her purse and briefcase, Alexis edged around her flight neighbor.

"I can't thank…um…you know…the help…it was needed. Please…well…please know I needed you…yes…well…thanks," he faltered.

"You are welcome," Alexis replied. Then, feeling sorry for any ill thoughts about this humble, stuttering man, she added, "I really hope your next flight will be better and that you won't be as afraid now to fly".

With that, she exited the plane and hurried to baggage claim.

Once outside the terminal, Alexis walked toward long-term parking. Several minutes later, tugging her one suitcase with her briefcase on top, she spotted her white Lexus convertible. Striding quickly, she popped the trunk as she approached but looked back over her shoulder. She had this niggling feeling. Was someone watching her? She tossed her cases into the trunk and looked about again. No one was around.

"Get a grip," she admonished herself and clutching her purse, she climbed into her car and was on her way out of the terminal parking.

Looking forward to driving on this sunny day, Alexis sped along Route 95 to the Dade County Courthouse Annex where her office was located. Her mood was lightening now that she had her thoughts to herself. Her job was the most important aspect of her life next to her family, of course, and she looked forward to getting back to her routine of delving into each new case with real gusto.

With the twenty-five minute drive out of the way, Alexis turned off Flagler Street and pulled into her assigned parking space in the parking garage and exited to the right. Walking past Jimmy, the attendant, she gave a quick salute and smiled and asked how his young wife and baby were.

"My wife's great but we've been a little worried about the babe, Ms. Saunders," he lamented.

"Have you checked with the pediatrician, Jimmy?" Alexis stopped and questioned, concerned for this nineteen year old's family.

"Yeah, we just took her yesterday and he put her on antibiotics and vitamins. He says she'll be fine but he is still worried about her not gaining the weight like she should be doing," he added.

"Well, if you need anything…formula or medicine…just anything, let me know," Alexis assured him and walked toward the elevator, making a mental note to buy more formula and diapers to drop off to Jimmy.

Digging into her large purse, Alexis pulled out her security card and swiped the black box at the door. Waiting for a few seconds, she glanced back and saw more cars pulling into the car garage. Nothing out of the ordinary, she thought and turned back as the door swished open. Pressing the fifth floor button, the elevator jerked upward.

As the doors opened, Alexis smiled and offered a greeting to the security man, George, and walked toward the receptionist's desk and its disarray.

"Hi Mary," she ventured to the sullen woman who barely acknowledged her, "do you know if Mr. Griffin is in at this time?"

"Yes," was all Mary offered and glared at her.

Well, okay, Alexis thought. I guess she's had another miserable day in her life and wants to make us all miserable. Well, enough of her…

Walking down the wide dark oak trimmed hallway towards her office, Alexis noted doors open in most cases, and a few coworkers looking up as she passed. The arched passageway held several smaller halls turning off toward the right with grand conference rooms, technology rooms, and a legal library adjacent.

Alexis couldn't get over the beauty and charm of this old building with its renaissance prints and large chandeliers hanging from the ornate ceilings. In her mind this was, along with the grandiose courthouse, one of the most gorgeous buildings in the state of Florida. Across the street another great structure, stood the History Museum of Southern Florida and around the corner on 2nd Street was the Government Center. All of them beautiful in their own way.

Stopping automatically at her door she turned the knob and walked in, depositing her case on the desk and her purse in her lower left drawer. Taking a deep sigh, she turned back out of her office and headed toward 'Big Ben's' office. She smiled as she thought of this 'gentle giant' who had offered her the job when she came to him. A large man, 295 pounds, 6 foot 2 inches of tanned brawn with dark brown hair and a dimple when he smiled, Ben was noted for his ruthlessness at trial but a real teddy bear when it came to his 'family'. As everyone knew in the district attorney's office, they were all family.

Walking up to Ben's secretary, bent over at her desk in front of the door, Alexis offered with a grin, "Anything I can help you search for, Betty?"

"Okay, doll face, you find the Trent files and take them into the dragon," she offered and levered herself upright while smothering a grin.

"Can do!" and Alexis marched around the desk to the open file case and went straight to the appropriate file.

Nothing out of order here, Alexis thought as she twirled, her knee length flared red suit skirt skimming her flawless legs. With a salute to Betty, she pushed open the double oak doors and strutted in to face Ben.

Upon her approach to the huge desk in front of the window, Ben looked up and perused her carefully. Frowning, he questioned with his courtroom demeanor, "I hope you didn't wear that outfit when you questioned the witnesses. They'd be too tongue-tied to respond...you look like an exotic model out of *Vogue*."

"No, sir," Alexis responded. "I wore my usual tailored drab suits. Most unimpressive. Had my hair in its usual back twist and minimal makeup too."

"Yeah, and that's supposed to put them off, I bet," he drawled. "Honey, you just have no idea how gorgeous you really are with your golden reddish hair, statuesque figure and a face L'Oreal is screaming to use in its commercials."

"Is this where I scream sexual harassment and pull out my hidden tape recorder?" she laughed. "You know I could get your job for this."

"Yeah, yeah," Ben lamented, "you're certainly on the right track. Speaking of being on the right track...what's going on with Lager, Thompson or D'Angelo cases?"

"Back to business, huh?" Alexis teased. "Well, the trip to New York paid off. Eric Thompson did have a lot to gain, so speaks his ex-girlfriend. As a state representative on the acquisition and spending committees, Thompson had first hand access to state and local projections and special projects brought about by the Democratic National Leader, Daniel Bachman, who is big in real estate throughout Florida. He is estimated to be worth 152 million alone and with his connections, he solicits contributions towards candidates who best see his way into viable developments. He not only profits on these by skimming and doing substandard work but apparently he's able to get big contributions for the DNC, part of which he launders for himself. Thompson, it seems, profits by a percentage of what he brings in to Bachman as he's able to bypass building committee rules and get through inspections by payoffs."

"So does the ex-girlfriend have any proof to back up her claims or does she have an ax to grind?" questioned Griffin.

"Only her word so far but I'm trying to dig up some info on men she said met with Thompson while she was staying at the house," Alexis replied. "She even mentioned the `Whisperer` whose nickname came up with an informant's info on the Lager case."

"I remember only one mention of that in looking over the Lager briefs," Ben conceded, "but nothing else has come up yet that I know of."

"No, but I'm working on that angle too...I still have a ways to go," she admitted.

"Then get out of here and prepare...I'd like to see about convening a grand jury within a month for Thompson," Ben growled.

Without answering, Alexis turned on her heels and glided out of his office back to her own. Once there, she glanced at the clock, noting she had quite a few hours left of the day to finally get some work done. She sighed and resolutely began the detailed work.

Nine hours later at 8:15 in the evening. Alexis rose from her chair and stretched. Grabbing her purse from the drawer and closing her briefcase, she scuttled toward the elevator. Pressing the button, she waited. A few seconds later the door slid open and in she stepped. The ride down was without stops and she arrived quickly at the garage.

Opening the door, she glanced about and noted that the small older attendant whom she barely knew was on duty now. She hurried toward her car and tossed in the two bags and locked and started the car. Backing up she then pulled forward and with a wave pulled through the exit onto the street.

Alexis barely noticed the night sky or the lights from various structures sending splatters of glare throughout the passing shadows. She concentrated on driving and the nearby traffic. Her father had always instructed her to be aware of her surroundings and she took this to heart. As she veered around a stopped car in the right lane, she noticed another vehicle's lights move with the same quickness. She first sped up then slowed suddenly, making a left turn as the light changed. The same lights followed, only the car went through a red light.

Uh oh! Alexis' head began pounding. Just remember your defensive driving techniques and you'll be fine. Only a few more blocks.

Coming upon a red light, Alexis geared down as if to stop. The car behind appeared to do so as well. Within a few feet of the red light, she noticed several oncoming cars to the left of the interchange had the green light. Holding her breath, Alexis floored the car and geared the Lexus up, making a right turn in front of the oncoming traffic. Horns honked. She swiftly cleared the next block glancing up to make sure the other car hadn't been able to turn into oncoming traffic as well. Then making a left turn before that light changed and another left into the alley leading to the back entrance of the Herman Professional Building parking garage. She zoomed upward to the third level, heaving a sigh of relief that no lights appeared to have followed.

Pulling between several cars, she hunkered down and waited. No lights appeared for a half hour. A few minutes later a small van pulled up about seven cars down. What appeared to be several couples enjoying an evening out exited the vehicle. Laughing they walked to the elevator and climbed in.

Guess it was time, she thought, to go home. Once there, she could unload some work and study up on some precedence necessary for upcoming trials.

The morning dawned red and golden skies. Clouds were negligible and clear skies until late afternoon was predicted. Alexis went through her morning routine…martial arts, treadmill, quick breakfast and shower. Dressed and on her way to work, she made a mental note of some important calls to make. Contact her private investigator, Jim Gérard, about any leads on various cases and let him in on the new revelation about the `Whisperer`. She had to get in touch with the Democratic National Committee and get names of members, patrons and upcoming functions. Oh, and she had to call home. She needed desperately to talk to someone with a calming influence.

Pulling into the parking garage, she waved to Jimmy and found her spot. Grabbing her bag and briefcase she scurried toward the elevator and swiped the card. Quickly she entered and the lift went upward. As soon as the doors opened, Alexis said a quick 'hello' to George and went on past reception without even a nod. There was too much to do today to even worry about offending Mary. She arrived at her office and desk without pause.

Dropping into her chair, Alexis put in a call to Gerard only to hear "This is Jim Gérard …Out of office…Leave a message." She left the message and moved on to her paperwork since 7 a.m. in Miami was too early to call the DNC or her family in Los Angeles.

Several times during her morning she was interrupted by colleagues. After an hour-long venture into the stacks of law books, Alexis headed down the hallway towards her office. Glancing toward the elevators, she noticed the sandy-haired man in the pristine suit at reception. Boy, one can't forget those shoulders or buns! she reflected. She had seen both often enough in the courtroom and had admired them from afar. Well…well. Wonder who "Wonder Boy" is here to see?

At that moment, Detective J.D. MacDonald, 'Mac' for short, looked toward her, his piercing gaze spoke volumes. He was here to see her, no doubt.

Alexis paused without breaking eye contact as she waited for MacDonald to complete his approach.

"I need to see you now," he stated. This was not a request but an order.

"Come this way to my office and be seated. I'll be right in," Alexis decided to command as well. She turned as he entered the office and went two doors down to the restroom to gather her composure.

Chapter 2

Detective J.D. MacDonald strode around the elegant office, noting a certain charm to the few simple decorations on the furniture...a large artificial floral arrangement in bright hues, a Chinese vase, and a framed family picture decorated the credenza. One wall lined with bookshelves had enough law books to be considered a library. On the walls hung only one large ornate painting of a seaside in the Mediterranean and various college and law school credentials.

Mac scanned to see if the painting was an original. He thought it probably was.

Along one wall was an oversized distressed leather couch and its two matching chairs stood in front of the desk. The desk was strewn with piles of paper, leather pencil holder, calendar, name plate and many discarded ink pens, paper clips, and pencils. A bronze 'justice' statue was the only adornment. Some crunched up papers dotted the floor around the wastebasket.

So, Mac thought with a chuckle, little `Miss Bombshell`, as law enforcement liked to refer to her, did indeed have a vice. She was not the total neat freak she appeared to be in public and in the courtroom.

He wondered what other vices she might have.

Suddenly Mac was aware of being watched scouring the room and he turned to see those lovely green cat eyes gazing intently at him. He was stunned, as always, with the visual impact she made.

An almost ridiculously straight posture; thick golden hair with red highlights that was always tied in a bun; a figure covered in a tailor-made gray suit that, however she tried, could not seem to disguise those feminine curves; and a face devoid of most make-up but was extraordinary in its beauty with high cheekbones and long-lashed eyes.

Yep, he thought and almost laughed in her face, she couldn't disguise her femininity if she tried. And right now she couldn't hide her 'pissed-off' mood either.

"So Detective MacDonald, what can I do for you today?" she drawled in her soft voice. "This is quite an honor to have our chief detective cross my threshold."

"Well now," he returned smartly, "I guess I'm here to ask you a few questions. Quite a change from the usual, wouldn't you say?"

"I'd say you know nothing about the 'usual`," she snapped back as irritation overcame calmness as a sudden urge to run her hands over those impressive pecs took hold of her. "Besides, maybe I should treat you to the same once-over you just gave me instead of answering any questions."

"Be my guest," he grinned as he raised his arms and turned slowly in front of her.

Unable to help herself from observing the magnificent 6 foot 5 inch form in front of her, Alexis noted the muscular legs *not* hidden beneath the suit trousers; bulging biceps even in the coat; large hands and fingers that curled slightly in strength; a chest to die for in its breadth; and a face that held amazingly blue eyes, square strong chin and dimples.

Yes dimples, Alexis thought as she fought to control a sigh. He, indeed, was quite the Adonis!

Turning back to her current situation Alexis thought the best route was straightforwardness. "With that done, let's get to the point Detective MacDonald."

Unable to hold back his existing erection caused by her perusal, Mac decided to turn away from her view and seat himself in a high-back chair. Never in his life had he been under such scrutiny when being looked at. But he liked it coming from Ms. Saunders.

"Have a seat yourself and we'll get started," he offered with a wave toward her massive leather seat behind the desk. "And by the way, the name is Mac."

"Mac," she conceded and offered, "Alexis…now, why are you here?"

"Right. You were on Flight 2132 from New York to Miami yesterday?" he queried.

"Yes," Alexis conceded.

"You were in seat 4A in first class?" he further questioned.

"Yes," she stated succinctly.

"Were you seated by a Charles Sirini?" Boy, he'd be lucky to get any answers of more than one syllable from this one, Mac thought.

"No," Alexis replied firmly.

"No?" Mac looked puzzled. "The airline manifest showed him sitting next to you?"

"There was a man I knew only as Chuck," she clarified. "The attendant stated his last name was Brown, I think. Let's get to the point. What is this all about?"

Getting straight to the point Mac answered, "You were seated next to a man who was found murdered in a terminal restroom shortly after his plane landed. Apparently after debarking he entered the men's room and about twenty minutes later was found dead."

Trying to look poised and not shaken, Alexis put on her best courtroom expression and in a level tone asked, "Am I a suspect, Detective MacDonald?"

"Mac. Remember? And no. We just need any information you might be able to tell us about the man."

"I know very little. I took my seat next to this man who began to talk incessantly. Apparently he is…or *was* afraid to fly. He had a panic attack just before takeoff. I rang the buzzer for the flight attendant who came and took care of the problem, after which he began his constant chatting while I just continued to work. Anything else…Mac?"

He reached into the pocket and pulled out a picture of the deceased. "Is this the man?"

Alexis glanced downward at the photo held before her and got a sick feeling in her stomach as she looked at the lifeless face.

"Yes," was all she answered.

"Anything else you can recall?" he insisted.

"No...oh, he said he was an accountant and had a relative who worked Fed Ex in New York..." she recounted slowly then tried to explain. "I learned a long time ago to tune out people as I was working and I'm afraid that is exactly what I did."

"Nothing unusual about the takeoff or landing other than fear of flying? Did you see him later in the airport? Anyone following him?" Mac certainly was persistent.

All at once her mind was pierced with that antsy feeling she had had when she left the airport. She paused.

"What's wrong, Alexis?" Mac sat up straight.

"No I never saw him again. But...I just remembered that as I was leaving the terminal I looked around just feeling that someone was watching *me* but of course there was nobody there," she answered primly, feeling foolish for mentioning it.

"You're sure?" Mac questioned.

"I saw no one," she reiterated.

"Okay, that's all for now but I'll be in touch." Mac rose and strode across to the door.

Opening it he glanced back, grinned and stated, "and looking forward to it!"

Whew...Alexis breathed while looking at the closed door. I definitely like it better when I'm on the other side of the questioning she thought. At once, however, the face of Chuck flashed through her mind and the dreadfulness of what happened to that man touched her. She was resolved to sift through whatever she could remember of the tidbits of conversation she had had with Chuck. She sank back into her chair, picked up a pen laying on the desk and with a legal pad pulled before her she closed her eyes and tried to remember. Time passed.

A knock on the door startled her. Alexis offered a `come in` and Ben Griffin appeared.

"You look lost in thought," he commented "and they don't look to be good ones."

"You're right," she acquiesced. "I just had a visit from Detective MacDonald."

Ben chuckled. "I guess he wasn't looking for a date, huh?"

Indignant, Alexis returned, "Of course not!"

Continuing his light banter, Ben said, "What do you mean, of course not! You two would make a striking couple. And remember, I've seen you in this building when he comes in and you can barely restrain yourself from jumping him."

"For Christ's sake, Ben…"Alexis was mortified about this picture he portrayed. Did everyone in the building recognize her lust for this man's body?

Ben held up a hand to stop her and lowered his voice intimately. "Now don't lie, Alexis. It doesn't become you. You don't really give yourself away to people. You hide your feelings well. But remember I've seen you go all stiff and veil your eyes to disguise them in court and other situations and I see you do the same thing when Mac appears."

"Just…just lets move on here, okay?" she pleaded. "Besides, the detective was here to question me about a man that was on the plane from New York with me. He turned up murdered shortly after I last saw him."

Serious now, Ben exclaimed, "He doesn't think you had anything to do with it does he? That's absurd!"

"No he doesn't," Alexis assured him. "He just asked me to try to remember anything about the encounter and that's what I was trying to do when you walked in."

Ben paused for a moment then looked at her solemnly, "I think you need to go home and relax and maybe something will come to mind. I'll tell Sally to reschedule any meetings you might have and to take messages."

"I can still do work. I don't need to go home," she protested.

"No, I insist. If you feel that badly though about leaving, take some work home with you," Ben conceded.

Grudgingly Alexis stood and began to fill her briefcase with work that was scattered about her desktop and grabbed her purse.

"If you insist," she surrendered.

Back in her car, heading toward home, Alexis' thoughts were in bits and pieces. She tried to mull over her flight from New

York. Nothing really stood out. Trying again to put her thoughts in a legal frame of mind she still came up with nothing. Images of Chuck's dead face intermingled with his nervous real-life image kept haunting her. She shook her head and thought that if she didn't get her mind on her driving she wouldn't be here to answer any more of Mac's questions.

Trying to concentrate on driving and all that was around her, Alexis let Mac's image take over in her mind.

Wow! What a hunk! This was the first time she had ever been on this side of one his powerful grins. On top of that, she had practically wet her silken panties when he had given *her* the once over. She had been bowled over by the impact as her nipples had hardened while thinking of those large capable hands skimming over them and pinching them lightly. She could only imagine what would ever happen if he actually did touch her.

In recalling this image Alexis felt the same wetness and hardening.

God, she thought, I'm going to have to do a whole lot better in disguising my reactions if I have to face Mac again.

And that, she assured herself, was bound to happen.

Arriving at her condo, Alexis gathered her belongings and with a quick glance around, hurried in. Walking through the doorway she again had a sense of well-being and a thrill of accomplishment for the image that assailed her. A massive dark oak chest painted in hues of pastels was ladened with photos of family and college friends. A large Chinese vase was filled with fresh flowers...one of her few unnecessary extravagances. A huge ornate mirror hung on the opposite wall with a five foot high pounded blackened brass urn standing beneath.

The urn, she remembered fondly, had been a gift to her father from the ambassador from Japan. She had taken a weeklong jaunt to Japan with her father where he was making a movie when she was a teenager. She had so admired the urn for its intricate design that the ambassador had given it to the family as a remembrance. Her father had promised her that after completing college he would pass this on to her. It now held a place of honor in her entrance hall and added a touch of sophistication and charm.

Alexis walked through the wood-trimmed archway. As Alexis turned on a gilded lamp beside the sofa and passed through her drawing room she noted her large bronzed glass-topped coffee table was still strewn with folders and notes from the night before. Several folders, she admonished herself, needed to be picked up as they were peeking out from under the bulky over-stuffed distressed leather couch. Several more were tossed carelessly on the matching love seat and she bent over to retrieve those on the seat and walked toward the master bedroom passing a wall of floor-to-ceiling windows that overlooked the ocean and a spectacular view. One wall held a conglomeration of prints and paintings of all sizes and a handcrafted sideboard of substantial design. Two damask high back chairs surrounded an oriental rug in front of the brass and marble fireplace.

Alexis continued down the long hallway carrying her material, the kitchen looming to the left and the guest bedroom opening to the right in darkness. None of the bright corals could be observed in the dark bedroom nor the golden shades of the kitchen accented by huge dark beams, cupboards and trim.

She passed through the entrance to her room, tossed the folders at the bed (barely noting when some continued to slide across the bedspread and went over the side) and began stripping off her clothes. Not bothering to pick up anything she flung herself on the bed and hit the response button on her answering machine.

(Beep: message 1) Hi Honey. Give me a call. I know you're back.

"Len Pretorious. Nope!" she said out loud. *"Ain't happenin'!"* She had to get rid of the moron somehow. What had ever possessed her to even go out to dinner twice with this man?

(Beep: message 2) Alexis dear…please call. We haven't heard from you in so long.

Yes, she planned to do just that and call her mom tonight.

(Beep: message 3) Hi Alexis. This is Len. You must not have gotten my message. Call me.

Persistent isn't he, she thought.

(Beep: message 4) This is Len. It's …

Alexis deleted that and two more messages from Len on the machine. She picked up the phone and dialed home.

"Hi mom," she smiled to herself as her mom's sweet southern drawl came over the wire.

"Before you ask, I'm fine, healthy, extremely busy with case-work and trials, and no… I'm not betrothed or secretly married," she responded before her mother could even get her standard questions out.

"All right," her mom Dee (Deloris) Saunders chuckled. "I guess I am redundant at times but since we see you so rarely, any-thing could be happening. Your dad and I were wondering if you could come from Miami in a few weeks to visit over the weekend. We'll even send the plane fare."

"Mom, you know I'd love to do that but I am truly swamped with work on several big cases," she commiserated.

"You know your dad and I aren't very happy with you working to put away such bad people." Her mom had sobered.

"Yes, and you weren't happy with me defending those same people either," Alexis reminded Dee. "You'll only be happy me doing real estate law or something equally safe."

Changing the subject, Alexis asked, "What's going on with sis and bro?"

"Okay, I get the message. Drop the subject. Cal is in Chicago on a fact-finding mission for the Marshall service and Jasmine is finishing up a movie that your father backed. The one filmed in Italy. They both are expected to be home for a few weeks and were hoping to have a family get-together," her mom stated op-timistically.

"Mom, I really wish I could but the work is…" As she was sincerely apologizing the doorbell rang. "Mom, I've got to throw on some clothes and answer the door. Call you later."

Alexis grabbed a pair of boxers and tank and scurried into them as she headed toward the door. "Yes?"

"I need to talk some more to you," Mac's imperative husky voice seeped through the thick door.

"Yes," she sighed breathlessly then steeled herself to face him. Get a grip, girl, she admonished herself.

Pulling open the door, she stepped back and waved him in with her arm. His gaze swept over her noting the hair still pinned neatly back but the figure she presented in shorts and tank with long arms and bare legs stunned him. Again his gaze moved up and down. He wanted to strip her naked and pull those pins out of her hair one by one.

What a true goddess with a shape that would make a Barbie doll envious!.. he practically drooled. Everything about her turned him; her looks, her sharp mind, her loyalty and dedication to her job

Turning away to hide his sudden hard on, Mac ambled through the entranceway into a large finely decorated room. He scanned every nook and corner that he could see from his stance.

"Wow! This looks like it came out of 'Home Decorating`. Pretty pricey neighborhood and digs!" He whistled hoping to annoy her enough so that she wouldn't notice how far his erection had pushed the front pant panel.

"Oh, knock it off!" she hissed impatiently. "Come into the kitchen and I'll make some coffee or tea."

Apparently his ploy had worked as she hustled him into the kitchen while turning on lights.

"Coffee please," Mac asserted.

Alexis began making the coffee, "It'll be a few minutes. Sit down and let's get this over with."

"Okay. Have you been able to come up with anything yet?" he questioned while lowering his colossal frame onto a kitchen chair.

"I did try for quite a while at the office but couldn't think of anything unusual. That's why Ben sent me home. To try to get my mind and memory on target without office distractions," she explained. "He understands how critical it is in these first couple of days after a murder to get any connections made and followed up. What can you tell me about the murder?"

"Thanks for the coffee," Mac offered as he accepted the freshly brewed cup from Alexis. Their fingers touched briefly in exchanging the hot mug and Mac felt a jolt of electricity. Startled and spilling a slight amount of the brew, he glanced up at Alexis and noted eyes widening. So she felt that same 'zing'? Mac mused. Taking a sip, he began to tell Alexis what little he knew about the case.

"We know very little at this point and time. He was carrying dual identification and used the name Brown for his airplane ticket. We do know he died from a single bullet to the head while he was in one of the bathroom stalls. Probably shot with a silencer. It looks as if whoever shot him waited until there was no one in the restroom and went into the next stall, climbing up on the seat and looking over the divider, the killer put one slug in his head. We have no leads as to why Sirini was on the plane to Miami. We have found no connection as yet to anyone in New York. We are still looking into that FedEx relative you mentioned but as yet, we're still coming up with a blank as far as a he is concerned."

"I'm sorry," Alexis apologized. "I still haven't thought of any pertinent details from the bits and pieces of conversation with the man. But I just got home and was getting ready to relax and try hard to think about what had transpired."

Finishing the coffee, Mac stood up and faced Alexis. Coming within a foot of her, he leaned slightly forward and intimidated her by giving her a lazy grin and offering in an indecent tone, "If you've come home to relax and try to remember, maybe I could help by giving you a massage."

God! When did this man develop such an evil streak! Alexis pondered as she thought back on all the different professional meetings and depositions they had been privy to. Mac had never looked this alluring when he was sitting in the witness stand and being grilled by her. I'll take that back, she amended, he had looked this tasty before but never had she been so enticed to give in to temptation.

"I think I'll pass but thanks for the offer," she stated primly. "Besides, I can't get too relaxed. I have too much work to do."

"Then, I guess I'll leave you to get back on track, but I'll leave you with a reminder."

Alexis was puzzled, "What reminder?"

"This," and Mac leaned into Alexis, and briefly touched her lips with his.

"Mac!" She protested as a spark of electricity seemed to zip through her lips.

"Yeah?" He drawled and turning on his heels Mac walked toward the front door. "I'll let myself out."

Alexis raised her hand and skimmed her fingers along her tingling lips. She wondered if her lips were swollen from the electrical jolt she had received when their lips had touched. The man was positively lethal. My God! Would she explode into nothingness if Mac would actually do more than just kiss her? The thought was daunting.

She needed to relax in a hot soaking bubble bath. She turned into her master suite bath and began filling up the Jacuzzi, adding her favorite fragrant scent. Stripping off her clothes she lowered herself into the tub and sank luxuriously into the foam. Laying her head back Alexis reflected on the day's events. Try as she might she could think of nothing out of the ordinary as far as Chuck Sirini was concerned. This just must have been a random shooting, she concluded then closed her eyes for a moment. She grabbed the wash cloth and ran it up and down her arms. Onward her hands moved sliding sensuously over her abdomen then breasts. Her nipples perked as once again Mac's image came to mind.

What would he look like naked? she pondered. Certainly his pectorals would be bulging, his stomach taunt. Would there be a few sprinkle of soft light hair or would it be dark and plentiful? Would it narrow downward to his groin …

My God! she thought, I shouldn't be thinking like this. Never having been with a man before in a sexual way because of her single-mindedness in obtaining her education and her determination to being top in her field of law, Alexis had avoided any true sexual relationships. Thinking back now she was sure her virginity had nothing to do with these but due, instead, to the fact that she had never wanted any man in that way until Mac had come along.

Quickly exiting the tub and bathroom after toweling herself briskly, Alexis strode into her closet and put on a lounging robe and entered her living room. With determination, she pulled out various files and concentrated on her cases.

It was dark out when Alexis became aware of her surroundings. Her grumbling stomach told her of her neglect to eat but after noting the almost midnight hour, she decided against a meal and instead searched her refrigerator for salami and cheese. Having consumed a few pieces of each she cleaned up her mess and climbed into her bed, knowing her day of exercising, eating and work would soon be starting.

Chapter 3

Morning did come exceptionally fast for Alexis. She approached her usual routine with renewed vigor. Her leg muscles were stiff and sore but not from her workout. They gave her a constant reminder of the sensual experience in the bathtub the night before. And, as usual, it gave her a mental picture of that handsome face. She forced the reflection from her mind and dressed quickly. She wanted to get into the office ahead of schedule to continue the work from the night before.

Glancing at all the various files strewn about, Alexis picked up most of them, loaded her briefcase and headed out the door. Once on the sidewalk, she headed out to the parking lot and glancing around, opened her door and climbed inside.

She wanted to remind herself to ask Jimmy if he could change the car's hard top so she could put the top down in this glorious May weather. Sunshine and blue skies were almost a daily occurrence now. Although the sun was yet to peak over the horizon, Alexis knew it would be a beautiful day.

Driving along Route 95 highway, the lights from cars were still glowing in the semi-darkness of the morning. As she headed into the city, one car's lights seemed to loom quickly in her rear view mirror and before Alexis could react, she felt a sudden jolt as the car rammed her bumper. The car swerved as she fought to control it. Pulling the wheel toward the left, she felt another more violent hit from that side which sent her careening off to the right. Over the birm she flew, the car jerking over the rough terrain. Alexis was aware of her head striking the side window and of repeated blows against the steering wheel. She felt pain in her head, shoulder, chest and abdomen as she fought for control. The car was suddenly going downward over an embankment and trees loomed in front. The Lexus glanced off several small trees and bushes before coming to a jarring stop.

Alexis' world went blank.

Words began to filter through her head. A light shown behind her closed eyelids. Alexis became aware of hands moving over her body and she let out a groan. She felt wetness running down her face.

Was she crying? she thought groggily.

"She's coming to. I have a pulse...62 and thready. Hand me the bp cuff." Alexis groaned again with movement of her arm. "Don't know if we have a break here...bp's low 88/50... Get me the neck immobilizer and the inflatable arm splint. I can't get a good look at the legs until we get her out of the car," a faint voice came through her haze.

Alexis felt herself slipping away with the pain and she tried to get some words out but only a garbled sound passed through her lips. Once again she felt nothing...there was only darkness.

The next awareness was of bright lights. Somewhere someone was moaning. Alexis shuddered slightly in pain and this movement only enhanced the level of severe discomfort. The moaning became cries of pain and Alexis realized that she was the source of those moans and cries. People were talking to her and touching her everywhere. Every bone in her body hurt miserably. Alexis felt moisture and gentle wiping with some sort of cloth on her face. Then gentle fingers tried prying open her eyelids. She felt suddenly cold as clothes were being cut off.

Alexis tried to protest this sudden exposure but was unable to express a coherent thought. She wanted to raise her arms in protest, to cover her nakedness, but was unable to do so. Questions were being addressed to her but she was unable to answer. Many voices intermingled as she laid on a hard surface, incapable of determining where she was. Someone was pressing gently on her ribs and the pain was so intense that darkness came again.

Alexis had no idea how much time had passed when she became aware of a booming voice in the background and protests coming from all around her.

"Sir, you can't come in here…" was one protest.

"Get him out now!" another ordered.

"Are you a relative?" questioned someone.

"Sir, we can't work efficiently with you in here," a male stated.

"I'm here and staying! Miami P.D. And yes…" growled the voice (God, where had Alexis heard that voice before?) "she's my fiancée."

Alexis dazedly wondered who in the world this man was talking about…And where had she heard that voice before? The fog that seemed to surround her thoughts began to lift slightly and she began to shake as reaction set in.

Mac was aware of such intense feelings as he viewed the limp body on the emergency room gurney. The people that scurried about tending to the patient were garbed in large green suits with gloves and plastic face guards protecting their skin. He couldn't believe that the dear fragile body lying on that cart with several IVs dripping into both arms was the same lady he had so tenderly kissed the night before. Alexis' face was bruised and swollen and blood was visible in the hair, temples and neck. She was obviously unaware of what was going on about her although occasional moans could now be heard coming from those pale lips. He could see bruises covering her slight frame and then a sheet was draped overtop her. This movement seemed to shake him out of his trance. His outrage at such injuries to her could not be tempered. He'd find whomever was responsible for this!

Detective J.D. MacDonald had been at his desk when he heard Sergeant Collier take the call about an accident on the highway leading into town just as dawn was breaking. Apparently multiple cars had spun out causing some minor damages to several vehicles in order to avoid a car that was careening off the highway. Traffic was at a standstill. An ambulance was being dispatched.

Continuing with his work, Mac was aware of the surrounding morning chaos in the station house. He heard voices calling across the room in jest while others were talking seriously about cases. A few doors down, several perpetrators of crimes could be heard calling out to try to get someone's attention. Probably drunks from the night before, Mac thought.

Suddenly Mac heard Collier repeat 'white Lexus' and 'bloody young woman' and he sprang to his feet and rushed to the counter.

"Who's on the phone?" he ordered.

Collier, startled, answered immediately, "Another call about that accident on Route 95...says it's..."

"Give me the phone if he's still on!" Mac grabbed the phone before Collier could answer. "Detective MacDonald! Who's this?"

"My name is Jake Ramsey. I came by this accident and I was reporting it. There is..."

"Is the car a white Lexus with a hardtop and female driver?" he broke in. "Can you see a plate?"

"The ambulance was just getting there when I left but I saw the car that hit her and wanted to..."

Once again Mac impatiently broke in "Did you get either plates?"

"Well. I stopped with others and looked at the car that was wrecked and the plate was R524L something or another or maybe it was R254L..." Suddenly Ramsey heard the sound of the phone dropping onto a hard surface. The detective was gone.

Mac was out the door and down the stairs in a flash. He ran to the secured parking garage and jerked open the door to his Buick Lasabre. Shoving the car into gear he reversed it then screeched forward, barely stopping at the gate. The attendant was stunned to see the car barely missing another vehicle going by the exit.

My God! the attendant thought, that policeman ought to be arrested for such recklessness. Mac had put on the flashing light but traffic was heavy and with the stopped traffic on Route 95, he had a lengthy drive to the scene of the accident. All the while his mind was on Alexis and his prayers were being sent to a higher being, something he hadn't done in a long time.

Finally Mac arrived on the scene after driving a good ways along the birm of the road. He jumped out of the car and, not even bothering to close the door, climbed up the incline and looked down. The Lexus belonging to Alexis was, indeed, the vehicle involved. It was pretty much totaled from what he could see of the mangled mess wrapped around a tree. Small trees were cut down in its pathway and glass was strewn about.

Cops were milling about and he strode up to one he knew as Fuerst.

"What happened to the driver?" he demanded. "Where is she?"

"Oh! Detective!" Fuerst seemed surprised to see him. "Nice seeing y..."

"Where's the driver?" Mac barked and stunned the officer as he grabbed his arm.

"Why, she just left in the ambulance...on it's way to Miami Memorial. Her name is Ale..." Fuerst was talking to air. The detective was already at his car.

Mac waited in the emergency room cubicle as the doctors and nurses worked on Alexis. They were checking responses and pupils. Two men were sticking some kind of sharp piece of equipment along the bottom of her feet and along the bloodied legs. An EKG was along side monitoring heart rate and vital signs. They were mumbling technical medical terms, many of which Mac understood.

He could stand it no longer, "Is she going to be alright?"

Several doctors looked up. The masked one at Alexis' head stated succinctly, "We think so but she's in pretty bad shape."

"Not critical though," he assured Mac. "We're just getting ready to send her to x-ray and then she'll be back."

"I'll wait," he stated emphatically.

"I was sure you would," the doctor said solemnly. "I'd better tell you it'll be awhile though. She's having a series of x-rays, an abdominal CT and MRI of the brain."

Mac nodded curtly and watched as they wheeled Alexis out the door past him. It took great will not to lean down and kiss her but he didn't want to pull on any of the tubing attached to her body.

While waiting, Mac reflected on past years. After graduating from M.I.T. he had enlisted in the navy and had spent six years in Special Ops in Central America and Afghanistan. He had enjoyed these special missions because he felt he was really helping his country with terrorism and crime. Yet years of being away from home, his four brothers and sister, as well as his parents, had taken its toll. He yearned to be back with family. And he was tired of the killing and subterfuge. He left the service honorably and was able to get on at the police department. His previous military record was sealed but the Miami Police Department had received excellent references from the U.S. Secretary of State and the Pentagon and on their recommendations, they had hired Mac. He hadn't let them down and within four years he was made detective. Now, six years later at the age of 38, everyone seemed to think he would be the next police chief or police commissioner.

Mac also thought back on the years he had known Alexis Saunders. He had first seen her nine years ago in the courtroom as a criminal defense attorney. He had heard from the men on the force about this new 'hot' attorney. She was apparently a 'bombshell' with gorgeous golden hair highlighted with red, and very kissable lips. But the grapevine had also said that those same lips could crucify a witness on the stand.

The first time Mac had walked into the courtroom as a witness, he was almost stunned into silence. She was indeed breathtaking! He had taken his place in the witness stand and after the grilling began from her, he was no longer enthralled. He got half pissed off because of her grueling tactics. He left the courtroom in a huff and went back to the precinct. The other officers just laughed at his mood and teased him that Alexis had 'cut him off at the balls`.

His second encounter with Alexis in testifying was just as arduous. He didn't like being interrogated like a criminal by a 'ball buster`. He ended up leaving that courtroom just like the first time in no better frame of mind.

It was about three weeks later when he had to meet with the District Attorney, Ben Griffin in the annex. Ben needed to depose him and as Mac entered the building he held the door open for several ladies who had approached the building and were laughing.

One was Betty, Ben Griffins' secretary. The other was prim and gorgeous Alexis Saunders.

Wow, he had thought. She didn't look so prim and proper now as he listened to her low voice teasing Betty. He followed them into the elevator and noted Alexis telling a joke, a somewhat scandalous one and then laughing at the punch line. He thought that at that moment he was in love.

Mac followed Betty and Alexis out of the elevator and down the hall to Betty's office. Just before arriving there, they both seemed to realize at the same time that someone was tagging behind them. They stopped simultaneously and turned toward him and while Betty greeted Mac, Alexis laughing face froze. She nodded primly to him and offered a greeting in that hardened courtroom voice of hers. Mac had nodded back and turned to Betty.

"I'm here to give a deposition to Ben Griffin," he offered and smiled charmingly.

"Of course, Lieutenant MacDonald. I'll take you to the room you'll be in and Mr. Griffin will be right with you." Betty had moved toward Alexis and smiled.

"You might as well come too as you'll be deposing at the same time for your client, Ken Hutchis." With that said, Betty had lead both Alexis and Mac into a large room and closed the door.

The room wasn't big enough as far as Alexis Saunders was concerned and she circled the massive conference table, placing herself as far away from him as possible.

Well, well. Mac had thought to himself. The little 'she devil` either had an aversion to him or…what?

"So you're representing Hutchis?" he queried solemnly. "Don't you ever get tired of defending these 'scumbags`?"

Something like hurt flickered in her eyes and Mac felt like he had thrown a rock at a puppy and wounded it.

"Someone has to defend the accused," Alexis countered and defended herself. "I do my job just like you do yours."

"Yeah, I know. You have quite the reputation for it," Mac tried to rile her.

"And just what does that mean?" she questioned haughtily.

"I was just making a statement of fact. You're known by the police for your brutal tactics in the courtroom." Mac knew this wasn't a nice or proper thing to say but he wanted to get a reaction.

And he did.

Alexis gasped. Her expressive eyes showed she was offended by what he had said to her.

Mac definitely felt like a cad for being so forthright.

"Look, I'm really sor…" he began apologetically.

"No," she was stoic in her reply as she stopped him from continuing with an upraised hand. "You may think what you will. All of you. But according to the law of our land, everyone is entitled to the best they can get in a defense attorney and I'm just providing exactly that. It doesn't mean that I believe in their innocence. It just means I want them to have a fair trial. If you can't understand this premise…then you have no understanding or respect for the U.S. Constitution and our laws and I certainly don't understand how you are able to be a policeman and enforce them."

"My goodness, Alexis," Ben Griffin had entered the room. "You seem to be breathing 'fire and brimstone` his way!"

"I'm sorry," Mac offered with a sheepish look. "It was my fault. I got a little testy around Ms. Saunders and said something I shouldn't have. Particularly…because she was right. I truly offer my apology to her and I only hope I can do my job as well as she does hers for her clients."

With that said, all three of them sat down and talked briefly for a few minutes until the stenographer came in. After the deposition was completed, Mac rose and shook hands with both Griffin and Saunders and left.

In the succeeding years, Mac had been grilled by Alexis Saunders in the courtroom and he had high regards for her. She was not only exceptionally attractive, but extremely intelligent as well. During the years she worked as a defense attorney she gained much respect in the courts, yet many in law enforcement were leery of her because she did so well in representing her clients. This changed, however, when she 'came to the other side` in becoming an assistant prosecutor. Even the police force couldn't sing her praises enough and it was always a fight as to whom would get to court when she was prosecuting. They all adored her even though she seemed oblivious to it!

Mac had to admit he was probably the most smitten of all. He couldn't take his eyes off her when she was in the room and he couldn't wait to hear that strong yet soft floaty voice when she talked. Just thinking of the years observing her and dying to touch her made him tremble a little. He could imagine slowly unbuttoning the blouse and slipping it slowly off her shoulders then reaching around back to unfasten the silky bra. He could practically feel her nipples perk as his fingers caressed the tips and then he would bend his head and his lips…

"Mac!" a voice broke into his thoughts, "What's happened here? How's Alexis?"

Mac realized Ben Griffin was standing in front of him and was urgently waiting for an answer.

"We're not sure how it happened yet, Ben," Mac's sober grim tone was enough to convey how serious a condition Alexis was in.

"What do we know? First, how's she doing?" persisted Griffin.

"Right now she's in having x-rays, an MRI of her brain, and a CT scan of her abdomen." Mac could barely keep the emotion out of his voice. He filled Ben in on details. "She's on O2, has several intravenous fluids going and is still unconscious. She looks bad Ben. How did you find out so fast about the accident?"

"Alexis never showed at the office at her regular time. She's like clockwork when it comes to being there. After about an hour and a half, I had Betty start calling hospitals. She wasn't anywhere at that point. Then Sergeant Collier called me and told me about the accident. He thinks a lot of Alexis Saunders," recited Ben.

"Yeah, well so does everyone at the precinct," Mac muttered.

"So I gathered," Ben smiled slightly then slyly stated, "and some more than others."

Boy, this guy misses nothing, Mac thought to himself.

Just then personnel were bringing Alexis back to the E.R. cubicle where she had first lain. Ben and Mac could barely bring themselves to look at Alexis battered face.

The orderlies got her gurney in position then reconnected her oxygen. Several doctors approached her cart and Mac was there to intercept them.

"Tell me what you know about Alexis!" he demanded.

"You are...?" questioned one doctor.

"I'm her fiancé," Mac insisted "and I'm the only relative around here."

Mac could not look toward Ben to see what his reaction to that news was.

"Well she has a hairline fracture of the left humerus. She has a severe concussion but has briefly come to. She has three cracked ribs on the left side but none did any internal damage...we're still keeping an eye on the spleen. She has multiple contusions, cuts and abrasions over face, arms and legs. No breaks in the right leg but we're going to recheck in about a week to make sure because something looks a little different on the x-ray. I'd say she's a pretty lucky young lady," the doctor stated after enumerating all the damage.

"Yeah, well...she doesn't look so lucky to me!" Mac proclaimed.

"She's going to need lots of rest. We'll be keeping her for a few days. Right now I'd say she's in serious condition if anyone asks," the doctor announced. "We're going to put a removable splint on that arm and stitch her up then move her upstairs to a room. She'll be somewhere on SICU step-down unit…that's Surgical Intensive Care Unit on the fourth floor. You can wait up on the floor if you'd like. And by the way, congratulations on your engagement although you seem to have yet to pick out the ring."

The doctor smirked and turned and walked away.

"Well he sure has your number," Ben teased. "I guess he saw through the ploy of being Alexis fiancée. That is…unless it's true?"

Embarrassed beyond words, Mac retorted, "I needed to be in here to see her. To see if she was okay. They wanted to kick me out."

"I quite understand," Griffin assured him. "Let's go out to the lobby and you can tell me what you know so far about the accident."

Seated, Mac really couldn't say much about the accident.

"I was seated at my desk when a call came in about an accident involving a white Lexus with a woman driver. I took the phone off Collier and the witness said he saw the car that had crashed into her from the side. I dropped the phone and took off to the scene. Alexis had already been taken away in the ambulance. I didn't even ask any questions of an officer that was on the scene." Mac was clearly upset. "I don't know if was an accident or not…maybe a drunken driver. I should probably go back to the precinct but I don't want to leave her."

Ben tried to console him, "Your feelings are understandable, Mac. You and Alexis go back a long way. There's nothing that the other police won't do to help find out what happened. They seem to admire the lady. So stay here and look after her for me. I'm going back to the office and look up the number of her parents. I'll give them a call. When she wakes up, give her my love."

"Thanks Ben. I think I'll call into the station to see what is known about the accident before I go on up to the floor. Maybe Sergeant Collier knows something already. I'll keep you informed as to her condition and the case itself." Mac stood to walk outside to use his cell phone and Ben walked with him.

"I'd tell you to give her a kiss for me but I guess that would be asking too much of you, huh?" Ben tried to tease Mac to get rid of that awful picture in their minds of Alexis as she had lain supine on the cart, unaware of her surroundings.

"Yeah," Mac sighed and gave what might have looked like a slight grin, "Maybe I can do that for you."

Mac turned to his cell phone and began to dial while Ben headed in the opposite direction to the parking lot.

Mac dialed the precinct and Sergeant Collier answered the phone.

"This is McDonald," Max stated tersely. "What have you learned so far about the hit-and-run on the Saunders' vehicle?"

"Hi, Mac. We don't know very much at this time. All we know is that a car went around her vehicle and crashed into the side. She apparently careened off the road, went up the incline then down over the embankment until the car was stopped by a tree. The guy you were on the phone with had apparently seen a large black sedan with Florida license plates hit Saunders car on the driver's side. He noted that the driver had been traveling at a high rate of speed, and zooming in and out of traffic. He didn't catch a license plate on that vehicle but he thought there was only one person in the car. Sorry Mac. That's all we know at this point. We are trying to get some information from several of the people that stopped to help at the accident scene," Collier related. "How's Miss Saunders doing?"

"She's hanging in there, Sergeant. A broken bone, severe concussion, cut up, but the doc says she'll be okay in the end," Mac relayed back. "I'll be in to my desk later. I'm not sure when. Call in to Surgical Intensive Care Unit at Miami General Hospital if anything comes up. My phone will be turned off."

With that, Mac went back inside the hospital and headed to the elevator. He took the elevator to the fourth floor, and went directly to the nurses station.

"What room will Alexis Saunders be transferred to?" Mac queried. "I'd like to wait there until she's brought up to the floor."

"Sir, we just can't let you wait there. You will have to wait in the visitors' room, which is down the corridor to the left," stated an elderly nurse with a scowl.

Mac pulled out his badge, flipped it open and tossed it on the counter in front of the nurse.

"I *said* I would wait in the room for her!" Mac growled.

With stormy eyes, the nurse turned away and came out from behind the counter at the nurses station. She stomped down the hallway and into what appeared to be a storage closet.

Another younger nurse turned toward Mac and offered with a hesitant smile, "Miss Saunders' room will be 422. She should be up on the floor within an hour."

Mac headed down the hallway toward the rooms labeled in the 400s. Once inside room 422 he walked over to the window and glanced down over the landscape. There were trees and flower beds of different colors, and benches placed strategically within this little park. It appeared to be a well-kept area and the people below in various dress were milling around. Some of the people appeared to be patients in their hospital gowns, and some were even being pushed about in wheelchairs.

The sun was shining brightly and there wasn't a cloud in the sky. It appeared to be a gorgeous day but Mac couldn't enjoy the ambience of the picture that was painted outside. All at once, Mac heard the door being opened and Alexis was being wheeled into the room.

Seeing this stubborn look on Mac's face, and remembering what had transpired at the nurses station earlier, the nurse signaled to the other people there as they pushed the cart next to the bed and began untangling IV tubes. They placed a board with rollers under one side of Alexis after lifting her and gently rolled her on to the bed, keeping her covered all the while. IV's were attached to polls and hooked up to a machine drip. No oxygen was being used. Through all of this, of Alexis had moaned occasionally, but appeared to be resting fairly comfortably... apparently she was benefiting from medication.

After all the personnel had left the room, Mac pulled a chair close to the bed and settled in for the long day and night. He was determined not to leave Alexis alone until he was sure she was all right.

Keeping vigil, Mac passed the time by observing Alexis and by strolling to the window to gaze outside. He noticed people in uniform going in and out in order to smoke or eat their lunches. At times, when Alexis moaned he would walk over to her and talk gently to her while caressing hands or her hair away from her face. Several times, he even bent down to give her a soft kiss on the forehand.

It was after nine in the evening, when Mac finally saw Alexis' eyes flicker. With a soft groan, she began to mumble and her eyes opened but appeared glazed over.

Mac stood by the bed and gently rubbed up and down her arm. He grasped her right hand and said softly, "Hi, little lady, how ya doin'. Come on Alexis, open those beautiful green eyes. Come on, darlin', it's Mac. Wake up."

Alexis' voice appeared weak. "Wha...What happened?" And with that effort, she groaned again.

"You were in an accident, but you're going to be all right," Mac explained.

"What kind of accident... I don't remember?" Alexis felt so lost because her memory was gone. She also felt as if she had walked in front of a Mack truck. She tried to focus and looked downwards at her body. "Oh my God! What's wrong with me!"

Mac clasped Alexis' hand carefully and soothingly murmured, "You *are* going to be fine. You have a concussion, a fractured left arm, some broken ribs, but the doctors don't feel that you have internal injuries. They are going to keep you here for observation to make sure of that. You do have some scrapes and cuts and did need to have stitches in your forehead."

"How did this happen?" Alexis questioned in a whisper. "Where did this happen?"

"You were on your way to work on Route 95," explained Mac. "A vehicle came up beside you, and apparently swerved into you causing you to go off the highway and over an embankment. Your car stopped at a tree."

"Do you know..." she began.

An argument outside the doorway stopped Alexis from talking further. Several people were arguing, it sounded like a man and women. The commotion stopped and the door to the room was pushed open. A tall, dark be-speckled man in a designer suit stood in the doorway and glared at Mac.

The stranger bellowed, "Who the hell are you!"

Mac glared back. "I was just going to ask you this same question."

"Len Pretorius," the man stated abruptly. "I date Ms. Saunders. Now who are you?"

"I'm Detective McDonald of Miami PD." Mac wasn't going to give him any more information than was necessary. This `yo-yo' could not possibly be part of Alexis' life. Mac always had a good feeling about people, and his feeling about this man with greased-up hair and overdone wardrobe was not good. Pretorious' face looked gaunt, frazzled.

Len smiled slyly, "So you're here to investigate the accident, Detective?"

"It's a little more than that, Pretorious," Mac emphasized. "I have a personal interest in this case. Much more than that, I can't say."

"This is a bunch of bullsh..." Pretorious' face was distorted in anger.

"Please..." murmured Alexis, pain obvious in her voice.

"Enough!" Mac took charge and swinging back to the bed, he picked up a Alexis' hand and glanced down into her face. "I want you out of here now, and you're not permitted to come back unless I say so."

"Now just one minute!" Pretorious barked. "I have every right..."

The door to the room suddenly opened. A handsome older couple stood at the doorway. The man's face was instantly recognizable...Michael Saunders. Mac has seen that face over and over again in movies and on television. He knew, because of knowing Alexis' background, that this was her father.

The woman in the doorway was no less lovely than her daughter. She too had been in several movies but none within the last twenty years or so but still had that Hollywood star quality.

"Alexis!" The woman ran to the bedside, and peering down into her daughter's face she cried softly. "Oh, my darling, I am so sorry this happened to you!"

Michael Saunders approached the bed as well, and standing close to his wife he looked down at his daughter and then up at

Mac, totally disregarding Pretorious. He apparently could tell that Mac in charge.

"What happened to my daughter?" he demanded. "Are you the detective that Ben Griffin told me about?"

Chapter 4

"Yes. I'm Detective MacDonald," Mac affirmed.

Looking steadily at the detective, Michael Saunders questioned, "What's my daughter's condition?"

"She has a fractured arm, a concussion, some broken ribs, and as you can see, some cuts and abrasions." Mac stated as matter-of-factly as he could.

"So how did this happen?" Michael persisted.

"Facts are still coming in. All we know the she was run off the road by someone in a dark sedan in the early hours of the morning. She went off the side of the road, and over an embankment. We have a witness that saw the car, but did not get a license plate number. I'm sorry that I don't know any more than that at this time. Ever since they brought Alexis in, I have been here with her." Mac stayed firm in his reply.

Breaking into the conversation, Len Pretorious interjected, "It was probably a drunk! I'm a very close friend of your daughter. I've been dating her and I..."

"I told you to leave Pretorious!" Mac growled.

"Maybe we should let him stay if he is seeing Alexis," Dee Saunders interrupted softly.

"Just one moment, Dee." With that, Michael Saunders turned to Mac. "When we called to the floor earlier, a nurse on the floor told me that her fiancé was with her. Just who was that?"

Pretorious was stunned into silence. This gave Mac a chance to respond quickly.

"That was me," Mac stated emphatically. "We just recently got engaged."

"I don't believe..." Pretorious started to object.

Mac strode toward Len Pretorious and escorted him out the door. Returning to the room, he faced Alexis' parents. He had a difficult time facing him because of his lie. All at once Dee Saunders came up to him and threw her arms around him.

"Sorry, but he's been annoying Alexis by hanging around her," Mac continued to lie while Dee hung onto him. "I thought it best to get him out of the room ASAP. Your daughter and I have known each other about nine years, and it's only recently that we realized what we meant to each other."

"I am so glad that my daughter has someone here for her," Dee sighed and released Mac. "I *am* surprised that Alexis never told us about you."

Michael looked Mac squarely in the eyes and stated, "I expect you to take good care of my daughter as well as finding who did this. Ben says you're a good man. Was it an accident?"

"We don't know at this time. It looks as if it might have been a drunken driver. The driver was traveling at high speeds and weaving in and out of traffic," Mac answered.

Michael studied Mac intently, looking for clues as to Mac's honesty and integrity. Apparently, he liked what he saw. He held out his hand to Mac and the two men shook. "Keep on it then. We need to find out what happened."

Dee Saunders smiled wanly. "Welcome to the family Mac. I'm really happy for you two."

Suddenly a moan came from the direction of the bed. They turned simultaneously toward the bed, and went over to where Alexis lay peering up at them groggily from the bed.

"Mom, Dad, what are you doing here?" She wondered in a faint voice. "Mac, what..."

"Darling, your parents just got here. Ben called them," Mac interjected.

"Oh my darling," her mom gushed. "We brought the jet here as soon as we heard from Ben. You are so lucky to be alive. We are here for you now, and whatever you need we'll get. And I'm so happy for you. Mac seems to be a wonderful young man."

"Mom?" Alexis was confused. How could her mom be saying she's lucky when she was just in an accident? "I don't..."

Her father stopped her from speaking further when he stated, "Mac here seems just the type of man you need. Strong and in charge. Both your mom and I are thrilled."

Alexis was even more confused. She looked at Mac's face and saw the concern mirrored in his eyes.

"I'm not sure what..." she began.

Mac stopped her from saying any more. "We know you are confused. You were in an accident and you have some injuries. They are going to keep you here at the hospital for a few days, and then you'll be able to come home. We'll find out what happened, if it was an accident or intentional. But you are not to be worried. I haven't been to the precinct yet to find out what they know, but I'm going to get to the bottom of this."

"What *is* wrong with me?" Alexis questioned. "I hurt all over, and my lips feel swollen... my head hurts!"

Mac looked upon her dear face. "You have a fractured arm, a concussion, some broken ribs, and some cuts. They had to suture a cut on your forehead, but it's up by the hairline."

Dee Saunders interrupted and tried to relieve Alexis' mind, "Honey, your face is in pretty good condition. Once the bruising and slight cuts go away, you'll be fine. We'll stay here until we're sure you're out of the woods."

"Mom and Dad, thank you so much for coming but I'll be fine once I'm out of here. I'm sure they won't let me out of the hospital until the doctors are sure I'll be okay on my own," Alexis assured them. "Right now. I'd really like to get some sleep, and I'm going to call the nurse to get me something for pain."

"Michael, I think it's a good idea that we leave," her mom assented. "We'll be back in the morning to see you."

Michael Saunders looked down at his daughter, "Remember we love you darling, and we know you're going to be fine."

Mac glanced at all three and stated, "I'll go out to the nurses station and get a nurse for you. Then I'm going to go back to the precinct and see what they know about this accident. I'll see you first thing in the morning, honey." And with that Mac leaned over Alexis and planted a very soft kiss on her lips. Turning, he nodded to Dee and Michael and left the room.

Both parents bent over their daughter, and one by one gave her a kiss on the forehead, then turned and left as well.

Back at the station, Mac noted that Sergeant Collier was now gone. A new desk sergeant, Jones, was on duty. He walked briskly up to the man and asked what was known about Alexis' accident.

Sergeant Jones pulled out what papers he had at the desk and handed them to Mac. "I think from what I hear they have some interviewing to do in the morning. Except for one guy, I don't think they have many other witnesses. Several people stopped at the scene, but they said they didn't see anything except Saunders' car going over the side of the road. We'll know more in the morning after they come in. Sorry Detective."

Mac took the papers over to his desk and began glancing through them. Not much was written up at this time, so he decided to go home and get a few hours sleep.

In his bed that evening he reflected on his relationship with Alexis. Or rather, his lack of relationship. He had little association with her outside of the court room. Yet, his feelings for her were growing so strong. He liked her strength, her determination, her intelligence... and yes, he enjoyed the look of her.

She will be okay, he thought to himself, and however much she fights it, he was determined to follow through to form some sort of relationship with her. Whether just friend or more. And he was hoping it would be more. With those thoughts, he fell asleep.

As dawn was peaking, Mac got dressed and headed to the hospital. He arrived there before seven and when he strode into the room, Alexis' parents were already there talking to her. Unbeknownst to her parents who were smiling at him as he entered, Alexis gave him a scowl. The dark look did not scare him. He went up to the bed, picked up her hand and gave a light kiss on her forehead.

"Hi there!" he offered softly. "You seem to be more alert today even though you look badly bruised. Your eyes don't look as glazed... not taking any pain meds?"

"I haven't taken any·as yet this morning," Alexis replied and tried to look a little happy because her parents were looking directly at her. "Uh! Well... Mom and Dad told me that you gave up our... secret. They are very happy it seems. Mom and Dad want to know all about us, but I'm just not up to it right now."

"We are just so thrilled! We have been waiting so long for this," gushed her mom. "Maybe it won't be so long after all before we become grandparents! It doesn't look as if Jasmine or Cal are any hurry to give us grandbabies."

"Mom, I think you need to hold on there. Mac and I *really* haven't discussed anything. I do need to talk to Mac... um... about the accident nevertheless." Alexis persisted and looked upward at Mac, her eyes glinting with anger.

"Now darling," her mom objected, oblivious to her daughter's temper. "I don't think you should be thinking about the accident. Just concentrate on you and Mac and getting well."

Her dad interjected, "I agree, Alexis. The worst thing you could be doing right now is trying to bring back memories of something that must have been so horrific. You need to relax, sleep, eat, and concentrate on what the doctor tells you to do."

Mac decided it was time to interfere. "I really would like to talk to Alexis alone for a few minutes. If that's okay with you? There are some details about the accident that might be able to help us find out what happened. Would you mind?"

Dee and Michael nodded and told them they would be in the cafeteria eating some breakfast. They'd be back in a little bit.

After the two left the room, Mac turned to Alexis to face her fury. "Okay, let's have it!"

Alexis could hardly control her rage, "Just what the hell is going on! What's with a fake engagement? What's with the sweet little kisses? I don't understand at all! *Whatever were you thinking* to tell such lies!"

Mac held up his hands in surrender, "Just listen and I'll explain."

"You had better explain!" she bit out.

"Look...it went down like this. You were in the ER, and they wouldn't let me see you. I told him I was your only living relative that was close...your fiancé. I got to stay with you because of that. Your parents came while Pretorious was here…" Mac explained.

"Len was here?" Alexis couldn't remember. She was dismayed to think that Len had been here with her in this condition.

"Yeah…and I wanted to get him out of the room for your sake," Mac further explained.

Alexis persisted, still pissed-off. "Why in the world did you tell my parents we were engaged?"

Mac tried to mollify Alexis, "Because when your dad called earlier they told him your fiancé was in the room and they questioned who was the fiancé. I kind of thought you would rather me be that person than Pretorius."

"Christ!" Alexis could think of no other words.

"It's just while your parents are here. Once they go home, we can tell them we broke up," he tried to appease her. "Your parents seem to appreciate that you have someone here for you. Why don't we leave it like that?"

"I don't know…" she began.

"Alexis, think of your parents, and let's leave it this way for now," Mac insisted.

"I guess you're right," she assented. "But as soon as they leave…"

"We'll take care of the problem," Mac completed her sentence. "Right now, I'm more concerned about how you are doing. Have any doctors been in this morning?"

Alexis grimaced, "No…but the nurse said it shouldn't be long before they make rounds."

"I'm waiting here until they come," Mac stated, "then I'm going back to the precinct to find out anything new on your accident. They are supposed to be taking more statements today. Do you remember anything from the accident?"

"Nooo," Alexis began, thinking hard, "wait a minute!…I do remember…yes…I do remember someone crashing into the side of my car. God! That's all…No!..I think the car hit me in the back first!"

"You mean he collided with your bumper first?" Mac's eyes held a glare. Alexis had never seen him looking this irate before.

"Yes, I'm sure he bumped into the back first," Alexis was sure she remembered what had transpired.

Mac paced the room back and forth several times, thinking. Maybe it still could be a drunk driver…but maybe, it was something intentional.

Mac tried to alleviate Alexis' mind, "Okay, I'll take it from here. Just try to take it easy and get well."

Alexis and Mac talked briefly about her parents, brother and sister. You could tell by just the way her eyes lit up how proud she was of all of them. Proud of her father's creative genius, her mom's loyalty and devotion, her sister's talent as an actress, and her brother's reputation as a just law enforcer. While they were talking, a physician entered the room.

"How's my patient doing today?" A name tag on the doctor stated `R. Robertson'.

Alexis gave a slight smile and answered, "I'm really sore all over, my arm is hurting somewhat, my head's pounding… but I'll live."

"I think we'll keep you a few days, because of your head injury, and then we'll let you go." Robertson continued to check hand strength, pupil reaction, and reaction to pinpricks in the feet and legs. He also checked for blanching of the fingernails in the left hand, where the removable splint was holding the break in the left arm intact. All the while Mac watched as the doctor touched `his woman'.

Alexis protested, "I really think I can go home. Today."

"Now wait just one moment," Mac disagreed. "You need to stay longer than that because of your head."

"I'm sorry, Ms. Saunders," the doctor agreed with Mac. "I can't let you go home at this time, but I will re-evaluate you tomorrow and make the decision then."

Just then the door swung open, and Dee and Michael Saunders approached the bed and glanced at the doctor and then their daughter's mutinous expression.

"Power struggle?" Michael teased. "I know my daughter, and I'm sure she's trying to get out of this place. But stick to your guns, Doctor."

"Well... I told Ms. Saunders that I'll determine tomorrow what is to be done. Her reactions are okay, but I'd still like to hold her for another 24 hours. On that I'm firm," the doctor emphasized and with that, he walked out of the room.

"Since we have that settled," Mac leaned over and kissed Alexis on the lips and as she opened her mouth to suck in some air, his tongue swept sensually inside., "I think I'll head back to the precinct to find out what's going on and get a little work done. I'll be back later darlin'."

A flustered Alexis looked up into Mac's devilish eyes, and returned as calmly as she could, "Okay."

Mac left the room and her parents began to grill her about her relationship with him.

Oh, God! she thought hysterically. I can't deal with this now.

"Mom, Dad, I really need to rest. My head is throbbing! Could I talk to you later about this?" she begged.

"Of course, honey," her dad agreed. "I'll go out and get the nurse, and she can give you some medication for your discomfort. Your mom and I will leave you now to rest and we'll be back later in the day."

Her parents kissed her and left the room. It was only a few minutes later when the nurse arrived and gave her a pain pill. She closed her eyes and thought of Mac and drifted off to sleep.

Upon returning to the station, Mac found the two cops who were conducting interrogations of witnesses. At one desk sat a wiry, balding man in his late 30s that was being questioned. He walked up to Officer Wade's desk and glancing at the paperwork in front of him he determined that this was the 'Jake' he had talked with the previous night.

"Do you mind, Officer Wade?" Mac interrupted. "I'm Detective MacDonald. What exactly did you see last night at the accident scene? Ramsey isn't it?"

"Yes... Jake Ramsey," the man replied. "I was a couple cars behind the white Lexus when out of the blue a black sedan weaving in and out of traffic passed me and darted around another car before running into the little Lexus."

"Where did it hit?" Mac interrogated. "Did you get the plate number?"

Ramsey looked at him questioningly, "Well... he hit the side of her car? And no... I didn't get the plate number. After he hit her, he just drove off."

"Nothing else you can think of?" Mac persisted.

"No," Ramsey answered.

Mac walked away to the other officer's desk. Officer Olivetti was questioning a very good-looking woman in her early twenties and as Mac approached, nodded to the detective.

"Excuse me, Officer Olivetti, I'd like to ask this lady a question or two." Mac turned toward the woman and introduced himself. "I'm Detective McDonald. What did you see last night regarding the accident of the white Lexus?".

Startled, the woman looked solemnly up the Mac and preceded to elaborate. "My name is Kathy Baker. I was driving south on Interstate 95, when a dark car that was weaving in and out of traffic roared past me. I was right behind the Lexus. He pulled in between us, behind the little white car and must have gotten really close, because the white car started fishtailing. And then he started going around her and hit her in the side."

Mac didn't like what he was hearing. "So you think the dark car hit the other car first from behind?"

"My gosh!" Baker was horrified. "I don't know! I guess that could explain the car going out of control! Oh my God!, could he have been trying to hurt the person in that car?"

"We're investigating, we don't know," Mac voiced a denial. "Did you get a license plate number?"

"It began with DUI because I thought the person was a known drunk and had required license plates as an offender. That's all I got." She appeared regretful she couldn't tell more.

"Was it a Florida plate?" Mac queried.

"Why yes, of course it was," the woman agreed.

Mac questioned further, "Anything else? Did you see a face in the windows? Anything unusual before or after the accident?"

Solemnly, the woman replied, "No, nothing."

"If you think of anything," Mac prompted, "please call me at this number." With that Mac gave her his business card.

Later that day Mac drove back to Miami General Hospital to see Alexis. When he entered her room, Ben Griffin was at her bedside. Her parents were sitting in chairs at the side of the bed. Alexis appeared disgruntled. The others in the room appeared somewhat jovial.

"What's going on?" Mac appeared suspicious.

Ben replied with a grin, "Just talking about relationships...yours and Alexis'."

"We are trying to get the lowdown on you from Ben. We figured that he would know how you two got to be an item, after all these years of working together on cases," Michael Saunders told him.

"Oh,...well, it wasn't love at first sight, let me tell you," Mac glanced at Alexis' face and noticed her mutinous expression. "Now was it darlin'?"

Alexis huffed, "I'll `darlin'` you!"

"Now don't get ticked off because I didn't kiss you as soon as I walked in," he actually laughed in her face. He walked up to her and this time, gave her a lingering kiss.

"Damn it!" She was ready to scratch his eyes out for taking such liberties in front of her boss and parents.

"Hush," Mac admonished and bent to seal her lips again with an even longer, drugging kiss. This one was pure sensual. Mac opened his eyes to look down into Alexis' passion-glazed eyes. He only wished that they were alone.

Dee, Michael, and Ben laughed with glee.

Ben stopped laughing and changed the topic, "I'd like to talk to you outside, Mac."

After exiting the room, Mac turned to Ben. "I presume that you want to know about the accident. One witness stated he saw a vehicle hitting the side of Alexis' car. Another witness believes she might have been hit in the rear first and then the side. This goes along with what Alexis told me earlier today. She remembers being tapped in the back first, before being rammed in the side."

"Oh my God!" Ben was appalled. "What now?"

"We've got a line on a partial plate. It began with DUI...the woman thought it was a specialized plate because he was a drunk driver and that's how she remembered the first three letters. But it was a Florida plate, and we don't have special plates for DUI here. So maybe the plate could have been DU ` 1 ` instead of DU ` I `. We're checking it out now through the DMV."

"Is there anything else we can do?" Griffin was concerned but knew that Mac would do whatever necessary to get to the bottom of this.

"I'm just waiting to get more information coming in and I'll let you know when I do," Mac turned to go back in to the hospital room when Griffin stopped him.

"By the way," he teased, "you're one lucky man. She's a beautiful and gifted lady."

Mac looked back over his shoulder and he lifted one eyebrow in puzzlement. Griffin beamed and Mac grinned back. There was no sense in denying that comment, and he hoped someday soon to be even luckier.

Back at the bedside, Mac chatted about non-consequential topics to the Saunders. He discussed different movies that he knew Michael had been involved in and talked to Dee about some of the movies she had starred in. He found out that Alexis' brother Cal was investigating a cattle rustling operation out West and that her sister, Jasmine was still filming the last few scenes of her movie. Michael Saunders had been unable to get hold of Cal to let him know of his sister's accident. However, Michael was able to get hold of Jasmine who was going to leave the movie set immediately to see her sister. He had been able to talk her out of coming, explaining to her that Alexis was going to be okay. Jasmine said that she would come as soon as she was done filming.

After an hour or so of talking, while Alexis lay there resting, the Saunders and Mac realized that Alexis needed to sleep. Mac declined lunch with the Saunders, declaring that he had to get back to work. He bid a farewell to Alexis and her parents and went back to the precinct.

Mac kept busy throughout the day and in the evening returned to the hospital to see Alexis. She was awake and watching the news when he entered the room. Her parents were not in sight.

"Hi sunshine," he dragged her attention from the TV screen. "How's it going tonight?"

Alexis looked upon his dear face and thought of all the sensual images that had crossed her mind during the daytime. She must be feeling better if all she could think about was being caressed by him, having him kiss and lick her from the top of her head to her femininity.

"Fine," she answered succinctly, embarrassed at her own thoughts.

"Oh my. Another bad mood? Let me take care of that." With that Mac put both hands on either side of her face and planted one long, open-mouth kiss on her lips. At first, Alexis lay acquiescent but then responded with a moan. Her mouth opened and tentatively her tongue swept into Mac's mouth. That was all the response he needed as his hunger overcame any restraint. His tongue came out in battle and it became a war. Mac groaned and a hand left her face and caressed down her neck to her hospital gown where it's settled on her breast. His fingers moved lightly over the nipple, which was already taut with wanting. He pinched it slightly and she moaned even louder. He wanted this woman with a desperation he had never felt before. He wanted to make her his woman. He wanted to spill his seed inside her.

All at once the door opened and a nurse came into the room and looked discreetly away. Mac backed away quickly. Both were exceedingly embarrassed, and the silence attested to that. The nurse approached Alexis and explained to her that she was there to discontinue her IVs. The nurse efficiently completed this task and left the room without another word.

Once alone, Mac and Alexis stared at each other in disbelief. Neither could believe what had just happened between them. The passion they had just shared was so intense that Mac still had a huge erection. Alexis' nipples were still protruding and excitement glazed her eyes. Both knew, however, they could do nothing about the situation.

Finally Alexis spoke, "I think you'd better go now, Mac. I'm really tired, and I want to get rest so I can be discharged tomorrow.

"Please," she begged after a pause, "I really need you to go."

"All right. You get your way for now." Mac smiled briefly at Alexis and left the room without another word.

Mac had the best sleep that he had had in a long time. Sensual images had played over and over in his brain throughout the night. He was ready to face Alexis and another day of hard work.

He grinned to himself as he approached Alexis' door to the hospital room. He glanced inside and frowned. Alexis was gone! Striding back to the nurses station he approached a nurse there.

"Where in the hell is Alexis Saunders, room 422?" he growled.

The nurse replied matter-of-factly, not dismayed by his bad humor, "She was discharged about 45 minutes ago. She left with an older gentleman and woman."

"That was about 6:45 this morning?" he figured.

"Yes…the doctor made rounds early and discharged her. She left shortly after just as we finished her discharge summary," the nurse elaborated.

"Thanks." Mac turned and left the building. Getting into his car, he headed toward Alexis' home.

Pulling up outside her condo, he noted a black limo in front. He jumped out of the car and bounded up the stairs to the door and knocked firmly.

"Come in," ordered Dee Saunders in a melodious voice. When she saw who it was, she smiled. "I knew you would be here early. I told Alexis we should wait and all of us come home together. She said she knew you would be working and didn't want to bother you."

"Yeah, my daughter can be pretty stubborn as I told you before," Michael Saunders approached Mac. "I hope you're not too upset with us. But when she called, she told us to get there right away…she wanted to come home. She's in the bedroom resting. We've only been here a few minutes."

Knowing where the bedroom was, Mac tried to walk calmly to the door and open it. Alexis lay fast asleep. She looked exhausted. Mac decided this was not the time to confront her and retreated. He told Dee and Michael, all the while smiling, that she was sleeping and that he was going on to work. He'd be back later.

Mac got back to the precinct, and Sergeant Collier waved him over. "We might have a lead on the car that hit Alexis Saunders.

Some kids spotted a car submerged in a shallow pond off Dressler Road. First thing this morning the Crime Scene Investigation Unit was there and pulled the car out. It was a dark sedan, late-model and had plate number DU17YP. It was reported stolen three days ago from Fort Lauderdale. There was damage to the car on the right side fender and the front bumper. But we don't know if it happened when it went into the pond."

"What about the owner?" Mac inquired.

"An upstanding businessmen, Carson Klein. He owned a small steel processing company in Fort Lauderdale. He's involved mostly, though, with construction projects now. Does a lot of charity work…both him and his wife. Nothing there to connect him to Alexis Saunders that we know of as yet."

"Give me a copy of that and I want to check it out with my connections there," Mac insisted. Collier handed him a copy of the report and Mac return to his desk and picked up his phone. He had some investigating to do.

Five hours later Mac knew little more. All his resources told him that, indeed, Klein was a wealthy entrepreneur with no criminal background. He was stymied.

Chapter 5

Alexis lay in bed trying to figure out what to do about Mac. Should she let herself have a relationship with him? How could they carry on a professional relationship if she became involved with him and it didn't work out? She had lusted after him for what seemed to be forever. What she felt yesterday was unbelievable and she longed to experience it again.

It was late in the day when she heard the doorbell rang, and her mom answering in a singsong voice, "Come in."

Alexis heard footsteps down the hallway along the hardwood floor. Her door opened and Mac stood there. Large as life. Her breath caught. As she gazed at him she could see such passion in his eyes. No one had ever looked at her like this.

Mac slowly walked toward the bed and sat down on the side. He just looked at her for a moment without saying a word. Not wanting to scare her, he bent to her lips and lightly stroked them with his own. He did not touch her with any other part of his body.

Pulling away, Max stood up and circled the room. "I was here earlier today but you were sleeping. I didn't want to disturb you. Are you feeling better? Is your arm hurting?"

"I guess my arm hurts the worst of anything. But I'm taking Tylenol, and that's helping. I don't want to take anything stronger than that. My head is much better, and even my ribs aren't real sore as long as I'm careful," she supplied him with information matter-of-factly.

"That's great! You'll be back at work before you'd know it," Mac figured it would be sooner than later.

"Yes. I already called Ben and told him that I could get back to work on my cases. He put up a lot of fuss, but I was able to compromise with him. I'm going to take off tomorrow and then go back into the office the next day. He has promised me a special assistant from the legal aid department who can do legwork and typing for me. Luckily, I'm right-handed so I can still jot down notes," she offered.

"What about the immobilizer on your leg? Isn't your leg fractured?" Mac questioned.

Alexis explained, "The doctor told me that he did not feel my leg was broken after a second reading of the x-ray. That's why the immobilizer is off. The only problem is my arm which the doctor states is only a hairline fracture and he explained that the removable splint can come off in ten to fourteen days. And before you ask, my ribs are sore but they will remain sore, whether I'm lying in bed or at work."

"Have you been up out of bed yet?" he wanted to cover every angle.

"Go out to the living room and ask my parents. I've been up several times to the bathroom, and even walked out to the kitchen," Alexis' look was one of mutiny.

"I give up. You seem to have all your bases covered," Mac surrendered. He was still concerned but he had no control over her life. *Yet.*

There was a knock at the door and Dee entered. "I've fixed a pot roast with gravy and mashed potatoes. It's ready to be served if you two are ready to eat. Would you like me to fix a tray and bring it in here?"

Alexis quickly responded. She didn't want to be alone with Mac in the bedroom.

"I'd really like to get up and eat at the table. If that's okay with you?" That wasn't a question that she expected to be answered as she rose from the bed and started out to the dining room. No one would dare thwart her.

Mac followed, staring at her backside in the loose pajama bottoms and tank top. What a sexy little thing she was. He longed to scoop her up and carry her back to bed. That wouldn't happen as long as her parents were here.

Apparently, Dee and Michael Saunders were aware of Alexis' plans to go back to work. As they were eating dinner, Dee broached the subject of Alexis being alone.

"I don't like you being here by yourself. Um…I couldn't help but notice that Mac doesn't have any of his clothes here. I…"

"Mom!" Alexis protested.

"Dee!.." Michael Saunders interjected.

Mac just folded his arms over his chest and stared at Alexis.

"Well…I am concerned. Alexis…" Dee insisted.

Mac interrupted, deciding it was his chance to voice his opinion. "I agree with Dee. Alexis and I have kept our separate households, but certainly I would be more than willing to stay here with her until she's better."

"That would be great!" Both Dee and Michael looked relieved. Dee continued, "Since you'll be going back to work we'll probably go on home. There is no sense staying here if you're going to be gone all day…as much as we'd love to see more of you."

"But…" Alexis began.

Mac looked at Alexis forbiddingly and declared, "It's settled, then. Don't worry. We'll be fine."

Finished with her meal, Alexis stormed into the bedroom and Mac followed, "What the hell do you think you were saying in there? You are going to *live* with me?"

"Calm down! I was just trying to appease your parents. I figured that if they thought I was actually here with you, they would be more comfortable going home. That's what you want, isn't it?" Mac pointed out.

Abruptly, Alexis realized that he *was* right. Her parents would now leave and she could get on with her work.

"I guess you're right," she conceded thoughtfully.

"So with that settled, I'm going to leave you. I'll try to stop back tomorrow, but I don't know if it will be in the morning or evening," Mac enlightened her.

"Fine," she offered stiffly.

Alexis still did not look in the mood to be coddled. He nodded briefly, turned and left her room. He said goodbye to Dee and Michael and assured them again that he would take care of her.

The next day dawned rainy and dreary. The forecast was unpleasant for the entire day. Just getting in and out of his car to work, drenched him. He sat at his desk, and did some work on a burglary case. They had found one partial fingerprint at the scene and it was in the database of national fingerprints. He could have the offender picked up and booked now. He opened the case material on Alexis' crash. He was still baffled about the car owned by Carson Klein. Why would someone steal a car in Fort Lauderdale, just to run Alexis off the road in Miami? And Carson hadn't reported the car stolen for over 24 hours. He began to put in calls to the bus station, train station, and airport searching to see if Carson Klein had any dealings in the Miami area.

The day progressed rapidly. It was late afternoon when Mac hit the jackpot, so to speak. He had found airport passenger records showing Klein, over the last four years, had been making regular weekly flights to the Miami area. Klein also had made many trips to New York City. Mac pondered...any connection there? He was going to have to determine who Klein's contacts were in both places. Mac left the precinct and set out in the pouring rain. He went to various taxi companies and limo services and asked to see their logs of pickups. By early evening Mac had conferred with most of the local services with no success. He still had a few to interview. He also wanted to go to the airport and check with the various car rental services. He'd have to do that tomorrow.

Mac placed a phone call to Alexis. When her mom answered, Dee informed him that Alexis was sleeping. Mac paused for a moment and then decided it was best to wait until the next day to see her. He explained to Dee that he had been caught up in work and wouldn't be over until the next day, but not to worry. Mac headed home, cold and wet.

The next day proved to be more fruitful for Mac as far as his investigation into Carson Klein went. He found that Ace Taxi

Service and Pronto Taxis had picked Klein up at the airport and had taken him to the building housing McMillan and Pretorious law firm. Drivers at both places were hired for the remainder of the day that he stayed in Miami. The logs proved a recurrent pattern of behavior, but outside of going to that building, the logs showed no other drop-offs and pickups because of being hired for the whole day. This had been the pattern since January 1 and any logs before that day were already destroyed.

Why would Klein come to Miami to seek legal services at the law firm where Alexis had once worked? Mac wondered. He doubted that Alexis knew Carson Klein. She had left the firm long before Klein had started his weekly trips to the area. What was the connection?

Mac also found out from CSI that paint on the dark sedan matched that on Alexis' vehicle. No fingerprints could be detected because of the vehicle being in water. So Klein's car was the offending vehicle in the crash. Mac still had a lot of work to do, but he decided it was time to call it a day.

Mac went directly to Alexis' condo. Upon arrival he noted a fiery red Corvette parked in front on the street. He knew her parents had left for LA, but didn't know anyone at the courthouse that drove a car like this.

Mac marched to her door and knocked. It took a few moments, but the door swung open and Alexis stood there with grim lips. What the hell had he done to upset her so much? Mac was suddenly aware of movement behind her. Towering over her, he could see Len Pretorious.

Christ! He thought he'd gotten rid of this jerk!

"Well, well," Mac drawled. "You've got a visitor darlin'. Am I interrupting something?"

Alexis glared at him. "Come in Mac. Len just stopped in to see how I was doing."

Pretorious was affronted and whined, "You know I'm here for more than that, honey. I *thought* you and I had something special going. I *thought* we were exclusive.

You've never really given me a chance…"

"Enough!" Mac took charge. It was time to get rid of this creep. He was nothing but a whiny basturd. "*I* take exception to you being here! Alexis wants no part of you, can't you get that through your thick skull! Leave *us* alone."

With that said…Mac stepped behind Alexis and put his arms around her waist.

"Please leave now, Len," Alexis implored.

Pretorious walked past the two of them, giving Mac a most hateful stare. "I'll be seeing you, Alexis," he stated defiantly.

When the door closed behind Pretorious, Alexis turned in Mac's arms. She looked up into his face and gave a weak `thank you`. She sagged briefly against Mac.

Alexis felt so right in Mac's arms. His arms tightened and he lowered to his face to give her the kiss he had been waiting for. They were alone and no telling where this could lead.

Suddenly Alexis pulled away from his embrace. She didn't want passion right now. She had to keep her head around Mac or she would be lost.

Mac was startled by her response. But he let her go without a word.

"What do you want, Mac?" she inquired.

"You," Mac answered honestly. "Since that's not an option, I have a couple questions for you. CSI has found the vehicle that hit you. The paint on the cars match the scrapings as well as the license plate begins with the three letters that were seen that night. The car belonged to a person in Fort Lauderdale. His name was Carson Klein. Does that name ring a bell?"

Alexis thought hard, "No, not at all."

"Had you ever met the man at McMillan and Pretorious?" he persisted.

"No, never…why would I have?" she asked, puzzled.

"Because he apparently has been commuting to Miami every week to see someone in that building," Mac explained.

Alexis was truly puzzled. "McMillan and Pretorious is a very large firm but I can't remember any clients from Fort Lauderdale. And why would that tie in with me? I haven't been there for more than five years. There are other businesses in that building as well so he could be there for a number of reasons."

Mac expected that answer from Alexis and her question was right on. What was the connection? "I don't know about anything yet, but I'm working on it. Now…I have a bag out in my car so I can stay here with you as I promised your mom and dad."

"Just a moment there, I thought that was just a ruse," she protested. "I am just fine by myself. No need to put yourself out. Besides, I spend very little time here in my condo…most of the time I'm at work. Since I am going back tomorrow, there is no reason for you to stay. Please, Mac, don't hassle me about this."

Mac decided it was time to put his foot down. She could be in peril.

Mac stated in a no-nonsense tone, "You lose, Darlin'. I'm here and staying. I'll go get my things and even sleep on the couch. But leaving you alone is not an option."

Mac reached out a forefinger and slid it gently down the bridge of her nose. "Be right back."

Mac turned and went to his car to get his things, aware that Alexis had trembled when he had caressed her. Well, he thought, another cold shower, I guess.

Alexis debated on whether to lock the door behind him but decided against the move. Mac would probably shoot the lock off to get inside.

When he returned to the foyer, Alexis conceded, "You can sleep in the spare bedroom. I'm not arguing with you but I will let you know that Betty is coming to pick me up and will be bringing me home. It's already been arranged."

"That's fine, Alexis. And you're safe with me. Goodnight." Mac decided it was best not to touch her. She had to learn to trust him and now was as good a time as any to learn that. He marched into the bedroom and closed the door.

Alexis returned to her bedroom, lost in thought. She had long relished the thought of Mac making love to her. Maybe if Len hadn't been in her home at the same time, she would have been able to carry through on what she wanted. But Len had come barging in to gripe about her seeing another man and being un-faithful to him. Alexis had tried over and over to tell him that the two dates they had shared did not make a relationship. He just wouldn't listen. He had always seemed obtuse when he visited the law firm to see his uncle and make passes at her. After refusing his advances so many times, she had relented and had gone out with him. He was a boring man she soon found. He did have money which he made in the importing/exporting business that his uncle had backed. But he severely lacked any knowledge of the world and appeared self-centered and shallow. No way could she be attracted to a man like this.

Mac was a different story. He was honest, had integrity, and a love for the law, and yet he was still a very sensitive and sensuous man. Just thinking of what they could be doing right now if she had let him stay in her bedroom made her tremble and press her legs together. She didn't know if she liked having this kind of response or not. It was frightening to be this tuned in to another human being. Eventually Alexis fell asleep.

The new day dawned sunny and bright. Alexis had slept in later than usual because she had foregone her usual exercise routine. She was still sore but was able to complete her bathing and dressing in almost the usual way due to the fact that she could remove the arm splint while she showered.

Ben Griffin had made arrangements for his secretary Betty Lawson to pick her up at 8:30 a.m. And as usual, Betty was precisely on time. Alexis made her way to the car and the two of them chatted while on their way to the office. Betty was appalled at what had happened to Alexis. She kept offering to stay with her while she healed, but Alexis refused.

Alexis questioned Betty as to what had been happening in the office. Betty explained to her that she had placed some messages on Alexis' desk for her to return. The commute to work didn't take long. They got out of the car in the parking garage and after waving to Jimmy and talking briefly to him, headed up the elevator.

George was the first to welcome Alexis but as she walked down the hallway, many of the secretaries and assistant prosecutors greeted her. She left Betty at her office door and settled behind her desk. She picked up a stack of messages and began returning phone calls.

She called Gérard at his PI office. She practically fell off her seat when he picked up the phone this early in the morning.

"Hi Jim, this is Alexis Saunders. I need to know what information you have for me."

"Hi…hope you're doing okay after your mishap. Heard you have a few broken bones and a head that was knocked about," he continued his fast talking without waiting for a reply. "Lager was involved big time in distributing crystal Meth. He worked out of several South American countries but his biggest involvement was with Cantonelli in Bogotá, Columbia. I have two collaborating witnesses that worked for him in loading the Meth on trucks and a foreman who oversaw the packaging. They also got paid extra for bringing in workers, usually illegals, into the Meth lab."

"So what's the connection with the murdered man, José Alfonse?" Alexis was puzzled.

"Bob Lager was dating a girl named Santana Regas. They had been seeing each other for a couple years. Regas was from Bogotá. I got this information from her roommate, Jill Westman, who says she's too scared to testify, by the way, and won't. Regas has a child two years old that is still in Bogotá living with her sister. The father of the child is José Alfonse. Alfonse hated Lager, so much so that he got Santana alone several times and beat her up after trying to get her to come back to him. From what Jill Westman said, Santana Regas was going to go back to live with José Alfonse because his cousin had taken the child away from Santana's sister and had the child in hiding in the outskirts of Bogotá. Alfonse promised Santana that he would bring the child into the U. S. if she came back to him. So Santana went to live with José. After a few months, Santana got in touch with Bob Lager. She was apparently still in love with Lager and told him of the plan José had hatched to disclose Lager's crystal Meth lab and dealings. That is apparently why Lager `iced' Alfonse," Jim divulged.

Alexis was ready with the next question. "So where is this Santana Regas? And do we have any witnesses?"

"Regas has disappeared. She might've been with Lager the night José was killed. No one seems to know yet. I'm still working on it. Jill Westman told me something I think you should know. Apparently, Santana had told Jill that José had contacted your office already with information on the crystal Meth set up. Santana also, it appears, told Lager the same thing. So

Lager wants to get a hold of the information you have on him and he's going to do it in whatever way he can," Jim Gérard confided.

Alexis was thoughtful for a moment. "Off the record, Jim…my secretary did get a call from José Alfonse. He had an appointment to meet me the day after he was murdered. He never showed and shortly thereafter, the police found his body. He never told us what the meeting was about…except that it was something illegal."

"You'd better watch yourself Alexis. Lager has a lot of money and a lot of thugs that work for him. He's not about to go down for murder or lose his operation," Jim offered seriously.

Alexis asked, "I will, but I can't be diverted from this case or any others for that matter. Now…do you have anything yet on the `Whisperer' or the D'Angelo case?"

"Yes" Jim continued. "Terrie D'Angelo was a steady customer at several of the local bars. A bartender at the Crystal Saloon on 1100th Street, and one at the Wrecking Station on 1500th Street said she was a prostitute. She was at these places maybe two or three times a week and picked all sorts of guys up then left with them. The men were the unsavory kind, if you know what I mean. At both places, the bartenders talked of a man that had a really deep husky voice…almost like he had had surgery on his throat. The bartender at the Crystal Saloon told me that Terrie left one night with him."

Alexis perked, "Was it the night of the rape and attempted murder?"

Jim Gérard answered tersely. "Don't know, boss. The bartender took a vacation with his family for over a week. He didn't hear about Terrie's rape and attempted murder for several days after that. It's too bad she's still in a coma and can't tell us what happened."

"Over the last two years, several of the girls in Miami neighborhoods that were raped and beat up described the rapist as having a husky voice. The newspapers labeled him the "Whisperer". They didn't know the man, his face was covered. But maybe it's the same man. Why don't you take pictures of those girls out of the archives and solicit the different bars around town for any information they can give you?" she instructed.

"Right on it!" Gérard snapped. "I'll get back to you."

And with that he hung up.

Alexis began going through her briefs. Her next call was going to the Democratic National Committee.

Ben came into her office about two hours later. "Are you getting some work done and how is your health?"

Alexis smiled and commented, "I really am fine, but this left arm is a nuisance. I will be needing some help doing some typing. But I can still write with my right hand. I got in touch with Jim Gérard. Let me tell you about what I've learned."

She told Ben all she knew about the two cases that involved Lager and D'Angelo. He kept shaking his head as he began to understand the various connections.

"We have no information on José Alfonse? You never met with him?" Ben acted worried.

"I never received anything from him ahead of the scheduled appointment. Unless it's laying around somewhere. That would have been ages ago, though. I'll check with some of the secretaries," Alexis affirmed.

"You need to be careful. Maybe Lager had something to do with your accident. You need to tell Mac what you've learned today," Ben instructed.

Alexis refused to be intimidated by thoughts of someone like Lager. "I'll be careful. Thanks Ben."

After Ben left her office, she placed a call to the DNC in Miami. Explaining that she was interested in joining, she requested a list of upcoming events and of patrons. She requested that these be sent to her home and gave her fax number.

It was late in the day and Alexis was exceptionally tired. She had worked long and hard with the legal aid all afternoon, getting her cases in order. She requested subpoenas for the bartenders that Gérard had told her about as well as Jill Westman. She was hoping to have more information over the next several days and send out more subpoenas.

Alexis walked down to Betty's desk and the two of them left the annex. On the way home they talked of beauty tips and fashion and laughed about some of the antics of their coworkers. Once home, Alexis kicked off her shoes, flopped back on the couch and turned on the TV. She listened to CNN to update her knowledge of world events.

Later in the evening, there was a knock at the door. Looking through the peephole, she saw Mac's face. Opening the door she peered up at him.

Mac walked right past her into the hallway and turned to her. "Ben gave me some of the low down on what you learned today about your two cases. I don't like it. If Lager thinks he can be brought down by you, he'll go after you. I'm going to try to find a connection to Carson Klein, if there is one. But it's going to take time. Until then, you still need me for protection and I'd better take you to a safe house."

Alexis stood rigid against his stare. "Don't be ridiculous. I have plenty of locks and dead bolts here. Betty is taking me to and from work every day. I only come home to sleep, and I feel safe here. Most of my day is in the annex or courthouse and they're both guarded...Please Mac... I'm tired and just want to go to bed. Let's just leave things as they are. You can even stay in the spare bedroom."

Mac took one look at her and decided now was not the time to fight. She looked whipped! But he was going to continue this conversation tomorrow. He turned and went out to his car to get his clothes.

They both found themselves in the kitchen together drinking coffee in the morning. However, Alexis was fully dressed and ready to work while Mac had on only a pair of dress slacks with the belt still undone. Alexis stared almost in a trance at Mac's gorgeous, well-defined muscular chest with a sprinkle of light hair then looked away. This brief moment was noted by Mac who recognized passion in her gaze and wanted to act on it. The doorbell rang and interrupted their silent yearning. Alexis hurried to the door where Betty stood waiting. She grabbed her briefcase and purse and left, saying a quick goodbye to Mac who was standing in the archway.

Betty refrained from teasing Alexis about the near naked hunk staying at her condo. Instead, she talked about fashion and some cases being prosecuted. Alexis responded but kept looking in the side view mirror to see if anyone was following them. No one. Once parked, Betty and Alexis headed up to their respective offices. Alexis went directly to the library to looked up some penal codes and laws, then on to her office.

Opening her door, she came to a stop. There sat Mac in one of her chairs. He gave her a slight grin and motioned her in. Alexis stomped past him and threw herself in the chair behind her desk. She tossed her briefcase to the side and her purse on the desk.

"I thought you have to work." Alexis stared rudely.

"Nope, not yet. My hours are flexible. Detectives can do that you know." Mac smirked.

"What is this all about? How did you get into my office?" Alexis had a piercing look in her eyes.

"Well now…you had to know we weren't finished yesterday. I think we have some things to say to each other. And some matters to settle." Mac was firm.

The door to her office opened and Linda Beller approached. "Do you have any typing…?"

Mac interrupted her before she could finish her sentence. "Not at the moment she doesn't. If you could hold her calls and any visitors or appointments, we'd appreciate it." He followed Linda Beller to the door and after she closed it, Mac turned the lock.

Alexis was astounded at his behavior. She was speechless. "You had no right to dismiss her like that. I do have work for her. Now if you would leave I'd like to continue with my work."

"Not until you tell me about your conversation with Gérard. Let's have it." He was still standing with his arms crossed.

Deciding it was better to get it over with, Alexis told Mac about her conversation with Gérard.

"Any more information that comes to you I want to know about. Do you understand?" Mac persisted. As soon as Alexis nodded her assent, Mac went on. "Now…there is a matter of you staying by yourself. No more arguments. I'm staying with you until this mess is completely over. I won't make you go elsewhere though. We'll stay at your condo. Got it?"

Alexis was furious. "I don't like being ordered by...!"

Mac dropped his arms at his side and began moving slowly toward her. As he approached, she could not even finish her sentence. He had such a devilish look in his eyes. He began circling behind the desk, and she walked backwards until she was in front of the desk. Suddenly she could go no further because Mac took two more steps until he was flush against her. He pressed slightly against her until his pelvis was crushed against her waist. As he leaned over, arms on either side of her, she leaned backwards. *Dreadful mistake!* she thought as her own pelvis pushed back against him. This arching had brought her into an even tighter contact with his body. She could feel him, taut and engorged, pressing into her belly.

Mac shifted his legs so that his erection was cradled at the apex of her thighs. He ground against her, rotating his hips. He could feel her heat already.

Alexis gasped. She couldn't pull her eyes away from a look of hunger on his face.

Mac stared back. He wanted to consume her. He slowly lowered his face and feathered kisses along her brow and down the sides of her cheeks until he reached her lips.

Alexis pulled away and stared confrontationally into Mac's face. "Mac, you're not going to divert me from my job...I have important cases to work on and I..."

Mac stopped her words with a heated look, then he plundered. Alexis' head was forced backwards as his lips opened on hers. His tongue invaded her mouth just as he was waiting patiently to push into her. The battle of tongues continued. All thought processes had stopped. The grinding of their hips did not stop. Both were soon lost to sensations.

Alexis grabbed onto his shoulders and began tugging his jacket off with difficulty, her left arm burdened with the removable splint. She picked frantically at his buttons with her one good hand, trying to undo them. Ripping several off, she finally had it partially opened and was able to run her right hand over his solid abs and pecs. She pulled at the shirt until it was out of his trousers. She ran her hand down under his belt and around the back until she could grab at the top of his buttocks. Her nails bit in. She gyrated her hips, spreading her legs as far as she could in her tight skirt.

She wanted this man now!

Mac had had no intention of going this far yet his fingers left the desk and moved to the silky blouse adorning Alexis' breasts. He wanted to see them…to touch them, suck them. He clumsily opened the blouse but couldn't get her top off because of the offensive splint. Mac yanked her bra down under her breasts and his mouth darted to the nipple and devoured it. His sucking pulled at an invisible string, making her wet. Over and over, he sucked and scraped at her nipples with his teeth. First one breast, then the other was given the same frantic attention. Mac's hands lowered to her skirt until he found the hem. He tugged and slid it upward until it rested at her hips. One hand slipped around the back and grabbed a buttock, his fingers slipping into its crease. The other hand slid forward until it reached her juncture. He had to move slightly away and stop grinding against her in order to move his hand to touch her heat. His fingers felt a sodden piece of material and moved back and forth against it. He lifted his head to suck at her mouth again.

Alexis arched her pelvis in order to get closer to the friction against her. She wanted more! Struggling to separate her legs even farther she tried pressing downward at the same time grinding against those fingers.

"Mac!" she begged against his lips and moaned as his fingers slipped under the wet panties.

Mac caressed and plundered her mouth. At the same time, his fingers began combing through the thick carpet of hair surrounding her opening. His fingertips dove inside.

"Oh God!" she hissed, breathless, as her body shifted to get his fingers to move inside her.

Mac moved his forefinger inward and she shuddered. He moved it back and forth, in and out as she swiveled her hips frantically.

Mac bowed his head to her breasts again and inserted two fingers inside her. God was she tight. Alexis squealed. His fingers began a rapid rhythm in and out.

Alexis clawed at his trouser belt. "Help me!" she begged.

Mac released her butt and used that hand to unbuckle his belt and unbutton his trousers. Apparently, he barely realized, he must be going too slow, because Alexis pushed his hands away and pulled his zipper down herself. She shoved his boxers and trousers down far enough to expose his bulging erection. She grabbed at him with eager hands and stroked with impatient fingers. He was ready to come. Alexis pulled at his erection and shifted herself. She wanted him. All of him.

Mac moved his hand away as Alexis lifted a leg and wedged it near his hip.

"Now, now..." and with that Alexis leaned back and dug her nails into Mac's buttocks.

Mac had waited so long for this moment. He had never wanted anyone in this desperate way. He grabbed Alexis' legs and plunged deep inside. Thrusting frantically with suppressed emotion, he was only vaguely aware of Alexis' moan of pain at the first invasion. He was lost.

After the initial pain, Alexis began to feel that spiraling feeling of sensual pull deep within her as Mac continued to stroke. She began gyrating and trying to match Mac's movements. She couldn't get enough of him. She felt her muscles began to contract. She came in a sudden shuddering explosion of exhilaration and intense feelings.

Mac felt Alexis' powerful climax which pulled him into his own.

They clutched each other. Mac ground himself into her and she responded back with the same movement. Mac placed tiny kisses all over her face, neck and breasts. After an undetermined amount of time, they became aware of their nakedness and positions.

"Oh my God! My God! What have we done!" Alexis was horrified at her behavior.

"We've done just what we wanted to do for the last several years," Mac responded in a deep sexually fulfilled voice. But he could tell the change in Alexis' mood...she was already regretting their sexual encounter.

Pushing away her lover, Alexis began pulling at her clothes, straightening the skirt and buttoning the buttons on her blouse. She glared at Mac,

"Fasten your pants!" she practically shouted.

"Alexis. We have to talk." Mac tried to remain calm.

"Your diversion tactics are not going to work again. This was a big mistake," she stated vehemently. "Just leave."

Alexis turned away and began fastening her clothes.

"Not a mistake nor a diversion, Alexis. I've wanted you for what seems forever and I believe you wanted me just as badly." Mac grabbed his coat, pulled it on and buttoned it as he approached the door. He looked over his shoulder at Alexis, but she still had her back to him. He unlocked the door and left the room.

Chapter 6

Mac returned to the precinct fuming because of Alexis' abrupt dismissal. Though he had some various leads he had to check up on, his attention span was nil due to the incredible loving earlier. He desperately tried to force his mind from the unforgettable image of Alexis in her nakedness in the throes of passion. He couldn't forget how her body had held him so tightly.

Sitting at his desk, Mac wondered…were there any connections…Lager, Alfonse, Sirini, Alexis? Was the attempted murder and rape of D'Angelo somehow connected? Who tried to run Alexis off the road and why? Or was it an accident? However much he tried, he found concentration impossible.

All his senses were still tuned to Alexis. He almost laughed out loud at her words running through his head…'you're not going to divert me from my job.' She was the minx who was doing just that to him. The thought of being buried within her was certainly keeping his mind off police business. Mac almost groaned out loud at his desk as he pushed his thoughts back to his work.

Alexis could not remain in her office. She needed to get out of the building and away from any remnants of sexual images that haunted her. She straightened herself, grabbed her belongings, and headed to Betty's desk.

"Would you tell Ben that I need to go home and work on some briefs I left there. I called a cab to take me home," Alexis was matter-of-fact so that Betty would not ask any questions about her appearance or demeanor.

"Is there anything you…?" Betty asked her friend.

"Nothing, thank you," and with that, Alexis turned and left the floor.

Once on the lobby level, she exited the elevator and paced through the lobby and out onto the street. Since she had lied to Betty. It was a matter of minutes before she could hail a cab. Inside, Alexis leaned her head back, closed her eyes, and relaxed on the way home.

Arriving at her condo, she paid the taxi driver and approached her door. About to place the keys in the door lock, she realized that it was already unlocked. Alexis cautiously opened the door.

Alexis immediately noticed her living room was in disarray as she stepped into the entranceway. She noted papers strewn all about, cushions pulled off the furniture, cabinet drawers and doors opened with contents scattered about. The furniture was even moved out of its position.

Alexis reached into her bag and pulled out her cell phone, dialing 911 straight away as she backed out of the condo.

"911…emergency services, how can we help you?" a voice answered the phone.

"This is Alexis Saunders, 11094 Bridgeton…I've had a break-in in my condo… please…wait someone's still in here!" Alexis heard glass shattering in one of the back rooms. She froze! Fear sank in and she stepped more quickly backwards and rushed into the open air. Glancing back, she continued to the curb and waited by a parked car.

Several minutes went by before she heard the sirens. A black-and-white jerked to a stop in front of her. Two policemen with guns jumped out of the car, one turning towards her. Alexis slowly raised her hands in front of her and called out to the policeman that she was the owner of the condo. The policeman lowered the gun but still held it with two hands.

It took only a minute to describe what she saw, and two policemen headed into her condo. Alexis stayed by the police car. It seemed like hours before a policeman returned. The cop that first held the gun on her walked her way with a grim expression.

"You were a very lucky woman. There was a burglar who apparently left through a broken window in the first bedroom. He's not there now. Let's go inside and look about and see if you can tell what he was looking for."

With that said, Alexis followed the policeman inside.

Several hours went by as Mac worked various cases. He still found concentration difficult but did manage to joke with other officers who came in and out at the precinct. He finally decided it was time to leave, and seek out Alexis.

Driving along Route 95, Mac deliberated as to what was the best way to approach Alexis. He knew she would have put up walls by now to keep him away from her, both physically and emotionally. Should he just blast his way into her home, take her in his arms and...no...Alexis didn't respond to that kind of treatment. Maybe, he should just consider talking to her about cases and ignoring the fact that they had made love. No... that wouldn't be a great way to deal with her either. He could always...

Mac's whole thought process stopped. He had arrived at Alexis's condo and outside on the street were two police cars with their lights flashing. He screeched to a stop and jumped out of his car barely closing the door as he left. Mac jogged up the walk and pushed open the door, only to have one of his fellow policeman point a gun at him.

"Stop right there!" insisted the policeman. Mac thought the cop's name was O'Brien.

"Whoa! I'm a detective! Let me reach inside and get my badge. You're O'Brien aren't you?" With a nod from the cop, Mac reached inside his coat and flipped out his badge.

Immediately Mac asked, "Is Alexis Saunders here? Is she okay?"

Alexis appeared in the archway heading into her living room. She appeared dazed.

"What are you doing here, Mac?"

"I came to talk to you, and saw the police cars out front. What happened? Why are they here...and are you okay?" Mac looked anxious and closed the space between, placing his hands on her shoulders.

"Mac, I'm fine…" Alexis began but was interrupted by the policeman.

"Detective, there was a B&E here tonight, but Ms. Saunders is fine. She started into her home and saw the place torn up. She left immediately dialing 911," O'Brien explained.

Mac noticed other policemen coming from the back hallway. He nodded to them and looked around at the mess before him. A third man, from CSI, walked back into the hallway with his kit and some evidence bags.

The man from CSI talked to the group standing there, "It looks as if the perpetrator came in the front door by picking the lock, then went out the window in the bedroom. I have a print on broken glass but I'll have to check it with the national database. I can't do much else now. I'll be back in the morning, but Miss Saunders will have to stay elsewhere until we complete the crime scene."

"She's coming with me," Mac was emphatic. "I'll bring her to the station tomorrow morning for any further information."

Alexis must be more upset than what she appears to be, Mac thought. She went with him without objections. Mac took her arm and led her to his car and assisted her in.

Alexis was numb from the whole experience of the day. Never had she experienced such highs and lows…making love with such passion and having her home and personal belongings violated.

Before she realized it, Alexis was on the way to Mac's place.

Alexis made a decision quickly and protested, "Take me to the *Hilton* on 22nd Street!"

"No way!" Mac was just as forceful. "You're staying with me! You need protection, and I'm going to give it to you."

"Your protection is not needed," she shot back. "I'm sure there are plenty of people who need your help…I am not one of them."

Alexis continued, "And to clear up another issue…your affections are misdirected too. Find someone else to push yourself on, just leave me alone!"

"Now wait one minute, Alexis." Mac come back with. "You were with me all the way in your office today…you even encouraged it. You have always been honest and straightforward so don't even go there."

Alexis could not deny what had transpired earlier so she chose another tactic. "I am not sleeping with you again, Mac."

Before she could go any further Mac interrupted, "I didn't ask you to…but if you remember, sleeping wasn't the issue."

"You know what I mean," Alexis bristled.

"*I* know what we both meant! Now, as for tonight…you *will be* staying at my place." Mac held up his hand to stop any words from her lips. "You can take my bed, and I'll sleep on the couch. No arguments please."

Alexis clasped her arms about herself and looked out the window with a mutinous expression. She remained this way for the rest of the time in the enclosed vehicle.

They arrived at a stately apartment building in downtown Miami. Its old red brick and long thin windows stretched for six floors. Mac proceeded to park in the adjoining parking garage and after walking down a flight of stairs, they walked a short distance to the double door entrance to his building. Using a swipe card, Mac opened the door for Alexis and ushered her inside. They walked down a short hallway, where Mac opened the second door on his right, leading to his first-floor apartment.

Alexis stepped inside the apartment but barely glanced around her. She waited for Mac to close the door and asked abruptly, "Where do I go?"

"This way," Mac led the way to his bedroom and pointed inside. He walked over to the dresser and pulled a T-shirt from a drawer. He returned to where Alexis stood and handed her the shirt.

"Would you like something to eat?" Mac queried. He was trying to stay as emotionless as Alexis was.

"I'm not hungry. Thank you. I would just like to get some sleep." Alexis turned her back on Mac, and waited for him to leave the room.

Mac wanted to deal with what had transpired at her office but decided to wait until morning. After exiting the room, he went to the hall closet and removed a blanket.

Making a bed on the couch, Mac finally drifted off to sleep.

Alexis was in no better mood in the early morning hours. She got up and showered and put the same clothes back on. Going to the kitchen, she noted that Mac was still sound asleep on the sofa. Opening the refrigerator door, she found eggs and bacon and began to cook breakfast.

About five minutes later Alexis realized she was being watched. Mac was standing in the doorway, slacks zipped partway and not buttoned and shirtless. A scattering of dark blond hair trailed from between his nipples down his chest in a V and disappeared behind his unzipped pants. His blond hair on his head was mussed and his eyes were narrowed with a lack of sleep. He tilted his head and looked at her questioningly.

"Breakfast?" Mac was hesitant as how to approach Alexis.

"I didn't eat yesterday and was hungry. I hope you don't mind. I made enough for both of us. It's just scrambled eggs and bacon because there was no cheese or anything else to make an omelet." Alexis was babbling in nervousness.

"Sounds great Alexis," Mac responded. "Should I bathe now or are…"

Alexis did not hesitate, "It's ready now. You can shower later."

Mac sat down at his table and began to consume what Alexis had dished out for him. "This tastes great! You're a good cook."

"This is about all I can do…my culinary abilities are scarce. I guess I was always too busy pursuing my career to learn much about the workings in a kitchen," Alexis apologized.

"I've always helped with the cooking, coming from a large family. Had to do dishes, clean house and do laundry too. I'm well-trained," he bragged with a slight smile and took several bites of food.

Alexis returned the smile, "I'm surprised that you haven't been propositioned into becoming a family man."

"Never said I hadn't been…just hasn't been the right lady." Suddenly the expression on Mac's face was sensual.

Huh oh. Alexis realized she had started something she shouldn't have. She wanted to stay away from any mention of relationships.

Alexis looked down at her plate and sampled her eggs without tasting a thing. She refused to look at Mac's features again.

"Well...I'm finished. I guess I'll go take a shower." Mac picked up his plate, carried it to the sink, and rinsed it. He twisted from the basin and as he walked by Alexis, he lightly touched her forehead with a kiss then ordered, "Do not leave. I will take you to your condo to get you clothes, and then on to work. You'll need to call Betty to let her know."

He continued out of the kitchen to his bedroom where he noticed the bed rumpled from Alexis lying in it. Stripping off his clothes he entered the shower where he stood under a cold spray of water to cool his raging hormones.

Alexis was sitting primly on the edge of the chair, waiting for Mac to provide transportation. He crossed the threshold of the living room and noticed her stiff posture.

They sure would not be talking about their love life today, Mac thought dourly.

"You ready?" Mac went to the door to open it. With a gesture of his arm Alexis stood and preceded him out the door.

Mac followed her outside, and together they walked to where he had parked his car in the garage. After helping her into the passenger seat, he returned to the driver's side and proceeded to Alexis' condo. No conversation was exchanged during the entire ride.

Arriving at the condo, Mac observed that the CSI unit was already on the scene. He quickly exited the vehicle and assisted Alexis out. Together they entered her home to find several people from the CSI unit loading up equipment.

One of the men Mac recognized as Ted Landis, a beat cop who had attended college to become specialized in crime scene investigations.

"Hi Mac, Ms. Saunders," Landis acknowledged. "We're just finished here so come on in. Apparently the perpetrators only made it into the living room and front bedroom. The other rooms seem intact. You're free to clean up around here.

"Ms. Saunders, if you find anything of interest missing please contact the police...I believe you know the drill," he ended with a grin, knowing she was an assistant D.A.

Simultaneously Mac and Alexis replied, "Thanks."

The three men picked up their equipment and bagged evidence and left the condo.

"I'm going to go change, then you can take me to work," Alexis informed Mac and turned towards the hallway leading to her bedroom.

"Wait one moment." Mac interrupted her pace down the hallway. "You're going to have to look around and see what's missing...or did you do that last night?"

Alexis stopped in stride and looking over her shoulder stated, "I have to work. I'll have to do that this evening. It doesn't look like anything's missing."

"Look, Alexis," Mac returned her steady gaze, "We have to find out who is responsible for this break-in. It might be related to your being forced off the road or one of your cases. I don't think this is a random thing."

Alexis started walking back to her bedroom and said over her shoulder, "And you look, Mac, I have several important cases to deal with *now* and I need to be in the office looking over my briefs and witness statements. Everything here will have to be dealt with later."

Stubborn lady, Mac thought to himself. I guess I'll just have to attach myself to her more closely until this investigation is closed. Deciding he would be at her office all day looking over her caseload, he used his cell phone to call into the precinct.

Fifteen minutes later, Alexis stood before him. Dressed in a pinstripe navy blue suit with a corral shell peeking out between the lapels and her hair a reddish gold mass pulled back in a loose bun, she looked like every man's dream...especially his.

"I'm ready to leave for the office," Alexis brokered no arguments. She picked up her handbag and the briefcase she had left the night before, and headed out to Mac's car. She climbed in without assistance and solemnly waited for him to get in the vehicle and take her to work.

Instead of dropping Alexis off at the entrance to the courthouse annex, Mac turned into the underground parking garage and found an empty space. Alexis rapidly exited the vehicle and started towards the elevator. Mac followed.

"What do you think you're doing following me?" a disgruntled Alexis questioned him. "No one is going to hurt me here in the annex... there are guards."

"I am aware of that. But I am coming with you today to look over your cases and see if I can pick up on any connection to what has been going on. And before you object, I have Ben Griffin's approval as well as my own boss'. So just shush and deal with it!" Mac disclosed shortly and entered the elevator with her as she compressed her lips into a fine line of mutiny.

The two of them arrived at her office with the lot of speculative gazes cast upon them. Alexis opened her briefcase on her desk, threw her purse in her drawer and without glancing at Mac she began to read through her cases.

Mac walked behind her desk and he peered over her shoulder at the various file folders she had tossed aside. He picked them up from where she had laid them, and walked to her couch to settle in for the day. Mac glanced up at her but she was ignoring his presence.

Alexis found it difficult to forget that Mac was in close proximity. Yet she had work that had to be completed so she focused on the papers before her. At the same time she picked up the phone to place a call to the DNC.

"Hi, this is Alexis Saunders. I am interested in becoming a member of the DNC and would like to attend the next fund raiser. I believe it's Saturday, according to a list I received from your office. Could I get a ticket for this event? I'll be glad to pay extra to have a messenger bring it to my place of work." Alexis noticed Mac rising from the sofa and signaling to her by holding up two fingers. She looked at him quizzically.

Mac mouthed the words, `two tickets' and pointed at her and himself.

Alexis opened her mouth to object but with the fierce look on his face she knew better than to protest his high handedness.

"You had better make that two tickets...yes I understand that's $500 apiece." Alexis almost laughed at the look on Mac's face when she disclosed the amount. "Yes, that will be Alexis Saunders and J. D. MacDonald. Send it to me at the Courthouse

Annex at 2508 Flagler Street…thank you so much. Have a good day."

"You have got to be kidding me…$1000 for this shindig?" Mac almost choked on the amount. "You want to be in the Democratic National Committee that badly?"

Alexis did grin now that she saw Mac at a disadvantage, "Don't worry Mac, I'll put in the request for the money from the D.A.'s office. And no…I don't really want to belong. I'm doing this for info on our case against Eric Thompson. You know, perjury, bribery, ethics charges and more. And perhaps even on an eventual case against Daniel Bachman."

"Daniel Bachman?" Mac was astounded. "The DNC chairman?"

"Yes, keep this under wraps though…we're working a possible case between the two and Daniel Bachman could go down…big-time," Alexis emphasized. She proceeded to explain the connection between the two. "I was in New York getting preliminary testimony from Eric Thompson's ex-girlfriend, Margery Gates. She states he, being on the acquisition and spending committees for the state of Florida, can access special projects brought to him by Daniel Bachman. With Bachman's clout because of having hundreds of millions of dollars, he importunes contributions that help his favored candidates throughout the state…those he personally selects to help him get his projects through the state and local bureaucracy. Through various scams and substandard work and materials, Bachman stands to make millions more with each new project he's involved in. He profits by skimming and doing substandard work as well as acquiring vast contributions for the DNC which he skims off for himself. We think that Eric Thompson does the laundering for a percentage of the profits he brings in to Bachman. Thompson, you see, is able to bypass building committee rules and get inspections to go through by payoffs."

"My God, Alexis!" Mac was mortified. "You have more people that stand to profit by something happening to you than most criminals."

"I have a job to do, Mac. And I have taken an oath to do it the best I can. I hate crooked politicians and the graft that I see being spread around them…and even lawyers that feed into this. While they profit, the people of Miami and all over the state of Florida suffer due to lack of funding for health care, schools, Medicaid and all other publicly funded projects. It's abhorrent!" Alexis preached.

"You are terrific at what you do and I feel the same about the corruption within our government," Mac asserted. "That's why I'm out on the streets, trying to protect the citizens from not only the thieves and muggers and murderers, but also from those in power and in our lofty professions."

"I *do know* you feel the same way," Alexis emphasized. With that said, she turned to her phone and dialed Jim Gérard.

Mac tried to grasp the implications of various short words and phrases during Alexis' conversation with Gérard but understanding was futile. He decided to wait until she was off the phone to find out what information had been given to her about her cases.

When Alexis hung up, she continued to jot down some notes. When she placed the pen back on her desk, he inquired, "Okay, I've given you time, tell me what you've learned."

Alexis looked up from her papers and nodded. "Gérard has been visiting local bars in our area. He's working on the D'Angelo case. He told me that one of his informants said that man with a slight New England accent and husky voice came to Miami about a year ago. This guy has been visiting various bars throughout Miami and the surrounding areas and that he is about 5 feet seven or eight inches, balding with long strands of dark hair at the back of his head and a one-inch puckered scar along the right side of his cheek. He says he's a mean-looking dude…quote that. He was in the Dirty Dog one night and beat up two of the patrons, drawing a wicked-looking knife and threatening the one man that was still conscious. Gérard said everyone on the street knows about this man now and they're leery of him and try to avoid him. One thing is unusual about this. Apparently, this man has met with a well-dressed individual with an arrogant demeanor. And some people noted an exchange of a thick envelope. It is extremely unusual to see someone of such apparent illustrious nature in a place like this."

Mac was intent, "Anything else?"

"Yes," Alexis went on. "This husky-voiced man has been seen with not just Terrie D'Angelo but another one of our murder/rape victims that has the same M.O. Maybe, just maybe, we can look in the case files, and go to other bars involved over the state to see if anyone in them remembers a man of this description with one of the victims."

Before Mac could interrupt, Alexis continued, "So my thinking is that we have one in the same person. Our murderer/rapist is apparently up for hire...for doing *what* we don't know yet."

Mac nodded in agreement. "I'll get on the street to see if any of my guys know anything. Can I use your phone to make some calls?"

"Be my guest," Alexis offered.

While Mac made some phone calls, Alexis went back to her paperwork. Phone calls completed, Mac returned to the sofa and scrutinized more legal cases. Alexis placed several more phone calls, including one to her parents telling them that she was doing fine. She was interrupted several times by colleagues and her temporary assistant.

The day passed in a whirl and soon it was after seven in the evening.

Betty walked through the door and approached Alexis. "Are are you ready to go?"

Mac shot to his feet, "What the hell is going on?"

"I made arrangements with Betty to take me home and get a few things and I'm staying with her for the next few nights." Holding up her hand, Alexis halted the words she knew would be forthcoming from Mac's lips. "No arguments, Mac! You can check out my condo the next few nights, I won't stay there. Starting Saturday, I will be in my own home. No one is going to frighten me away from my normal life."

Mac looked steadily at Alexis. He knew that in life, there had to be give-and-take and right now was the time to give. He would have extra patrol cars watching throughout the night, however. He nodded his okay.

Alexis turned to her desk and picked up some briefs, placing them neatly in her briefcase. With her purse in hand, she left the building with Betty.

While driving Interstate 95, Alexis was even more conscientious about the traffic surrounding them. She practically flinched every time a car passed them. However, they made it to her condo and back to Betty's home without incident.

By the time Saturday came, Alexis was exhausted. Having the constant stress of wondering if someone was following her, feeling it necessary to make conversation with Betty during the evening, and wondering when Mac was going to make another amorous move, kept her on tenterhooks. Along with these stress-producers, she had looked throughout her home to see if anything was missing. Apparently nothing had vanished. What had they been after in breaking into her home?

Alexis worked for several more hours Saturday morning along side of Betty. Betty kept remarking on how attentive Mac was to Alexis and how charming and handsome he was. As if Alexis wasn't already aware of his attractions…Ha!

Returning to her condo in the afternoon, Alexis took a long soak in the Jacuzzi, and sipped a glass of wine…for courage? She would be attending the DNC ball at the Center for the Fine Arts around the corner from the Dade County Courthouse on Flagler. Just dressing up in finery and meeting dignitaries in no way bothered Alexis, she had done this often enough during her growing up years with a world famous actor/director/father. No, it was the idea of being with Mac on a date. The anticipation was making her almost breathless with sexual tension. She was going to this in order to make contacts with Daniel Bachman and his cronies but it was inevitable to have some sort of intimate contact with Mac. The amount of contact was going to be up to her.

Alexis dried off and pulled on a satin robe, leaving her cast tossed aside. She approached her refrigerator and peered inside. Pulling out some cheese and grapes, she took some crackers down from her cupboards and sat at the counter and picked at the food. Alexis was certain she would be drinking token wine this evening while she made her rounds among the guest. She felt she needed to have something in her stomach to counteract the alcohol.

At 5:30 Alexis began to primp for the evening. She took careful measure with her makeup and lightly touched her wrist with her favorite perfume, *Curve*.

Now what to do with her hair? she wondered. She was tempted to go with a French twist which was the standard `do' for evening for her. But the rebel in her made her toss her red/gold mane loosely about her shoulders.

Walking to her wardrobe, Alexis pulled out the gown she had chosen. It was a Dolce and Gabbana gown she had worn several years ago to the Oscars when her father had picked up two more for best film and director. This was her favorite three quarter length silk gown of emerald green which crossed at an upward angle over her right breast and was held there by six tiny straps that draped over her shoulder and spread out across her back. These straps attached low in the back where her buttock started to curve. It was a dress of simplicity, yet elegance as it hugged her generous curves.

Alexis was just finishing putting on her diamond drop earrings and specially-designed Bulgari diamond necklace that had been graduating gifts from law school from her parents when the doorbell rang. She quickly picked up her Prada handbag and headed to the door. Glancing through the peephole, Mac's appearance was striking. Mac in a tux was quite a true visual experience! She was in deep, deep trouble.

Opening the door, Alexis stepped back.

"I have my purse. So we can just leave," she stated almost nervously.

Mac stilled for several moments. He hadn't actually looked at Alexis in such a thorough way, even when they were making love like rutting animals. He had seen her in casual clothes with her hair in a bun or in suits of an unembellished kind. Yet, he had never seen a more stunning and breathtaking individual.

"I'm speechless," he struggled to get out some words. "You are unbelievably gorgeous! No cast?"

"Not any more and thank you for the compliment. You are a sight to behold yourself. Exceptionally handsome, may I say." Alexis countered softly. As Mac took a step towards her she said softly, but briskly, "We'd better go...I really do need to get there to start meeting these patrons of Bachman."

Mac tilted his head, gave grin and held out his arm for her.

Alexis could feel her head swimming already, but took his arm, and together they walked outside to his car. They were silent throughout the drive to the Center of Fine Arts. After assisting her exit from his vehicle, Mac placed his hand gently on Alexis' lower back and escorted her through the door and into the elevators taking them to the top gallery. Upon arrival, they turned in their tickets entered the vast foyer.

Chapter 7

People milled about and within the small walls of artwork and statues. There were artistic ventures from all over the world. American painters were represented by Kent Rockwell and Arthur Davies. Spain had sent several paintings by Pablo Picasso and England was represented by Edward Lear. Paintings by Edouard Manet and Fernand Leger were lent to the exhibition by the French government as well as sculptures by Gaston La*chaise. Throughout the crush of people, one could see the best in artistic interpretations.

As Mac and Alexis roamed the extensive area, they could see the notables of Florida high society. Movie stars, rock stars and top business executives were talking to several judges and lawyers she knew from working at the courthouse. She and Mac barely conversed as they circled among the people and the exhibits. Going around a wall into another section of art, Alexis finally spotted Daniel Bachman. She tightened her fingers on Mac's arm and nodded her head slightly towards the businessman. He was conversing with a someone she did not recognize. Taking Mac by the hand, she led him to a series of paintings by Ernst Ludwig Kirchner, Franz Marc, and Wilhelm Lehmbruck.

She whispered in his ear, "Listen carefully."

As they studied the paintings, Alexis caught only isolated words from Bachman who was facing them. `Get him to...I don't want…do what we have…money is essential…I need that…'

Bachman's wife approached at that point in the conversation and after a few words, drew him to several people standing further away.

"Did you get anything out of those few things we heard?" Alexis leaned toward Mac and whispered.

"Not really, but he does sound intense," Mac whispered back. "Let's continue to mingle."

Mac and Alexis continued to amble, all the while nodding and saying a few words to acquaintances they recognized. They tried to remain aware of Bachman's location at all times. Music by an American pianist and composer Scott Joplin could be heard in the background, giving the whole production a glamorous and romantic edge. A waiter approached in black tie and offered them champagne.

Sipping the bubbly drink, Alexis was startled to see Len Pretorious approach her.

Pretorious stopped beside the two and lifting Alexis' hand, kissed the palm. Alexis rolled her eyes at Mac while Mac almost snorted his champagne.

Pretorious straightened and remarked, "You look absolutely gorgeous, darling. You need to be on the arm of someone at the top of our society, someone with dignity and class…not someone who totes a gun for a living."

Before Mac could retort, Alexis tilted her head and rebuked him. "I don't know about that, Len, I feel very protected with this hunk around me."

With that she smiled devilishly. "Besides, I've always been fascinated by a man having a big gun."

While Pretorious sputtered indignantly, Mac burst out laughing. "Let's go, pumpkin, for *that* you get something special tonight."

Mac placed his hand on her bare back and shepherded her away. Alexis could feel the vibes coming off Mac. He was turned on. She had started something she didn't know if she could finish with this very sexual male. His eyes as they gazed at her held a magical quality. His hand was scorching against her back. His whispered words held longing. They stopped in front of some paintings by Rene Magritte. They were very sensual artworks, some of them being nudes.

Alexis became aware of Mac shifting against her from behind. She felt his lips caress the nape of her neck.

"Uh..Mac," Alexis barely choked out. "We are here for a reason…"

"No reason why we can't enjoy ourselves," she felt his lips again.

"Uh…you're trying to divert my attention again and it won't work…stop it…" Alexis didn't know if she was begging him to stop or go on with his caresses.

Alexis glanced about her to see who was looking at them. She noted that they had chosen an area close to where Bachman was standing with another man. This man looked out of place, wearing only a brown suit that looked as if it came off the racks and had never been pressed. His face had several pockmarks in it and a scar on the cheek and was balding with greasy straggly hair. Alexis nudged Mac and turned slightly.

Mac looked into the intent face of Alexis. He realized it wasn't a look of passion. He quickly scanned the room, and saw Bachman only a few feet away. Realizing they needed to listen, he stepped slightly back and turned his ear towards the conversation.

"I don't care what it takes," Bachman's voice was furious. "You've screwed this up and I want it fixed."

Bachman shifted and turned his face slightly away from where Mac and Alexis stood. Conversation was now difficult to understand. "Get…done…no witne…you've…two weeks."

"Did you get a look at that guy?" Mac questioned Alexis, intent on watching the man leave Bachman's side. "He matches the description…about 5'8", long stringy hair at the back of his head, and a scar on his cheek. Stay here…I'm following him."

Alexis watched in dismay as Mac took off after the guy. She wanted to follow him but was afraid she'd get in Mac's way so she stayed where she was and kept track of Bachman. When he moved to another section of portraits, Alexis followed.

"Would you like to meet Dan Bachman?" Len Pretorious was suddenly standing behind Alexis. "I see you looking at him...I could introduce you to him."

"Thank you, Len. I am thinking of becoming a party member and I would like to speak to Mr. Bachman." Alexis wasn't sure it was a good idea to approach Bachman, it might keep his contacts from coming up to him while she was there. Many in the community knew she was the assistant district attorney and several knew she was investigating him.

Len took her arm and led her over to where Bachman was standing with several men. "Dan, let me introduce you to Alexis Saunders. She and I have been dating."

Alexis glanced at Len with exasperation. She then turned to Bachman and offered an extended hand. "Nice to meet you, sir. This is a very nice gathering you have here to benefit the DNC."

Dan Bachman stepped closer and Alexis felt slightly intimidated by the intent look in his eyes. "Thank you. It did turn now rather well. Len, you found herself very lovely lady. Consider yourself lucky...she's as beautiful as she is intelligent. I am rather surprised to see you here, however. You have never declared a political preference up to now. I do wonder what brings you here?"

"Perhaps I came to see who makes up the Democratic Party in Florida," she countered. "After all, maybe I will be seeking some political position in the future and would like backing from some of your constituents."

Bachman's eyes narrowed, "Then, perchance you had better stop trying to defame members of the party."

Bachman had practically hissed the warning and Alexis knew at that point that he could be an evil foe. "There has been no denigrating going on, sir. I just look into facts offered to the DA's office and, if enough evidence is available, I prosecute misdoings."

"Alexis...you don't..." Len Pretorious interjected.

He was interrupted by the deep voice of Mac who had come up behind Alexis and encircled her with his arms. "Good evening. This looks to be a solemn group. I'm J.D. MacDonald, Alexis` fiancé." With that said, he held out his hand toward Bachman.

"Fiancé? I was under the impression…" began Bachman and peered at Ken Pretorious.

"Yeah, well, Pretorious here gives off a lot of different impressions. All of them wrong," Mac declared as Pretorious seethed. "I imagine you know everybody in the room, Bachman. A strange assortment of people here…there was one man I noticed that didn't quite seem to fit. Balding, long hair at the back, scar on his face?"

Dan Bachman straightened and with a pinched look on his face proclaimed, "I don't know whom that would be. There are many people here I don't recognize. If you'll excuse me, I need to attend to some other matters."

As Bachman scurried away, Pretorious opened his mouth to speak. Before he could say a word, Mac took Alexis' arm and led her away.

Alexis was perturbed by this move. She had wanted to get more information from Bachman before he had gotten pissed off. "What the hell were you thinking? You came right out and confronted him. We'll never get to know his close contacts now."

"I think we have a better chance of finding out now that he knows we're on his trail," Mac informed her.

"You can't possibly think that he had anything to do with those girls' beatings, rapes, and murders. He may be a crooked politician, but he wouldn't murder women," Alexis protested.

"You saw the two of them talking. That guy fit a description of a possible murder suspect." Mac shrugged as he reminded her.

"Only loosely. We'd need more than that to tie him into this," Alexis asserted. "I have been watching politicians and attorneys that I know are here tonight. They all seem to be avoiding personal contacts with Bachman. I'm not aware of what the others do for a living, but the people I believe he's been in contact with are business people."

"What about `dear Lenny`? He seemed to know Bachman pretty well by the looks of it," Mac stated sarcastically.

Alexis conceded, "I *was* really surprised when Len was able to introduce me. I did not know he knew Bachman since Bachman wasn't a client of McMillan and Pretorious when I worked there. Len didn't work there in the law firm, but his office was in the building. He only came to the firm when he wanted to talk to his uncle. I really wouldn't know the connection between the two, because Len is into shipping and Bachman is real estate and construction."

"That's something we need to look into. But for now, let's grab another glass of champagne and look about for awhile longer." Mac took Alexis' arm and together they strolled about, sipping champagne and watching for Bachman's whereabouts.

Approximately forty-five minutes later and after exchanging lighthearted banter, Mac happened to stop Alexis in front of a very sexually explicit painting of nudes by Rene Magritte. They both gazed at it in awe. It was powerfully striking and brought to mind their past intimate experience in Alexis' office. Mac stepped closer to Alexis and placing both hands on her waist, he touched his lips tenderly to the nape of her neck. She trembled and Mac slid his hands forward to her lower pelvis.

Alexis could not stop her reaction. She pushed her pelvis slightly forward to increase the contact with Mac's fingers. She leaned slightly backwards until she was up against his hard chest. She could no more stop this movement than breathing. Alexis could feel the tension in his body and his fingers dug into her in reaction to her indrawn breath. Mac shifted to press his hardened manhood against her.

They stood this way for several heated moments, then Mac released Alexis and took her glass away. He placed the glasses on a nearby stand and taking her hand, escorted her to the elevator.

A bemused Alexis stood to the side as the door closed on them, leaving them alone. Immediately Mac pressed Alexis against the wall of the elevator and his mouth ground down on hers. They were oblivious to their surroundings as their lips and tongues dueled. Her fingers implored him to get closer by grabbing his tux shirt. His hands feathered across her bare back and butt and pulled her up into him. They couldn't get enough of each other.

The elevator doors opened and Alexis hastily pushed away from Mac. They stared at each other, both breathing heavily, with the look of sexual hunger on their faces. Mac grasped Alexis by the hand and led her to his car in a deserted corner of the parking building. After assisting her inside Mac circled the vehicle and got into the driver's seat. He angled toward Alexis and leaned across the console. His palm's encircled her neck and pulled her close, his lips crushing hers in uncontrolled heat. Alexis' hands fluttered to Mac's shoulders then her arms pulled him closer in a loving embrace. They strained together as their hands wandered over torso, back, hips, and neck and face. Alexis groaned in passion and Mac in turn muttered a `Yes`.

Mac's hands roamed over her bodice, tugging at it until it was below her left breast. His fingers at first caressed the tip and then tightened slightly on it. He plucked and pinched until Alexis begged, "Please...your mouth, please Mac."

Mac lowered his lips to her nipple and sucked vigorously. Alexis arched into his mouth in silent plea for more. He lapped at the breast and opened his mouth wider in order to take in more of it as Alexis entreated for more. She took his hand and moved it to the junction of her thighs. Mac pressed hard as Alexis spread her legs as far as she could in the confined space. He could feel the heat coming from Alexis' womanliness as she rotated her hips against him. Mac shifted his hand in order to grasp the hemline and tugged at it until, with Alexis' help by jerking her hips upward, it was settled around her waist. Mac's hand descended until his fingers reached the silken thong. It was hot and wet as Mac's finger slid underneath.

Alexis squealed and rotated her hips quickly, begging for more as Mac tantalized her.

"Darling...Lexi," Mac implored fervently.

Alexis was lost in ardor. "Mac, oh God, please Mac!"

Mac halted his caress long enough to disengage both hands and work open his buckle and zipper. Alexis pushed a hand under his boxers and stroked. Mac's hands surrounded Alexis' hips and pulled her awkwardly across the console until she faced him perched on his lap. Alexis lifted her hips and moved until they were one. They both stilled with the tightness and exhilaration of the sensation. They looked deeply into each other's eyes in the dim moonlight. They both gave a small grin and fastened their mouths together hotly.

Mac began to move gently then more rapidly at Alexis' urgings. They had no concept of time and place as this frenzied coupling continued. Alexis could feel the shuddering begin from deep inside as her with Mac's frenetic movements and she shouted, "Yes! Yessss! Oh Yessss!"

They lay replete in each other's arms, while Mac pressed kisses along Alexis' neck, jaw and brow. He murmured, "I have never experienced anything like this. Lexi, Lexi…you are so dear! This was incredible!"

Alexis was exhausted yet, as Mac's words reached her consciousness, she realized she wanted him again. Changing position slightly, her movement caused an answering reaction from Mac. He moaned and …

Suddenly, voices interrupted their impassioned movements. They stared at each other and realized that they had to get out of here before someone saw them. As Alexis struggled to disengage herself from Mac, he placed his hands around her waist and lifted her back to her seat. Alexis tugged at her dress until it covered her lap. Neither talked as Mac turned the ignition on, barely taking time to pull up his zipper. He headed out of the garage while reaching out to grasp Alexis' left hand and clasp it to his thigh.

It was a silent ride along Interstate 95 until they reached Alexis' condo. Both were aware of their barely suppressed emotions. Mac assisted her out of his car and together they hurried to the door. As Alexis removed her keys from her purse, her hands were shaking. Mac grabbed the keys from her and unlocked the door, pulling her inside. He twirled her around until she was plastered against the door, his hands working the back zip of her dress. He drew the dress downward until it puddled at her feet while Alexis' fingers were busy pulling apart his shirt and dragging it off his shoulders. Her fingers then worked his zipper as she wrenched his pants downward.

Struggling to kick his pant legs off his feet and stay upright, Mac's hands moved rapidly all over Alexis' body. She was ready and unable to wait any longer, Mac lifted her high, spreading her legs around his hips and impaling himself. Alexis could do no more than hang on for the ride. When the spasms were over, Mac carried Alexis with her legs still draped around his hips into her bedroom, where they collapsed onto the bed. Mac shifted slightly and pulled a blanket over the two of them. They lay in each other's arms and fell into an exhausted sleep.

It was the early morning hours when Alexis was pulled from a delightful dream by nuzzling at her shoulder blades and neck. She was spooned with Mac with one of his arms supporting her head, a strong warm hand cupping her breast but how long they stayed like this... Alexis did not know. She remembered afterwards, Mac placing kisses along her nape then...nothing. She had fallen back to sleep.

Alexis and Mac awoke almost simultaneously, after hearing noise in the living room. Startled, Mac grabbed the blanket and tossed it over a Alexis' naked form. Footsteps stomped toward the bedroom as Mac tried to locate his clothes. Whoops...clothes were in the hallway...no help there.

As her bedroom door was pushed open further, Mac was ready to throw himself across Alexis for protection.

"Uh...sorry...I guess I should have knocked!...Uh...you want to cover up, man?" A blonde, muscular giant of a man stood in the doorway. He had high cheekbones and dimples showed as he smiled. He looked surprisingly like Alexis.

Alexis gurgled, *"Oh God! Cal! Get out of here now!"*

Cal tipped his hand to an imaginary cowboy hat and pivoting walked back out of the room.

"That was...?" Mac knew without asking.

"My *brother!*" Alexis was practically hysterical. "Get dressed while I do the same."

"That would be fine, but I have no clothes in here." Mac watched with growing sexual hunger as Alexis struggled to cover her naked body with a shirt and shorts.

Alexis glanced at Mac's face in exasperation then grinned. "Stop it! You look like you want to devour me. I'll go to the hall and get your clothes and toss them in here."

With that she hustled out of the room.

Entering the living room, she observed her brother sitting nonchalantly in the leather chair, his right leg slung casually over the arm. She walked by into the hall and picked up Mac's strewn clothing and returned to her bedroom long enough to throw the clothes inside.

Alexis's stood before her brother with her arms crossed. "What are you doing here, Cal? And couldn't you have knocked?"

Cal grinned, "Right, sis. Sorry, but I did knock only there was no answer. Since I knew about your troubles, I used my own key to come inside and investigate."

He sobered and stood just as Mac came down the hallway in only his unzipped tux pants. "I really was worried."

Mac strode forward and offered a hand to shake. "No need to worry, I'm here to take care of her. But it is great to meet another member of the family."

"Yeah, and I hear the family is gaining another member. Mac, isn't it?" Shaking hands, Cal looked up into the towering male in front of him.

"Yep," Mac affirmed.

"I thought I was tall but compared to you..." Cal left the sentence unfinished as he gazed up from his 6 foot 3 inches..

He turned to Alexis. "Mom and dad told me about your engagement. I was kind of surprised since you never said a word to either Jas or myself when we've had you on the phone. Kind of sudden, isn't it? Going to be a shotgun wedding?"

As Cal smiled at the two of them, Mac replied, "Don't worr..."

He peeked at Alexis' horrified expression on her face as he began to speak and his words stopped. His heart did a quick pause as he realized the reason for her shock instantly.

How many times. Mac wondered, had they made love without using protection? Three or four times? More? Mac had not even thought to slide a condom on. He had been too focused upon getting inside Alexis and fulfilling both their needs. Suddenly he remembered how tight she had been that first time, how surprised at first she had seemed by the sensations of love making. Her shock now only confirmed his thinking...she had been a virgin and had probably not been on birth control.

"Uh...Cal...Alexis and," Mac hem and hawed.

Alexis gained her composure. "Cal, Mac, why don't I make us some coffee."

She turned and walked to the kitchen and began preparing the coffee maker. Cal and Mac entered the kitchen and began talking about their jobs. Cal also asked about Alexis' accident. All the while Mac kept glancing at Alexis to see if she was upset.

"We are assuming it was not an accident but we don't have any other real leads... except we do have the abandoned car. We're looking into Alexis' cases to see if there are any tie-ins. That was the first incident involving her, then afterwards, we had the break in here," Mac explained.

Alexis suddenly remembered another incident. "Wait a minute! I forgot about being tailed by a car and having to pull some fast moves to avoid it a couple weeks ago."

"What the hell...why didn't you tell me?" Mac was livid. "When exactly did this happen?"

Alexis was pensive for a moment. "It was the day I flew home. It wasn't until late in the evening, around nine o'clock. I had left the office and was driving home when I noticed headlights appeared to be following me. My father had sent me to defensive driving school a few years back as a teenager and I used some moves to get away and pulled into a parking garage. I stayed there about an hour or so then went home."

Mac gazed intently at Cal. "That was the day of the murder at the airport. I wish I had known that there was a possible second attempt to hurt Alexis."

Cal stared at his sister, "You have to let Mac know every little detail that you can remember, Sis. Don't leave anything out. What about protection for her, Mac?"

Mac almost chortled. He knew that Cal had meant police protection, but the instant Cal said the word, Mac thought of his not using condoms when loving Alexis. Peering at Alexis, her worried expression signified her own similar thoughts.

"Don't worry, Cal. Your sister will have me staying with her every night until this is solved." Mac was emphatic and as he looked fiercely at her, dared Alexis to refute the statement.

"I will leave you alone now and go back to my hotel room," Cal insisted. "How about supper at the Marriott...six o'clock okay? I leave to go back home at 6:45 in the morning."

"Sounds great. Alexis and I will be there," Mac confirmed.

Cal shook Mac's hand and glided over to where Alexis stood and gave her a hug and kiss. He then left the condo, leaving Mac to confront a brooding Alexis.

Mac took Alexis by the shoulders and looked deeply into her eyes.

"Is there anything else you can remember, honey," he questioned her softly as he rubbed her shoulders.

"Not really...there's been nothing else," she answered hesitantly, loving the feel of Mac touching her.

"Okay. Keep trying to remember." Mac turned to another subject. "Uh...you and I have to talk about us personally. When Cal mentioned `shotgun' to you earlier you got a crazy look on your face. In all the times we made love, I never used a condom. Are you protected?"

"I...I..." Alexis faltered. She couldn't look Mac in the eyes and lowered her face.

"Right...you just answered my question." Mac tilted up her chin and pressed a sweet kiss on her lips. "We are in this together. I think you know I have great feelings for you and I want to be with you. Whatever happens I will be by your side."

Alexis stepped backward out of Mac's arms and returned primly. "Whatever happens, I will deal with it by myself. I've never told you that I was using birth control. Your altruism is appreciated, however."

Mac stepped up until he was chest to chest with Alexis, "Oh no, sweetheart, if we made a baby, I'm right there with you. There will be no abortion, and there *will* be a wedding."

Alexis placed both hands on her hips and spit out, "I know that I won't have an abortion. I don't believe in them for myself. But a wedding...? We don't know each other well enough."

Mac placed a hand low on her pelvis and stated in a sexy low voice, "We know each other well enough..."

"Look Mac..." Alexis began but Mac interrupted her by placing a finger over her lips.

"I think that for the sake of your family and mine, we had better get you an engagement ring for your finger. That's the first step in setting things right. Besides, it will give a signal to those looking for you that you have in-house protection by a cop," Mac alleged.

"I'm going to get cleaned up, I don't want to argue with you." With that Alexis went into her master bath. She stripped off her clothes, turned on the shower and grabbed a towel. She entered the cubicle and stood facing the shower head, letting the warm water wash over her face and body.

Alexis had never once thought about birth control in the heat of the moment or after. And boy, was there ever heat! She and Mac had started a fire every time they touched each other. One kiss could bring her to her knees. Could she imagine going to bed with Mac every night? She knew what he was like as a lover, but a father and husband?

Alexis smoothed her hand down over her belly and imagined it growing with child. Lost in thought, she was brought back to reality by a very large hand pushing hers aside as it covered the same spot. She quivered.

Mac massaged gently over her pelvis. "Kind of mind-boggling, isn't it?"

Alexis peered over her shoulder at Mac's eager face. He bent his face and took her lips in an all-consuming kiss. She arched backward against his naked form and her arms curved backward to clutch his hips tightly. Mac pushed his hand down to her pale curls and began making love.

Minutes later, they remained in each others arms under the warm spray until Alexis began to shift away. Mac let her go as she hastily picked up the bar soap and moved it over her upper body. As she rinsed, Mac did the same. They finished simultaneously and Mac grabbed the towel and began drying Alexis off. She watched as Mac toweled himself swiftly then dropped it to the floor. He swept Alexis up in his arms and carried her to bed.

"I'm sorry, Alexis," he apologized, "I didn't do a very good job of protecting you again."

"It's my fault too, so don't blame yourself. I could say no. Let's just get some sleep because I'm really tired, Mac." She pulled back the bedding and they crawled under together. Mac hauled her against him and she rested her head on his shoulder. Her hand was tucked against his chest. As she fell asleep, she was aware of Mac slipping his hand downward to cover her lower belly.

They had been sleeping for several hours when Alexis woke and gingerly crept out of the bed. Grabbing up some clothes she went into her second bedroom to work at her computer. She had been working for an hour when Mac came into the room. He stood behind her for several moments before placing his hands on her shoulders.

"Can I do anything to help you?" his voice was tender, as he massaged her shoulders. "Do you want anything to eat?"

"Nothing, thank you." Alexis was firm. "I have a lot of work I need to dig into. I have to be in court tomorrow for the Lager case."

"Gotcha!" Mac got the hint right away. Alexis was in her no-nonsense attorney mode. He went into the living room and began making some calls.

Alexis remained holed up with legal work for the remainder of the day. Cal called and reneged on their dinner plans. He had to return that night for an important case.

So instead, Mac fixed a salad and steak for supper but Alexis took only bites and returned to work. It was midnight before Alexis crawled exhausted into bed beside Mac who took her in his arms and fell asleep.

Chapter 8

The next day dawned rainy and cool as Alexis prepared for court. Mac drove to the courthouse and dropped her off on his way to work. Stopping briefly at her office, she picked up court materials and headed to Judge Masters' courtroom. Jim Gérard was waiting for her.

"Alexis, I've been trying to get in touch with Detective McDonald. He had contacted me a while back about several of your cases plus what he has been working on. I have located a man named Manny Contini who used to work for Fed Ex in New York," Gérard informed her.

Alexis knew that Mac was interested in locating this man, "Okay...I can let him know or go ahead and call him at the precinct."

Gérard was insistent, "You don't understand yet. Contini was the cousin of Charles Sirini whom Mac was wanting to find. He has been in hiding ever since he heard of Sirini's murder. He met with Sirini in New York and his cousin told him about being afraid because of doing the books for people with mob connections. Sirini was being followed. The guy that was following him had a very husky voice and fit the description of our `Whisperer'. Sirini said this guy had sat down beside him several times at restaurants. And you'll like this…Sirini told Manny that one of his clients was Bob Lager."

"Oh my God! Lager could been responsible for Sirini's murder!" Alexis was horrified at the thought. "I need Rodrígues here to testify. Can we get protection for him and bring him to Miami?"

Gérard shook his head, "That's why I have been trying to contact Mac. I can't persuade Contini to come here but I thought if Mac could talk to him, maybe we stood a chance of getting him here."

"Call Mac. We need this man to testify," Alexis said urgently and Gérard nodded and left. With that she began unloading her briefcase as people began to fill the courtroom.

An hour later, all stood within the courtroom as Judge Masters entered. The bailiff called the court to order and Alexis approached the selected jury members, all the while feeling deadly glares at her back coming from Lager.

Alexis began solemnly, "Good morning. Today and in the days to come you will have a very important task before you. You will be entrusted to listen to facts presented to you by the district attorney's office as well as rebuttals from the defense team and come to a conclusion of guilty or not guilty as instructed by Judge Masters in the case of the State of Florida versus Robert D. Lager. The state will be presenting evidence showing Robert Lager did, for all intents and purposes, seek to perpetrate crimes against the people of the state of Florida and the United States by engaging in a continuing criminal enterprise by producing, packaging and shipping and distributing crystal Meth. The state shall prove that Robert Lager was indeed the principal administer, organizer, and leader of this enterprise. Through evidence provided by those working with Robert Lager, as well as those in law enforcement, the prosecution will prove beyond a reasonable doubt that he was engaged in this unlawful activity. *And* should be punished as such. Through expert medical testimony the prosecution will also prove how detrimental crystal Meth is to our society. It causes severe headaches, paranoia, suicidal thoughts and suicide itself. It's now a horrible drain on our emergency services as crystal Meth is the most often abused drug of choice. Over the last 5 years, E.R. visits are up 73% due to crystal Meth and hospitals have seen a 56% increase in E.R. costs. Crystal Meth also takes a much longer rehabilitation period and thus, dreadful costs. Crystal meth is a drug effecting all our lives drastically and because of this, the defendant when found guilty should be given the maximum penalty as prescribed by law."

Alexis returned to her seat, glancing at the back of the courtroom and noting that Mac and Gérard were seated at the back. The defense attorney, Ronald Handler, rose to address the jury.

Handler began casually leaning on the jury box, "Mornin'. The prosecution will be unable to provide any direct evidence that links my client with a crystal Meth lab. They have only persons testifying who hold a grudge against my client. They will fail to provide any written evidence that connects Robert Lager with criminal statutes. My client is therefore innocent. The prosecution must convince you, the jury, that the defendant did engage in a continuing criminal enterprise as described in the law. This, my esteemed colleague, Assistant D.A. Saunders will fail to do."

When Handler returned to his seat, Judge Masters began instructing the jury as to their duties and responsibilities. He educated the jury as to their prudent behavior during the trial and afterwards and explained some of the technicalities of the law. The jury sat there appearing engrossed in his words.

When the judge finished, Alexis stood and called her first witness…Samuel Otte, a foreman at the Meth facility who took direct orders from Lager.

Alexis ambled over to Otte after he was sworn in, "Mr. Otte…can you tell me please where you are employed?"

The day continued as Alexis and Handler cross-examined the witness. The whole time, Alexis was aware of Lager's piercing gaze upon her. One o'clock in the afternoon, Judge Masters called for a recess until the next day and as Lager was led out in handcuffs, Alexis was aware of his calling out her name. She turned briefly to him and tensed as he lifted both hands and pointed them at her while pretending to shoot her with a gun. She inhaled sharply and turned away, gathering her materials.

Leaving the courthouse and walking along the walkway to the annex, Alexis was aware of footsteps behind her approaching at a rapid pace. She swung about and came face to face with Mac and breathed a sigh of relief.

"Hey there, are you okay?…You look worried." Mac placed his hand along her back and pulled her to him.

"Yes, I'm fine. I've just had a long day." She didn't want to go into the incident with Lager.

"Sorry I couldn't stay long today in court. I had some leads to check out. Are you up for dinner today?" Mac looked tenderly at Alexis.

"I don't…" she began then looked at his dejected face. "Okay, what time?"

"Can you be ready at 5:30?" he questioned with that endearing smile.

"Well, I won't have time to go home to change. Just pick me up here," she assented. Mac leaned over and briefly touched her lips with his own and turned and left.

Mac was standing in the doorway of her office before she realized the time. "Are you done now?"

As she gathered her belongings Alexis beamed, "I'm ready. I can use a good meal."

Together they left the building and headed out of downtown in Mac's car.

"Where are we going?" she inquired as they left the metropolitan area and headed into some palatial estates on the outskirts.

"Just another minute and you'll see. I hope you like great Italian food?" Mac lifted her hand and kissed the back.

"I love Italian. But…" she started as they drove into a private estate driveway and pulled up before a beautiful colonial home. "Where…"

"This is my parents home and we're having a family dinner." As she began to protest Mac grabbed her shoulders and held her facing him. "I knew you would balk at the idea of meeting my family but I thought it was time. Particularly if there's a baby involved. And before you protest," he pulled a small black box out of his coat pocket and handed it to her, "I want you to put this on your finger."

"Mac, I can't" Alexis was astounded as she opened the box and saw a brilliant emerald cut diamond surrounded by bagets that extended along the band.

"Yes. You can, honey. If you are pregnant, we are going to do right by this baby that we made. And that begins by establishing a relationship immediately with our friends and family," he coerced her. Taking the ring out and placing it on her finger, he hushed her protest with a deep kiss. Bemused, Alexis stared at her hand while Mac jumped out of the car and went around to escort her up to the house.

"This home is beautiful, Mac," Alexis exclaimed as they headed up the sidewalk. "You never told me your family was well off."

"It never came up," Mac insisted gently. "Besides, my grandparents made the money by opening a chain of restaurants nationwide and the family has had good luck with it. I even have a nice trust fund from my grandparents already set up which I will turn over to my children. I plan on living on what I make and off investments I've done."

"Oh, that's nice," Alexis didn't know how to respond since it might be her child that would benefit from the trust.

He rang the bell and in a heartbeat the door whipped open, and a large gathering of people stood on the other side.

An older woman with silver/blonde hair took her by the arm and pulled her inside. She beamed widely and introduced everyone, "Hi there sweetie! I'm Nora MacDonald, mom to this young man that brought you…and this is Steve, his father. These are his brothers Mark and his wife Julia; Jason and his wife Maxine: Brent and his wife Carla and his sister Meredith. His brother Paul and wife Deb aren't here tonight."

As everyone took turns hugging her and kissing her on the cheek, she looked desperately around for help from Mac.

Mac extracted her from the arms of Brent and introduced her, "Mom, Dad, and everyone here…I'd like to introduce you to Alexis Saunders…my fiancée."

Everyone gasped in wonder and began to chatter. Meredith exclaimed, "My God, Mac! We were excited about you bringing a date home but this…"

His Dad declared at the same time, "We are so happy Mac finally found his perfect woman."

His Mom pronounced, "This calls for a celebration."

Brent remarked, "I never thought I'd see the day, old chum!"

The comments were deafening and Alexis was practically mauled with more hugs as Mac experienced the same fate.

"Okay, you guys, give Alexis a break. You are going to scare her off," Mac admonished and took her in his arms and with a laugh remarked to the glowing faces surrounding them, "Let's move inside and eat and be civilized."

The large family pushed through the vast hallway, past the curving stairs and into a large elegant dining room. As they began to take seats, Meredith squealed and grabbed Alexis' hand, "Oh, Mac, you've given her a beautiful ring. God, Mac! It must be two carats for just the center stone!"

All the women present surrounded Alexis before she was seated and admired her ring. Finally she was settled into a chair and was able to speak, "I'm overwhelmed by all of you and your taking me into the…uh…family this way. This was truly a…a…"

"I think what Alexis is trying to say is that your enthusiasm for us is overwhelming and how about giving us a break and we'll answer your questions later," he finished with a genuine laugh. "I love you guys, but as a group you are overpowering!"

Nora agree instantly, "You're right, Mac. Everyone sit down and I'll bring out the rest of the food."

Minutes later, everyone was seated and after a prayer, they began passing the food.

"What a wonderful celebration we're going to have," Steve remarked cheerfully as he uncorked a bottle of champagne. "Pass the glasses and we'll all have a toast."

As the glasses were passed around, Mac stopped his sister from picking up Alexis' glass, "Uh, Alexis won't be drinking tonight. I mean…she doesn't drink," he stammered and everyone looked curiously at the two of them.

"Of course, dear, no problem," his mom remarked and as Alexis looked up she saw a hint of real pleasure and gentleness in her eyes.

As the meal began, Alexis and Mac were inundated with questions. Mac decided the best tactic was to tell all.

"Alexis is an Assistant District Attorney. We've known each other a number of years and have been dating for quite some time." Mac come to a decision that it was best to stretch the truth so if a baby was in the works, everyone would be more settled with the idea of the two of them together. "I decided it was time to make Alexis an honest woman. Period. End of story."

"How did he propose?" Meredith questioned excitedly.

"In his car," Alexis replied truthfully as everyone groaned.

Mac's sister-in-law, Carla, chastised him, "I thought you would be more romantic than that Mac. No flowers or special dinner or special place?"

"Now wait a minute," Mac teased Alexis, "we've had some pretty good times in that car, haven't we!"

Alexis was mortified at his innuendo as his mom rebuked, "Mac, you shouldn't kiss and tell!"

Brent mocked, "I'll bet that Mac did more than just kiss!"

His dad interrupted, "Okay, every one, let's eat and behave."

Meredith wanted to know more details, "So do you know all about Mac's military past? Is that part of the reason you fell in love with him?"

"Actually, Mac doesn't talk about his past." Alexis glanced sideways at him. "Although we've known each other for about six years."

"We're very proud of him," his mom beamed and over Mac's protest began, "Mac graduated from M.I.T. then enlisted in the navy. He doesn't like to discuss it but he spent six years in Central America and Afghanistan. What did they call you dear, Special Ops? He was discharged from the service and was hired here at the police department."

"Okay, enough already," Mac growled.

The table talk turned to Alexis' job and she answered a multitude of questions. After dinner, they retired to the living room.

"So do you have the date picked out?" Julia asked expectantly.

Simultaneously Mac and Alexis answered.

"No...not...," Alexis squeaked.

"I was thinking fairly soon if...," Mac voiced firmly at the same time.

"Well," Mac's dad remarked and chuckled, "I guess we have a first argument coming."

"I need to go to the ladies room," Alexis had to get away to gather her composure so she stood up.

"I'll take her upstairs to my old room," Mac told the roomful. With that said Mac took Alexis' hand and led her upstairs. Once in his room he turned her to him.

"Mac," Alexis was agitated, "I don't like lying to your family. We have to stop this! We aren't really engaged so we need..."

Mac placed his finger against her lips to hush her, "As far as I am concerned, we are engaged. Remember, we have yet to use protection. We're not bringing a bastard into this world. We will legitimize this baby!"

Mac bent over and pulled Alexis tightly into his arms, kissing her with all the passion he had. His tongue swept into her mouth as he ground his hips against her. She sobbed and clung to him. Mac backed Alexis to the bed and fell on top of her. His hands worked swiftly to unbutton her blouse and unhook the front closure of her bra...

They both became aware of a knock on the door.

"Is everything all right?" Nora sounded concerned through the closed door.

"We'll be down in a minute, Mom," Mac leaned his forehead against Alexis, then kissed her gently on the lips. He slid down her body and cradled her belly with his hands as he kissed it through her clothes. He glanced upward at Alexis and offered a gentle smile. Alexis was bemused by the look in his eyes

Mac assisted Alexis with her unbuttoned blouse and together they returned to the family. All eyes were on them and the signs of their ardor couldn't be missed. Alexis blushed. Mac chuckled in embarrassment.

"Well now.." his dad began.

Alexis interrupted in haste, "I really should be going. I wasn't prepared to spend so much time away from my briefs. I'm in court tomorrow and need to get prepared. This was lovely meeting you all but I do really do need to cut this short."

Mac agreed, "I've got to get Lexi home so she can get some rest. We'll make arrangements to come back soon, I promise."

Everyone strolled to the door and after much hugging and kissing, they left.

During the drive home, Mac held Alexis' hand against his chest. They talked about the information given to them that day by Gérard.

"I was impressed by you today, as usual. You're a great prosecutor," Mac remarked casually. "All of the police force are enamored with your work and your presence. We're glad you're on our side now."

Alexis felt a thrill at his words. "Thanks, Mac. I really appreciate that."

As they pulled up at her condo, Alexis noted the car in front along the sidewalk. "What the hell...?"

"What's wrong?" Mac questioned briskly.

As she got out of the car, Alexis angrily replied, "That's Len Pretorius' car."

She hurried to the door with Mac at her heels only to find it unlocked. As she shoved open the door, Mac drew his weapon and pushed her behind him. The lights were on.

"Pretorius...Pretorius. Come out with your hands up! This is Detective MacDonald of the MPD!" Mac shouted as he held his 9mm Baretta with both hands.

"Whoa! Wait! It's Len!" He came out of the spare bedroom with both hands raised and a peculiar look on his face. "Don't shoot!"

"What the hell are you doing breaking and entering Alexis' home?" Mac's voice was terse.

Pretorius continued to walk closer. "I came to see you, Alexis, to talk to you and I found your door open."

He implored her. "I was afraid you were hurt inside so I came in."

"Stop right there, Pretorius, I'm arresting you for unlawful entry!" Mac started towards the man.

Alexis grabbed Mac's arm and begged him earnestly, "Wait, Mac, he was just worried. Leave it be. I don't want to press charges."

Mac peered into her face and resignedly put away his gun. "Get out of here, Pretorius and don't come back or I'll have Alexis press charges for harassment."

Len blustered, "Now wait, you can't do that. We know each other, we've…"

Mac seized Alexis' left hand and held it out before Len. "Yes I can. She's mine and I want you to leave her alone. No more contacts. Understood? We're engaged and it's final."

Glumly Pretorius nodded and turned to Alexis, "Congratulations, I guess. If you ever…"

"She won't!" Mac broke in. "Go!"

As the door closed behind Pretorius, Mac suggested, "Let's go look to see if anything is missing."

An hour later, Alexis went toward Mac, "I don't see anything gone but I think some of my papers have been looked through."

Mac nodded and replied, "Let's pay close attention over the next day or so and see if anything is missing."

Alexis went to the computer in the spare room and settled in, "I have some work to do. I'll be to bed later."

Mac went to the master bath and showered and climbed into bed thinking all the while that something was amiss. It was after midnight when he felt Alexis warm body curl into his and he held back a grin as his arms cuddled her. Things were working out well.

The Dade County Courthouse courtroom was filled to capacity the next day. Alexis approached the witness stand to interrogate Doug Spangler, a warehouse shipping clerk at the bogus front, A.C.E. Coffee LTD., a focal point for packaging and shipping the crystal Meth for Lager.

"Please tell us your name and what you do for a living." Alexis commenced.

The witness sat higher in his chair, all the while glancing nervously at Robert Lager. "Uh, Doug Spangler. Umm, I work in shipping. I'm a shipping clerk."

"Where do you work?" Alexis persisted.

"A.C.E. Coffee," he mumbled.

"Please speak up," Judge Masters encouraged.

"A.C.E. Coffee," he stated louder.

"Who is the owner of A.C.E. Coffee, Mr. Spangler?" Alexis questioned.

"I object, Your Honor, Mr. Spangler would be making an assumption," Ronald Handler, the defense attorney proclaimed.

"Your Honor, Mr. Spangler has worked at A.C.E. for a number of years. He should know who the owner is," Alexis protested.

"Overruled but rephrase your question, Counselor," the judge ruled.

"Thank you, Your Honor. Can you tell me who is the man who comes into A.C.E. and issues orders to all the people there practically every day? Is he in the courtroom?" Alexis finished.

Spangler pointed shakily to Robert Lager and answered in a low tone, "Right there…Robert Lager."

Alexis concurred with a nod and continued, "In the capacity of your job, what do you do?"

Spangler shrank in his seat and looked toward Lager, "I…I look over daily manifests and make sure we have the appropriate number of containers sealed and crated and ready for shipment."

"Where do these shipments go?" Alexis looked at the jury, waiting for an answer.

"Ah…all over the U.S. and some overseas," he acknowledged.

"Do you know what is in these containers Mr. Spangler?" Alexis questioned.

"I object, Your Honor. The prosecution is asking the witness for speculation," Handler stated loudly.

"Your Honor, Mr. Spangler has direct visual knowledge of the contents of these containers," Alexis objected.

"Overruled. You may continue, Ms. Saunders." Judge Masters concurred.

Spangler choked as he continued, "Eck…Um…crystal Meth."

"I object, Your Honor!," Ronald Handler again demanded. "He's not a chemist…"

"If you please, Your Honor, I will explain in the next question and answer," she pleaded.

"Overruled. Ms. Saunders, I have been patient…please finish with this line of questioning," the judge ordered.

"And how do you know this, Mr. Spangler?" she persevered.

"I…I was curious to what was in these containers of coffee and opened several cans, then hid them since I had opened them. Later I took them home to a buddy and asked what the packets were. I was told they were crystal Meth." he replied nervously.

"I object, Your Honor, the witness or his friend aren't chemists and wouldn't know," Handler blustered again.

"If you please, Your Honor, the prosecution can show cause and tie everything together in just a couple more questions," Alexis protested.

"Overruled. I'm giving you some latitude here, Counselor. Be careful." Judge Masters agreed.

"Whom did you take these packets to, Mr. Spangler?" Alexis continued.

"To a friend of mine, Sergeant Tim Walker of the Miami Police Department. He had it analyzed…" Spangler responded but was interrupted.

"I object, Your Honor. Mr. Spangler doesn't know what happened to the packets after giving them to the Sergeant. He wasn't there," Handler persisted.

The judge concurred with the attorney, "Sustained."

"Mr. Spangler, can you tell me if you opened containers just once, as an isolated instance, or more than once," Alexis inquired.

"I did this to six different shipments over a three week period. Sergeant Walker and a Detective Manuss asked me to," the witness enlightened.

"Why did you even look the first time in these containers, Mr. Spangler?" she queried.

"Well…I happened to see some accounting papers that were left on the top management's desk in Mr. Spangler's office one night when I worked late and had to have security let me in their office. I've been taking accounting classes for almost two years at Miami Technical College and the papers had me curious," he complied with the question.

Alexis pressed the witness hard now, "And what did these papers reveal?"

"Well, they were hand written accounting ledger papers for A.C.E. lying beside the actual A.C.E. ledger book only there were discrepancies. The one ledger showed transactions amounting to millions of dollars for solitary shipments and the other ledger showed only a small part of that money in transactions for the same shipments to the same places on the same dates."

"And this made you suspicious?" Alexis questioned.

"Yes, because I knew that no way could a shipment of coffee amount to those figures. On top of that, I could compare the opened ledgers and realize someone was fixing a second set of books." Spangler looked terrified now as he viewed the hardened angry face of Lager.

"I object, Your Honor, the witness has not been formally admitted into evidence as a person specializing in fixing the books," Ronald Handler once again protested.

"Sustained. The jury must disregard Mr. Spangler's view as to `fixing the books'," Judge Masters concurred. "Is that all, Ms. Saunders?"

"That's all, Your Honor," Alexis returned to her seat while the defense attorney approached the witness for cross-examination.

The courtroom drama continued throughout the day with a break for lunch while Ronald Handler tried to discredit the witness. By 4:30, when the judge recessed for the day, Alexis was feeling very good about the trial.

Alexis returned to her office where Mac found her about two hours later.

"Are you ready to leave?" Mac wanted to get some food because he hadn't eaten all day.

"Sure am," Alexis strutted over to Mac and took his arm as she chatted about the trial. She was in a great mood.

"Let's order in Chinese," Alexis suggested as they entered her condo and threw her purse and briefcase on a chair. As Mac agreed, she continued on to the bedroom. "Go ahead and call. Since it's early, I want to strip the bed and put clean sheets on it."

"You don't want to dirty them first?" he laughingly protested.

"They *are* dirty and I haven't had a chance to change them," she disregarded his suggestion and began stripping the bed. She pulled the bedding loose on one side and went to the other. After ripping the sheets off, she began to make it up with new. While pulling the fitted sheet under the mattress at the upper corner near the wall, she noted papers in a folder stuck down between the nightstand and bed. She pulled them out and began to browse through them.

"Oh my God!" she muttered to herself then called out loudly. "Mac, come here quickly!"

Chapter 9

Mac came charging into the bedroom, "What's wrong?"

"Look at these," she insisted as he sat beside her on the bed. "This was a folder of some case notes I haven't been able to find. Look at all these extra sheets of paper that don't belong to me."

As she leafed through several dozen sheets that looked to be from a ledger, she pointed to the scrawl at the bottom of each page, "What do you think this signature reads?"

Mac looked closely at several pages and looked directly at Alexis, 'It looks like its `C. Sirini'."

"That's what I thought too. It looks like this is an account ledger involving millions of dollars for some company called L & D or P," she concurred.

"Wow! This might tie in with his murder and it might be what your burglars were looking for. Lay the papers back in the folder and I'll take it to C.S.I. tomorrow for fingerprinting. They're going to need your prints to exclude but I'm assuming they're already on file," he contended.

"Yes they are," she agreed and handed him the file. Alexis stood and began to finish making the bed as the doorbell rang. "That must be the food. Let's go eat."

The evening continued with Alexis working on notes for the trial the next day. Mac made more phone calls and did some paperwork himself and cleaned up the kitchen. When bedtime came, Mac glanced up to find Alexis had fallen asleep on the coach where she was working. He strode over to her and looked at her tenderly. He wanted this woman so desperately in his life. He wanted a loving home and children and all the activities and outings that came with a family.

Mac bent over and lifted Alexis in his arms with her barely acknowledging the move. He carried her to the bed and pulled off her clothing. Removing his own garments, he laid down beside her and took her in his arms, pulling the bedding over them.

It was eight o'clock in the morning when Mac woke and realized they had both overslept. He leaned over Alexis and nuzzled her neck. Alexis didn't move. Mac reached across her and kissed her thoroughly as she began to wake up. Her eyes peeked open and she mumbled, "I'm too tired, Hon."

Mac almost laughed out loud. He was definitely progressing if she referred to him as `Hon'. "Hey sleepyhead, it's eight o'clock."

Alexis eyes popped open and she scrambled to the side of the bed. "Oh my God! I have to be in court at 10:00. I can't believe I slept this long! I never sleep past 5:30."

She ran into the bathroom naked and Mac followed while she quickly stepped into the shower. "Don't come near me Mac! I don't have time for fooling around."

Mac teased, "No `fooling' intended. I was planning some serious business here."

"I don't have…" Alexis was interrupted by Mac dropping his boxers and climbing in the shower too. She could feel her nipples hardening as she gazed at his tremendous physique.

"Here, let me wash you quickly to save time," and his hands cupped with soap began to move over her.

"Maaaac," she whimpered as his hands glided over her tender breasts and moved down and behind her to wash her buttocks. His hands moved between her and she felt fingers gliding over her womanhood. She couldn't help herself as she urged, "Please!"

Mac grabbed the shower nozzle and lowered it to rinse her off between the legs. He reached outside and grabbed a towel and began drying her off briskly. Lifting her to him, he stepped out and placed her on the countertop and they came together in passion.

Mac wanted her with everything thing that was in him, yet he foolishly left behind protection in his haste.

He muttered, "I have no condom…I'll need to go…"

"Mac, I want you now…now!" she implored and he granted her wish.

A short time later Mac looked intently upon her and remarked, "I'm sor…"

Alexis leaned forward and kissed him. "Oh Mac! I couldn't have stopped you because it's what *I* wanted, too."

Before he could continue, she had slid off the counter and scurried into the bedroom. "I really have to fly! I can't be late!"

They arrived at the courthouse with a half hour to spare. Mac watched her walk in before taking off to CSI. He was going to be busy trying to figure out just what those Sirini documents meant.

When Mac returned to the courtroom, it was mid afternoon. Ronald Handler was just finishing his rebuttal questioning of Spangler. Alexis called Lieutenant Tim Walker to the witness stand.

"State your name and what you do please," Alexis addressed Walker.

"Lieutenant Timothy Walker, Miami P.D." he replied earnestly.

"Do you have occasion to know Doug Spangler and in what capacity?" she questioned, turning toward the jury.

"He's been a longtime baseball coach for little league and I have had several nephews as well as two sons coached by him. He is also an elder of my church and works for various charities around town and heads a scholarship committee for those needing assistance," Walker mentioned.

"So would you say Mr. Spangler is a `pillar of the community`?" she inquired.

"I object, Your Honor. She's leading the witness." Handler began but the judge interrupted.

"Sustained," Judge Masters agreed.

Alexis corrected, "Can you tell us anything about Mr. Spangler personally?"

Walker nodded then, "Yes, he is well thought of by our congregation who voted him in as an elder. He is well liked by the children and parents as a coach as he allows all the kids to play and is gentle and encouraging with all. He is excellent at obtaining donations for our charities and allows several people to audit all the books to make sure everything is legal and aboveboard."

"Is he a wealthy man?" she wanted the jury to know.

"I object, Your Honor. How would the lieutenant know?" Handler rasped.

"Sustained," Masters agreed again.

"How does Mr. Spangler appear to live?" she persisted.

"In a modest home, drives two used vehicles, buys clothes at Kmart and other department stores," Walker answered. "I've been with him when he has made many purchases because our boys are friends."

"What happened on the night of September 21, 2004?" Alexis had set the stage and was ready for the technical questions.

"Doug... Doug Spangler called my house and asked him to meet me in the Jose' Marti' river front park at the concession stand. He handed me some coffee containers that held packets of a white substance. Doug told me he had gotten them at work and that there were hundreds going out in shipments every night. I opened a packet, sniffed then tasted a fingertip of the powder. I thought it was crystal Meth but I told him I would have it tested at CSI."

"And what did the test confirm and what did you do?" she looked directly along the jury members.

Walker looked at the jury and responded, "CSI confirmed it was crystal Meth and I contacted Detective Manuss. We then set up a meeting with Doug Spangler and made arrangements for him to get us more samples over the next week or so."

"That's all the questions I have for this witness, Your Honor," Alexis relinquished her position and returned to her desk.

Before Ronald Handler could cross-examine the witness, Judge Masters broke in, "I think we'll take a recess for the day and return tomorrow at 10 a.m. Thank you jury, and I'd like to remind you that you are not to discuss the case with anyone. We're adjourned for the day."

Alexis picked up her notes and began placing them in her briefcase, all the while sensing Lager's anger as he crossed in front of her. She glanced up as he mouthed the words `you're dead`. Alexis shivered as he continued on by and as Mac appeared beside her.

"What did he just mouth to you?" Mac was insistent.

"I think it was `you're dead`," she intended to be honest with Mac.

Mac was irate, "So help me God, if…"

"Mac just leave it be. He's in jail and I'm going to make sure he stays there," Alexis placed a hand on his arm to stay him.

"Let's go, We're going to dinner. I have some news for you after talking with Gérard. He's been trying to get in touch with you," Mac hastened her along.

Forty-five minutes later, they pulled up in front of a liquor establishment on the upper East side. "Danny's" flashed above the door. They entered an exterior entranceway and opened a door leading into a smoky, old-fashioned bar. People were lined up at the bar and sitting along two bars extending into the single room. Round Formica table tops edged in metal were scattered about and surrounded by metal and black leather chairs. It reminded Alexis of the `Danny's Grill` she had been in while visiting her college roommate, Stephanie, in northeast Ohio. There was a lot of laughter and comradery amongst the patrons as music filtered through the air. Local and state sports memorabilia filled the walls.

Alexis smiled and remarked as Mac led her to an open table, "This place is quaint. Just like a place in Ohio I used to visit. I think it was Philadelphia…no…New Philadelphia."

"It is nice. I'm starved! Let's order." A waitress had approached and took their order from a menu placard on the table.

"Now, what's up!" Alexis quizzed Mac.

"CSI confirmed fingerprints of Sirini on the papers, as well as an unidentified print. So we can justifiably say that they were Sirini's papers. We can't find an L & P company in Florida. We're now looking nationwide and elsewhere. Also, Gérard called me since he couldn't get in touch with you. He said he has been in contact with Santana Regas. Apparently she had contacted her friend, Jill Westman who then contacted him. Santana is in Mexico City and he went down to talk with her. She is terrified of Lager because he murdered José Alfonse in front of her. She was able to slip away from Lager in a pretext of shopping. She's afraid for her child who is still missing from her sister's in Bogotá, Colombia. She has already stated she won't come back to testify against Lager because of the child."

"We have to get the C.I.A. involved to find that child and bring back Regas to Miami. We'll need the F.B.I. to get her in witness protection for now and possibly the remainder of her days," Alexis ruminated. "We'll also have to act as if nothing is going on. We don't want to show our hand before we have all the evidence for a murder charge."

Their dinner arrived and they began to dig in. Mac continued along with some more information that stunned Alexis.

"Terrie D'Angelo is awake now and we believe she can identify her attacker," Mac's excited voice stilled the fork going to her mouth. "She said she wasn't in the Crystal Saloon the night of her attack but had met the man there before and left with him. She said she had come here to `Danny's` that night with girlfriends for a night out...she wasn't here to pick up a John. But the same guy approached and offered her a thousand dollars to leave with him so she did. All she got for her troubles was to be nearly killed and brutally raped. He never gave her the money because he thought she was dead. She's going to work with the sketch artist to work a composite sketch tomorrow."

Alexis was thrilled, "Things are coming along just fine! Oh, Mac! I would just love to put those two men behind bars for life!"

"Well, let's eat and check with the bartenders here to see if they know anything. Then we'll go home," Mac dug into his food with gusto.

The bartenders' candor was refreshing for a change. They were more than willing to talk about customers but none could remember someone who resembled the `Whisperer's` description. Mac and Alexis vowed to bring back a sketch after it was completed to try to jog their memory. They left and returned to her condo for the night. The long ride home in the night had exhausted Alexis. She collapsed on her bed where Mac found her sound asleep only a few minutes later. He removed her clothes once again and covered her. He went out to her computer to do work on the Internet, returning to bed several hours later.

Morning dawned dreary and rainy. Both Mac and Alexis slept in again. Frantic, Alexis begged Mac to make coffee and while he did so, she took a hasty shower, thus avoiding Mac joining her. Mac returned to the bedroom as Alexis was pulling on her satin underwear. She held a hand out to stop his approach and begged, "Please don't make love to me right now, Mac. I really have to get to the courthouse early!"

Mac laughed as he walked up to her with coffee, "Alright, Lexi, you've made your point. But I am taking a quick kiss."

With that, Mac gave her a drugging kiss.

"You are making a case for yourself. This could become addicting," she giggled like a schoolgirl.

"That's what I'm counting on," he smirked. They finished a quick cup of coffee and headed out the door.

Alexis had to almost run to the courtroom that morning. She sat quickly and in a matter of two minutes the bailiff called the court to order and Judge Masters appeared. Ronald Handler recalled Doug Spangler and the questioning began.

The day seemed endless to Alexis. At the lunch break, she went over to the annex and sat at her desk just looking at the various cases lying about on her desk. What was the connection? There seemed to be some ties here but she couldn't figure out what they were. Sharply at 2:15, Alexis scurried out of her office and headed to the courthouse. Defense Attorney Ronald Handler recalled Walker to the witness stand but Walker finished off in a positive tone for the prosecution. His testimony could not be shaken. Alexis was overjoyed at the results. She called her next witness to the stand, Tate Benson.

"State your name and occupation, please," Alexis instructed.

"Tate Benson," he practically growled. "Foreman at A.C.E."

"What does a foreman do at A.C.E.?" she was not going to tolerate his attitude.

Benson glowered at her and wouldn't look at the defendant, "A little bit of everything."

"Could you be more specific?" Alexis persisted.

"I load stuff!" he retorted.

Alexis pleaded with Judge Masters, "Your Honor, the witness is purposely being vague and hostile."

Judge Masters agreed, "Mr. Benson, you appear to be an intelligent man. I will hold you in contempt of court if you do not properly respond to the prosecution's questions."

Alexis tried again, "What are your responsibilities...in what area of the plant?"

Benson grudgingly replied, "I make sure all the skids are loaded correctly on the trucks."

"Define `skids`," Alexis would get something out of this man. They had made a deal for his testimony...he would not be prosecuted for his help in giving up information on the crystal Meth dealings.

"It's wood pieces or planks that you line up products on to keep them off the floor. It keeps together pieces of cargo for shipping," he mumbled but still loud enough.

"What is the cargo that is shipped at A.C.E.?" she continued.

"Cans of coffee," he answered sullenly.

"Have you ever seen exactly what is in each can of coffee?" please answer this honestly, she thought.

"Yeah, I...um...I also go with the boss to the packaging facility on Elm," he explained.

"This packaging facility on Elm...what precisely does it package and why don't we know about it?" she queried.

"It's in the slums. Well...um...only the boss and two others have keys to this place and only certain hired people work there. They package coffee," he stated hesitantly.

"Mr. Benson, have you seen anything besides the coffee being placed in these cans?" she wanted him to state what he promised.

"I object, Your Honor, the prosecution is trying to lead the witness into an answer," Ronald Handler was flustered.

"Overruled, answer the question, Mr. Benson," the judge ordered.

"Mr. Benson, have you seen anything besides the coffee being placed in these cans?" she repeated the question.

He finally admitted, "Yeah, I've seen them put packets in the coffee. The coffee hides the smell from D.E.A. dogs. It's crystal Meth."

"I object, Your Honor," the defense protested loudly.

"Sustained," Judge Masters agreed. "The jury will disregard the referral to a particular drug by the witness."

Alexis changed her tactics, "Mr. Benson, who is the `boss' at A.C.E. that you refer to?"

Benson took a long moment before he answered as Alexis held her breath. "Robert Lager…that man in the defendant's chair."

"And what did Robert Lager tell you was in those packets?" please, she thought, please answer truthfully.

"He said it was crystal Meth," he had come through for the prosecution.

"Is there any other way you know the packets contain crystal Meth?" she asked gently.

"Yeah, Lager used to give me some packets for my own use and to sell for money," he continued. "He did this so I would bring in illegals to work at both factories. It was my payment."

"I'm done with the witness for now, Your Honor," Alexis returned to her seat as the defense attorney began his questioning.

At some point during the remainder of the afternoon, Alexis became aware of Mac returning to the courtroom. At one point he grinned as she looked over her shoulder.

The trial ended for the day as Judge Masters called for the return to session for Monday morning.

Alexis gave a deep sigh of relief. She would have a three day weekend to relax and sleep.

"By the way, Ms. Saunders, I couldn't help but notice the ring on your finger. Congratulations! Who's the lucky man?" Calvin was speculative.

Mac was suddenly smiling beside her with an arm draped around her waist, "That would be me! And I certainly agree that I'm lucky!"

Calvin shook his hand and looked crestfallen, "Well, you know there's going to be many an unhappy man in these buildings." He apparently was making it known that he was included in the group.

"Well, thanks, Calvin...I'll see you on Monday," with that said, Alexis grabbed her briefcase and Mac escorted her out of the building to his car.

Mac and Alexis stopped at a steak and seafood restaurant on their way home. She hadn't had the heart to tell Mac that she just wanted to go home to sleep. As the maître d' escorted them through to a back room, Alexis heard loud laughter and what she thought was her father's booming voice.

"Oh, hell!" she muttered to herself then turned toward Mac. "Don't tell me...Mac?"

"It's okay, sweetheart," he clasped her right hand and led her into the room where her sister, brother, parents and all of Mac's family sat. He leaned toward her and whispered in her ear, "My mom set this up. She contacted your mom about an engagement party. I wasn't to tell you and I couldn't put them off."

"Hi, everyone! I got the bride-to-be here and on time," Mac proclaimed loudly and laughed. He ushered her to the center of three tables aligned in a `U' and pulled out her chair.

Alexis peered about the room and was stunned by this surprise. She couldn't utter a word. She noted that even Ben and his wife and Betty and her date were there.

"Uh...I think we've left her speechless!" her dad exclaimed and he got up from his chair and walked over to her and gave her a hug and kiss. It was like a dam opening as the flood of people encompassed her area and delivered kisses, hugs, and well wishes.

As everyone eventually settled back in their chairs, Alexis finally found her voice.

"I can't believe this. I am amazed you could put this together so quickly. I mean, we have only been..."

Mac interrupted her, "She means we are thrilled to have you all here to celebrate our impending marriage. I have two glasses of champagne in front of us. Why don't we raise them and toast to my lovely bride!"

Bemused, Alexis took the glass that Mac offered her and sipped from it as everyone chanted `here, here'.

Mac's brother Paul whom she just met offered another toast, "May you have a very happy, healthy and prolific life together to take the pressure off the rest of us."

They all raised their glasses and `cheer' and `here, here' was offered by all as Alexis practically choked on her drink.

Chatter broke out as the men teased Mac and the women asked questions about a wedding date and babies. Finally, after about fifteen minutes of endless questions, the waitresses appeared and began to take orders. Alexis had gotten a reprieve from the questioning.

Mac leaned and whispered in her ear again, "I'm sorry I couldn't tell you. They just called this morning to surprise us. I thought it better not to warn you in advance in case you tried to avoid this."

"Mac, what are we going to do?" Alexis wailed softly in his ear.

"You're going to marry me and live happily ever-after," he whispered back and showed his devilish grin.

The evening wore on as delicious food was delivered and consumed at the table. Toasts were made again and again and Mac became more audacious as the taunts and laughter flowed. He was encouraged to steal blood-curdling kisses from Alexis and even she had to laugh at the high spirits and outlandish behavior from everyone.

The infectious mood began to make Alexis weary. How long could she keep up the pretense to her family and friends and Mac's as well? These were dear people at the table whom she did not want to hurt. What if there was no baby? Would Mac's relationship falter? She was lost in thoughts about waking up without Mac at her side when his voice interrupted...

"Hey, sweetheart...uh, Lexi..." Mac startled her into the present. "Hey guys, I think I'm going to call it a night for the two of us. Lexi seems to be in la-la land."

"Maybe you can get a wedding date out of her in this weakened state," Meredith chimed in as everyone laughed.

Alexis blushed as Mac pulled her toward the exit, "Well, I guess I'll see you later," she responded and smiled at these lovely people.

Alexis leaned her head on Mac's shoulder as they headed home. Neither talked as romantic music came softly through the speakers. Alexis dozed off but excitement kept her from a deep sleep. As they pulled up to the condo, she woke easily and Mac escorted her to the door and through her home to the bedroom. The both stripped quickly and got under the covers, lying face to face. Mac's hands glided over her face as he pressed tender little kisses all over. Alexis suddenly clutched his head and stopped his mouth as she thrust her tongue deep within his. Mac responded with a groan and pulled her tightly against him as she sighed in content. They remained cuddled throughout the night.

Chapter 10

Alexis felt great the next morning. She had her energy back and felt like eating. Up before Mac at 5:30, she did some workout routines in the living room. Returning to the bedroom, she crossed over to where he was lying asleep on his stomach. He looked so manly with a shadow of a beard and his bare torso exposed down to his hips. She hesitated briefly then decided to hit the shower. Alexis was able to bathe and dress and make it to the kitchen before she was aware of someone stirring in the bedroom.

She yelled down the hall, "What do you want for breakfast?"

"Eggs I guess…anyway you want to make them!" he hollered back. "Keep it light 'cause I'm not feeling up to par today."

Alexis cooked scrambled eggs and threw some bacon in the microwave for herself. Within five minutes, Mac was lumbering in, freshly showered, jeans on, and drying his hair with a towel.

"God! I am tired today and a little bit sick at my stomach," Mac proclaimed.

Alexis looked at him closely. "You do look pale. Why don't you go back to bed and sleep."

"Yea, I feel like I could sleep all day," Mac shook his head as he sat, "but I can't. I have some witnesses I want to question on Monday and I want to have some notes in order."

"Sit down then," she offered as she set his plate in front of him. "Maybe you need some food in your stomach."

She sat as well and while Mac picked at his food. She scarfed down a plateful.

"What's on your agenda for today?" Mac questioned.

"I would really like to go back to the office and get some calls in and see if we've been able to get any assist on bringing Regas and her kid back from Mexico and Columbia from the C.I.A. or F.B.I. I need to call Gérard again." Alexis picked up the plates and rinsed them off.

"Why don't you start calling from here while I check some things out on the computer. I can access my official line from here. Then we'll go to your office." He went to the second bedroom and got down to work.

Alexis dialed Gérard who answered immediately.

"Got any news for me?" Alexis was all business. She had to get a break in just one of these cases.

"I was going to call you today at home," Jim Gérard assured her. "You'll find this very interesting. I met with Mac about Carson Klein and I have a call into Mac about the investigation he ordered."

"Wait a minute and I'll get Mac on the other line," she hurried to the bedroom and told him to pick up a phone. As soon as Mac was on another line, Alexis ordered, "Go ahead, we're listening."

"I went to Fort Lauderdale to talk with Carson Klein and his attorney. He hadn't been very forthcoming to the detectives Mac sent to interview him previously. I put some pressure on him...told him he was going to loose everything he had, including his freedom if the police were able to put together any ties with him and the guy who stole his car. I inferred that he could be tied to attempted murder and if anything happened to you in the future...possibly murder. He freaked out. I told him if he knew anything, he should come forward because the prosecutors might cut him a deal. He immediately jumped on it but I told him he had to tell me all he knew before I sent in the police and the D.A. to make any offers." Gérard paused. "Klein was making monthly trips to Miami to meet with Daniel Bachman. They met at an unoccupied suite of offices on the third floor of your ex-office building. It was usually Bachman, Eric Thompson, himself, and a guy that kind of stood there but didn't say anything. He only was there a couple of times and no one introduced him. He said they all used a private elevator to the floor and that they came from the back parking lot. He doesn't think anyone ever saw them together."

"Can he identify the third person now?" Mac questioned.

Gérard immediately answered, "No, he didn't look at him enough to get a sketch artist to work with him and draw the face, but he said he could recognize the man in a picture or in person. I told him if a deal was cut and we'd bring him in for questioning, then we'd have him look at the books. Anyway, he said it was Thompson who asked him to leave a car out the night his was stolen. All Thompson told him was that he had a friend that might have need of it and if it was gone when he got up the next day, he should report it stolen."

"Why did he wait so long to report the missing vehicle?" It was Alexis' turn to question.

"Klein was scared when he woke up and found the car gone. He said he just didn't want to be involved, but his wife made him call…she threatened to call it in herself when a day had passed," Gérard explained. "Then later when he found out it was used to run you off the road, he's been doubly frightened. That's why he and his wife left for a vacation to Italy shortly after questioning."

"So I have nothing if there were no witnesses to the meetings," Alexis was thoughtful.

Jim Gérard halted her musings. "Wait…listen to this. Klein says he's always been leery of Bachman because he's shafted a few people in business from what Klein had heard. So after the first couple months, Klein said he started carrying a mini recorder in his pocket."

Mac was enthusiastic about the news. "Does he have tapes we can have and are they protected?"

"Yep," the P.I. chirped. "He said his wife mailed them to someone reputable and they would be turned over to the police in the eventuality of their deaths. But get this. We have a real connection here to Charles Sirini. I guess that both Bachman and Thompson used Sirini to doctor their books and they are the ones who turned him on to Klein to start doing his books."

"Why did Klein even get involved with Bachman or Thompson?" Alexis shivered with excitement.

"Remember, he's an entrepreneur and his dealings over the last year and a half were composed mainly of real estate deals involving Bachman and his cohorts. He had lost a lot of his money in the stock markets over a two year period before he met Bachman and was trying to get back his wealth. This seemed the easiest way and...after all, he and his wife were used to running with the affluent and he wanted to stay in that elite crowd. He was able to give me a list of seven transactions with Bachman including state and local building projects," Gérard finished.

Mac couldn't say enough praises to Gérard for all his hard work in getting this valuable information. "Hey, buddy, I owe you big time. If we have Klein to testify as well as those tapes, it'll pretty much be a done deal in taking down Bachman."

Alexis interrupted, "Wait a minute. Yes, we can probably make a case but will it stick? After all, Klein is a man who had lost a lot then was making a comeback with Daniel Bachman's assistance. He could be thought of as disgruntled for something that perhaps Bachman had done to him? Will the tapes be enough? The defense might be able to refute his testimony?"

"Not if we can find that unidentified third person in the room in those meetings." Mac added, "Or...if we can get Eric Thompson to turn *against Bachman* to get a lighter sentence on his charges or future charges. After all, we do have testimony from Thompson's ex-girlfriend of his graft in office and how he profits by getting projects for Bachman pushed through special committees."

"Yes, and we'll need to see if we can locate the whereabouts of Sirini's accounting office or the actual books he did for Thompson and Bachman," Alexis concurred. "This would go a long way in putting both behind bars."

Gérard signed off with, "I'll see if I can find out anything further on Sirini or the location he worked out of. Take care you two."

Mac and Alexis met in the hallway. They embraced each other with a hug and Mac, though wan, smiled.

"Why don't you go and lie down while I do some work." Alexis urged Mac down the hall into the bedroom where she pushed him on the bedspread. "Sleep, Mac."

Alexis opened her briefcase in the spare room and began working at the computer desk and making phone calls. Throughout the day she looked in on Mac's sleeping form but left him alone. She decided not to go into the office until the following day.

Shortly after eight in the evening, Mac woke up and entered the living room where she was sprawled on the sofa with legal briefs surrounding her. She peeked up at him as he entered and Mac noticed a decided difference in her demeanor. She appeared somewhat distraught and thoughtful.

She gave a slight smile. "Feeling better?"

"Yes." Without delay, he strode over and sat beside her. Taking her hands he inquired, "What's up, babe? You look like you've lost your best friend."

Alexis pulled her hands away and stood facing him. She twisted the ring on her finger. "Mac, I...well I have something to tell you. There's no need to carry on this fake engagement. What I mean is..."

Alexis turned away, unable to continue for a moment. "You see. There is no pregnancy. I started my period."

Mac jumped off the sofa and walked in front of her, staring her in the face. "The pregnancy issue isn't a *concern*. So what if you're not pregnant. We should still get married. We're greatly attracted to each other. We admire and respect what we both stand for. I *care* for you and I believe you care for me. These are all reasons to keep our engagement. Besides, you still need protection."

Alexis pulled away from his outstretched hands.

Mac was getting royally pissed off at Alexis' conduct as she continued. "I didn't say you couldn't protect me. Go ahead. Stay. But I don't think we should continue this affair. We hardly know each other and got into this intimate relationship too fast."

Alexis picked up some papers and headed into the second bedroom. "I also wanted you to know that I called my father and had him arrange for me to get a new car on Monday. I hate you having to be locked into picking me up and taking me daily to work."

"You can't drive alone. I insist I be with you." Mac was adamant.

"We'll compromise, Mac. I'll drive my car to and from work and you can follow me. If by chance you do get tied up on something to do with all your cases, then I'll have the ability to come home on my own. Since you'll probably rarely let this occur, nothing should happen to me because most of the time you'll be with me." Alexis thought this sounded like a good plan.

Mac apparently didn't. "I don't like this Alexis...but I see by the set of your jaw and the obstinate look in your eyes that I'm not going to be able to talk you out of this stupidity. We'll leave it alone for now but *we will* talk about all of this again soon."

As she sat at her desk and Mac answered his cell phone, Alexis was aware of such severe depression. When she had gone to the bathroom a short time before she had noted a slight amount of blood on the tissue. She was disconsolate...there would be no baby for her and Mac. And as strong as their lust was for each other, this was no reason to base a marriage on it.

Alexis retired early that night, asking Mac to please use the other bedroom. He complied with her wishes but didn't sleep well with her in the other room.

Alexis rose early again to get in a workout. She showered and dressed in another gray smart suit and entered the kitchen. Mac was already there and making eggs for their breakfast. He still looked pale but greeted her with a smile.

"Hey there," he remarked. "I wasn't sure what to fix but I thought eggs would be good."

"Sounds fine, Mac. How do you feel?" She was going to be pleasant whether her heart was breaking or not.

"I feel kind of weak but otherwise `fine'." Mac continued to scramble the eggs and put them on two plates. "When do you get your car delivered?"

"I'll have to ride with you to the courthouse today...they're delivering the car there to the garage." She took a bite of the eggs and continued, "I should be able to leave..."

Alexis was interrupted by the phone ringing. She lifted the nearby phone off its cradle and replied, "Saunders."

Alexis listened and answered with a few succinct words and hung up.

Turning to Mac she explained, "Court is cancelled for today and indefinitely. The judge's daughter had an emergency appendectomy and bowel resection. I guess the judge has to fly out to Utah to help her out. They'll get back to us about resuming the trial in a day or so."

"What will you do?" Mac queried.

"Work on other cases and see if the feds have anything yet on Santana Regas and her daughter. I'd love to be able to file murder charges on Lager before this trial is finished." Alexis walked out to the hallway and picked up her briefcase from where she had left it the night before. "Leave the dishes, Mac. Are you ready to go?"

Mac had followed Alexis and as she turned to him, he nodded his assent. "Let's go, I'm ready. But before we go out that door I'm going to insist on something. You are to continue wearing my ring for everyone to see. That should deter people trying to get to you if they think we're together all the time in a relationship."

"Fine, Mac. And I guess for the sake of the families who just had a party for us we should continue to let them think we're still engaged." Alexis was thinking that this would give her an opportunity to keep Mac by her side. She just couldn't imagine not being with him. Lying in his arms at night, conversing about their daily lives, and eating intimate dinners together had given her a feeling of completeness that she had never experienced in her life.

Mac dropped Alexis off and after making sure she was inside, he went to the precinct. He immediately contacted Eric Thompson and told him he wanted to meet with him. Mac called into Alexis' office and left a message that he had Thompson coming in at two in the afternoon the next day. Next call went to Gérard who was not in the office. Mac left a message there and went down to the CSI lab.

"Any connection noted yet on the rape/murders here and around Florida with the Terrie D'Angelo case?" Mac questioned the technician named Sam Jameson.

"We found a hair from the Clearwater victim that was clutched in her hand to have the same DNA as the blood in the mouth of Terrie D'Angelo from when she apparently bit her victim," Jameson replied. "There's been no hit, however, with the national DNA bank of known criminals. We also have three of the victims who apparently fought and have some threads of old rope found on their tops along the sleeves near the wrists."

Mac frowned, "That doesn't make any sense. I mean about the DNA bank. A murderer and rapist doesn't just begin to commit crimes without any priors."

Jameson responded quickly, "We have no prints on this guy at any of the murder scenes. All we have is similar MOs. You know, prostitutes, the drugging, sand from the beach although the bodies are found in town, and some old rope fibers that connects three of the cases."

"The guy gives these hookers a date rape drug after meeting them at a bar. Perhaps he hires them out once for sex and then waits until the second date to rape and possibly murder them." Mac was thoughtful. "He always takes them to the beach to do it then drops them off in town in an alley. He's probably tied them all up at the wrists but only those awake and fighting have resulting fibers on them. Thanks Jameson, I'm going upstairs to make some calls."

Mac entered the office of Dick Rumswell, the precincts computer geek. "Hey, Dick, any news on the company I asked about, L & D or L & P?"

"I've looked everywhere known for that company and can't locate anything except a large cattle operation in Oklahoma that seems real legitimate and a flag company in Ohio that seems reputable as well. Nothing else is showing up anywhere in the U.S."

Rumswell looked steadily at Mac, "Okay, by the look on your face you want me to look overseas too. Gotcha! I'll get right on it."

Mac grinned as he pivoted and peered over his shoulder at the man. "You know me so well, Rumswell!"

Mac returned to his desk and called down to Jameson, "I've been thinking. Why don't you contact the Pentagon and see what we can get from them. Use the chief's name and see if we can get into their computer banks to run DNA on military men on file. If there's a problem, call me and I'll see if my former connections can get me answers."

"It might take me awhile but I'll try," Jameson countered.

"That's all I can ask. In the mean time, I'll let the chief know what you're doing." Mac hung up and headed into his boss' office.

The morning passed quickly for Alexis. She contacted the lawyer of record for Carson Klein and told him they would be willing to work out a deal if he would come in and give testimony against Bachman. She left a message for Gérard to call her to see if he had located Manny Contini, the cousin of Charles Sirini to see if he could give any more information on Sirini. Paperwork took Alexis through the lunch hour which was interrupted by a call from Ben Griffin.

"I need to see you in my office now," he commanded.

Alexis was swift in gaining entrance to Ben's office. As she closed the door, she noted two men in tailored suits lounging in leather seats.

"Sit down, Alexis," he waved a hand toward a high back chair. "This is Quinn and Carlony. These men are from the FBI."

Alexis nodded toward the two with anticipation making her sit up straight with her hands curled in her lap.

Ben continued, "The FBI is here to inform us that through a joint effort with CIA operatives, they've located and absconded Santana Regas' child from his capturers and are holding him in custody in a safe house in Houston. Regas herself is proceeding there with FBI assistance and will be there in two days time."

Alexis leaned forward anxiously, "How soon can we get her here for a deposition?"

"That might not be possible for a while," Quinn, the taller and older of the two gentlemen interrupted. "She's under witness protection and probably won't be returning to Florida any time soon."

"But we need her testimony in order to bring Lager up on murder charges!" Alexis protested.

"Then you'll have to get her testimony at her secret location. We can't have her position compromised." Quinn was firm about this point of contention.

"Okay, I can understand that. I can offer up her written testimony to the grand jury but she'll have to actually return for testimony at the regular trial." Alexis waited with baited breath for his reply.

"All right," the younger man, Carlony, conceded. "But I can't give you a date for you to depose her yet. We'll have a lot of arrangements to make in order to guarantee her safety. We'll get back to you."

The men stood and briefly shook hands with Ben and Alexis and walked briskly out of the room.

Alexis threw her hands up in the air in victory and shouted with glee then raced over to Ben and hugged him. "Oh my God! Can you believe this? We're going to be able to get Lager on murder charges!"

"Settle down, Alexis," Ben cautioned. "We have to get all our ducks in a row. And we need to keep this secret. No one can know what we're in the process of doing. Understand?"

Alexis nodded somberly. "I'll go now and dig up what we do know about the José Alfonse murder."

"You do that, Alexis but don't let down on our case against Lager for crystal Meth trafficking and distribution." Ben waved his hand and Alexis exited his office.

Walking down the hallway Alexis made a detour to the ladies room, then picked up a soda from the pop machine. Opening the door to her office, she went rigid with surprise to see the visitor behind her desk looking out the window.

"What are you doing here, Len?" Alexis made no move to fully enter the room.

"Now, don't get huffy, Alexis," Pretorious soothed. "I just came here to apologize for any problems I may have caused you and MacDonald."

"Why would you think you have caused any problems?" Alexis was puzzled.

"MacDonald seems to get ticked off every time I'm around you. You two seem to be an item now and I don't want to interfere with this." Len was glancing about the office.

Alexis was perturbed. "You overestimate yourself Len. You and I had no relationship *thus* you can't possibly interfere between Mac and me. Just leave me alone and don't bother coming around. That's all I ask. Now please go, I have work to do."

Len came from behind the desk and walked past her. The expression on his face was one of barely controlled fury. She held her breath. Alexis had never seen Len behave this way. It was almost frightening to behold. As she closed the door behind him, she exhaled slowly and headed to her desk.

Suddenly her phone rang, startling her from her reverie. She picked it up and answered, "Saunders."

Mac's voice pulled her back to the present. "Alexis, did you get my message about the meeting with Thompson?"

"I did, Mac, tomorrow will be fine. Anything else?"

"Yes, we're getting some DNA matches with two of the murders in Florida but nothing is matching in the national database so I'm having CSI check with the military. This might take a while, however. I'll go over the evidence with you this evening. Also, we've been unable to locate L & D or P in the U.S. I'm having someone check overseas for a company by that name," Mac finished brusquely. "What time do you think you'll be ready to leave today?"

Thinking of all the information she had acquaint herself with regarding the Alfonso murder, she decided to make it a late night. "It well probably be late… maybe eightish. Is that alright?"

"That sounds fine, Alexis. Just make sure you don't leave until I come into the building to get you." Mac signed off and hung up.

Later that evening Mac arrived at the annex to follow Alexis home in her new red Mercedes convertible. Upon arriving at the condo, Mac parked beside her and teased, "Well, I must say, you are easy to spot on the highway now. The cops will be looking for speeding when you're in that car."

"Yeah, you're probably right. This is rather neat isn't it? My dad ordered this fully loaded. It even has a GPS system in it."

Alexis smiled. "This reminds me of a car my dad had when I was young that he used to let me drive before I even turned sixteen. I used to have a blast driving all over our estate."

"Why you little hellion!" Mac took in the interior of the vehicle. "Here you are upholding the law when you used to break it regularly."

Alexis giggled as she walked away. "Now wait a minute. Driving before I had a license is the only illegal thing I've ever done."

Mac disagreed, "Honey, you are a walking advertisement for `illegal` if I ever saw one!"

Entering the condo, Alexis dropped her briefcase and purse and headed toward the kitchen.

"How about toasted cheese sandwiches and a salad? I want to eat and get out of these clothes and relax while you tell me all you learned about my cases today." Alexis removed a pan and began assembling food, not expecting Mac to object to the menu.

"Sounds good to me." Mac headed toward the bedroom. "I'm going to get cleaned up."

They ate quickly after Mac cleaned up, then Alexis went to her room and hastily showered and changed into a tank top and shorts. Back in the living room she took papers out of her briefcase and began jotting down notes. As Mac walked into the room, she put them aside and demanded, "Okay, shoot. What did you find out today."

As Mac went over the details of his day, a small part of her mind was occupied elsewhere. She had a niggling suspicion that she shouldn't tell Mac about what happened in her day. Better not tell him about Santana Regas and her son being in U.S. custody. He might object to her leaving town to depose her. Better not tell him about her visit from Len Pretorious either. After all, he had threatened him with bodily harm the last time they had met up at her condo.

When Mac finished, he waited for her to respond or ask questions. When she didn't he looked at her, puzzled. "What's going on, Alexis? You're awfully quiet."

"Nothing." She found it difficult to look him squarely in the eyes. "I'm just trying to take in all that you've told me."

Mac glanced at her, suspicion foremost on his mind. "I see. Well, any progress on your end of the cases?"

Alexis prevaricated, "Not really. I made some phone calls today but I have to wait for return calls."

Mac questioned, "From whom?"

Alexis could honestly answer that, "Well, Gérard for instance."

"I'm waiting for his call back too." Her simple answer seemed to satisfy him.

Alexis worked on cases that evening as Mac relaxed and watched television. Occasionally, she would feel Mac's eyes upon her but refused to look back. Both turned in early that night with Mac giving a chaste kiss on her forehead as they turned in to their respective bedrooms. Alexis had desperately wanted to press close to Mac as his lips touched her forehead but she did not want to force him into an intimate relationship again. If they came together again, it would be because they both desperately wanted each other and wanted some kind of commitment.

The remainder of the week progressed rapidly, with little or no new information. For Alexis, court was still adjourned, the feds still hadn't contacted her regarding Santana Regas for getting testimony, Carson Klein's attorney still hadn't been able to work the deal he wanted for his client, and Gérard left a brief message for Mac (not Alexis) telling him that he was in New York trying to find Contini again. Mac's week was just as fruitless. Thompson cancelled his meeting with Mac and Alexis for Tuesday, CSI hadn't been able to reach the right people in the Pentagon to get a possible DNA match, and they still couldn't locate a company called L & D or L & P. All in all, they were both feeling irritated and this frustration continued throughout the weekend. They did little talking and instead, watched TV, shopped for groceries, and went to a movie thriller.

Neither was happy about the way the last week or so had gone by. Except for the brief kiss on the forehead Monday night, the only touching that took place was when Mac assisted her out of the car or through a door. Both felt bereft of emotion yet neither made a move to change the situation.

Chapter 11

Monday dawned bright and warm and after exchanging polite conversation, Alexis and Mac headed to work in their respective cars. Mac paused briefly on 2nd Street behind Alexis as she turned in to the parking garage. As soon as she was inside, he pulled back in traffic and headed to the police station.

Alexis was in her office for an hour when a knock on the door startled her. Before she could respond the door was pushed open and the two FBI men she had met days earlier stood before her.

The younger man, Carlony, was curt, "If you want to question Santana Regas you're going to have to come with us now."

Alexis stood and gathered her belongings. "Great! We can stop in to see Ben and go to my condo so I…"

Quinn was just as short, "No. We leave directly now. We'll call Griffin when we're in the air."

"But…" Alexis was interrupted again.

"I'm sorry, Ms. Saunders, but if you want to get testimony you'll have to do it our way. Remember, she's under federal protection now." Quinn waited patiently for her response.

"Right." Alexis picked up her purse and case. "I understand. Let's go."

Alexis was whisked out the door with the two gentlemen on either side. She did receive some curious looks as she passed people in the hall. Even George, of security looked at her questioningly and asked her if she was all right. Noting that George had put his hand on his jacket where he kept his gun, Alexis reassured him that she was fine. The two FBI men only smirked at the ploy and didn't seem fazed by the security man's action.

She climbed inside a dark sedan in the parking garage as the men peered about them for anything unusual. They left the garage and headed to the airport. Alexis was taken through a security door and through the airport to the area from where private airplanes leave. Guided to the tarmac, she was led to an unidentified plane and assisted on board. Taking one of the six leather plush seats inside, she was instructed to put on her seat belt and within minutes they took off. The trip took 3 ½ hours to Houston and Alexis closed her eyes and relaxed during the flight. Neither of the men had been inclined to talk except when they offered her a drink.

Upon landing in Houston, they escorted her to a rather tacky hotel called The Hasty Inn and checked themselves into two side by side rooms. After asking Alexis what she wanted to eat, Carlony told her it would be brought to her room.

Alexis became disturbed. "Now wait a minute. I'm in some crappy hotel and I'm apparently not allowed to go outside. I have no clothes or nightwear and not even a toothbrush and comb. How long am I here for and when do I see Regas?"

Carlony smiled briefly. "Sorry, but you can't go outside until tomorrow and that's when we'll take you to Regas."

"We'll get you some toiletries and nightwear and whatever else you want. Just tell us." Quinn stood up and got a piece of paper. He walked over to Alexis and handed her the paper to write on.

Alexis gave them both a glare but wrote down what she needed. She decided to add lightweight sweats and sports bra and underpants to the list. She might as well make one of these men a little bit embarrassed by making them purchase women's unmentionables. As Quinn glanced at the list he walked over to Carlony and handed it to him with a smile.

"I've got seniority. You go." And with that he laughed out loud.

Carlony just gave Alexis a wry glance and left the room. She thought that perhaps these two might actually have a sense of humor.

Later that night and alone in her room, Alexis wondered what Mac was doing now. She did not want him worrying about her, and she was sure he would be as soon as he found her gone. Would he have contacted Ben Griffin in order to find out what had happened to Alexis? Would he be livid because she had not called him first before leaving? The thought of what he must be going through, made her ill just thinking about it. She wanted desperately to call him, but Quinn had told her she could contact no one. With thoughts racing through her head, Alexis fell into a restless sleep.

The weather was beautiful in Houston the next day. Alexis was agitated, yet excited about meeting Regas. She paced her room in the lightweight jump suit as she waited for Quinn and Carlony to get her. About an hour had passed before there was a knock at her door. Carlony called out to her to open the door. As she opened it, she noted they were both checking out the surroundings.

Driving through Houston they zoomed in and out of traffic and down narrow alleys. After a half an hour on the road they pulled into the drive of a modest two-story home. Leaving the car, they approached the door and knocked. Several minutes went by before the door creaked open.

A long-haired bearded man in jeans waved them in and showed them into the living room. Another balding man and a Latino woman sat watching television and conversing. Quinn introduced everyone and Alexis asked Santana Regas to join her in the kitchen.

Alexis pulled out her legal pad and a small tape recorder as she and Regas sat at the table. Alexis began her interrogation in her most soft and coaxing tone.

"I'm the Miami Assistant D.A., Alexis Saunders. I understand this is difficult for you. I hope you're comfortable here and feel safe and secure. I am assuming your child is here with you." As Santana nodded an affirmative, Alexis continued. "I will start asking you questions and just answer them as honestly as you can. I'll be taping this conversation for accuracy. I will only be taking notes, this is no legal deposition at this point. We will have to do that with the court stenographer at another time. Can you tell me about your relationship with both Bob Lager and José Alfonse?"

"José Alfonse is the father of my son." Santana answered slowly with a thick Spanish accent but using good English. "We were together a year in Bogotá, Colombia, before I got pregnant with my son. José did drugs and often got violent with me. I put up with this for about a year before I was able to secure passage to the U.S. I left my son with my sister until I could afford to bring him to the U.S. I was working at a bar in Miami when I met Bob Lager. He was kind to me and bought me clothes and got me a decent apartment. He never hurt me, but I had seen him get angry with many men that came to his place. We were together for over two years when José found me. He said he still loved me and wanted me with him, but I refused to go."

"What happened then?" Alexis asked as she jotted notes.

"José followed me and begged me to come back. This went on for about six months but I was afraid to tell Bob that José was in Miami. Bob knew something was wrong, but he didn't figure out what at first. Then José told me that my son Pedro was no longer with my sister, and that he could guarantee his passage here. But I had to go back to José in order to get my son back. What could I do? I was desperate to have my son in my arms." Santana began to cry.

"But Alfonse did not bring your son to Miami," Alexis made a statement.

"No. I had to go back living with José before he would bring him here." Santana dabbed at her eyes with a napkin from the table. "I left my apartment and moved in with José without telling Bob. We lived in a shack on the outskirts of Miami for…I think it was three months. José kept promising me that Pedro would be here soon. He drank, did cocaine and got so high that he began beating me again. When he broke my nose, about a week before he was killed, I went back to Bob's place and told Bob why I had left."

"How did Bob react?"

"He was furious! He promised me he would take care of me and get my son into the United States. He had always been so kind to me and made me feel secure. I trusted him. Maybe I even loved him," she tried to explain sorrowfully.

"How long before Alfonse found you?" Alexis scribbled furiously.

Santana paused, "It was two days later at my old apartment when I was getting my clothes together. I was moving in with Bob. The next thing I know, José burst into my apartment and grabbed me. He told me I had to come back to him or he would turn information over to the police about Bob's business dealings."

"Did you know anything about Bob's business?" Alexis asked cautiously.

"I swear I didn't know anything! I didn't know he was making drugs!" she wailed.

Alexis soothed her, "I believe you Santana. What happened when Alfonse made his threat?"

"I went with him. I was afraid," Santana replied, her eyes downcast. "But José hit me several more times over the next few days before I was able to get to a phone and call Bob. Bob told me to leave and he would protect me. I told Bob that José would go to the police about his business if I left and Bob got really angry."

"So he threatened José?" Alexis continued writing.

"He said to leave but before I could, José found me where I was talking on the phone. He pulled me away and grabbed the phone and told Bob to `go to hell`. He said he had proof...a tape... of Bob's...what's the word? Illegal stuff? José said he was taking it to the District Attorney," Santana's voice wobbled.

"What happened then?

"Several days later Bob and some men broke into our place. They beat José badly and tried to get him to tell them where the tape was. It was awful! Then Bob pulled out a gun and shot him in the head." Santana began to sob.

"So you actually witnessed Lager killing José. You went with Lager then?" Alexis continued the questioning.

"I didn't know what else to do," she pleaded. "What would you do? I just saw Bob shoot somebody and I didn't know he could do something like that. It was horrible. So even though I was scared, I went with Bob."

"But you disappeared after?" Alexis probed.

Santana hesitated before answering. "It was several days later. I told Bob that I wanted to go to the store. He let me. I called my old boss from the bar and he helped get me out of town to a cousin's in New Orleans. They helped me get in touch with a distant relative in Houston. They were able to get me into Mexico."

"You do know you'll never be safe until Lager and his men are permanently behind bars, Santana? Will you testify to what you've told me?" Alexis held her breath.

"I have to. You know, you guys promised to protect me from Bob and to get my son back. I need your help to protect Pedro. Yes, I will testify, and then I'll disappear,"

Santana assured her.

Alexis stood and hugged Santana and gathered her pad and recorder. "We'll protect you. I promise."

Alexis was feeling exhilarated with all the information she had gotten today. Quinn, Carlony and Alexis quickly left and headed for the airport. Once on the private airplane, Alexis was permitted call Griffin. She informed him of the meeting with Santana Regas. Then Ben explained what chaos she had caused by leaving without telling any one. He said that Mac had stormed into the offices demanding to know where you were.

"Since I hadn't heard from Quinn yet from the plane, I had no idea where you had gone. Some people said you had left with two men but I couldn't say if they were the FBI or some unsavory sort. He was frantic, to say the least and called the precinct to put out an all points bulletin for you," Ben explained.

"Oh God! I'm so sorry Ben! I wasn't allowed to call or leave a message for you and Mac," Alexis protested.

"I know that now after talking with Quinn. I should have realized that you wouldn't tell Mac about our meeting with the FBI either," Ben said softly.

"Of course I wouldn't. We were both told not to tell anyone," she insisted.

"Well, as soon as I talked with Quinn I told him I had to call Mac and notify him of what was happening because of the APB that was out. I explained that he was your fiancé as well as a cop with integrity." Ben chuckled, "Quinn told me to go ahead then."

"Is Mac okay?" Alexis could just imagine how frantic Mac must have been.

Ben remarked, "Yes, but don't be surprised if he meets you at the airport. I'm to notify him when you're headed home. As a matter of fact, put Quinn on the phone and I'll find out when you're due home. I'll talk to you tomorrow at the office."

Alexis called Quinn to the phone and handed it to him. She adjusted her seat in a reclining position, closed her eyes, and dosed.

Alexis was tense as they arrived at Miami Airport several hours later. She gathered her belongings and climbed down the stairs to the tarmac following Quinn and Carlony. They had taken several steps when a man appeared from behind a luggage carrier and ran up to Carlony firing a gun.

Carlony fell to the ground as Alexis screamed in alarm and Quinn reached for his 44 magnum, pushing Alexis behind him. As Quinn pulled the trigger, the man dropped and rolled, taking Quinn's feet out from under him. Quinn crashed to the ground and groaned as his head hit the cement. Alexis stepped forward, dropping her possessions as the assailant began to get to his feet.

Alexis kicked out with her foot, catching the assailant in the face. He cursed as his head whipped back and he fell on his rear, dropping his gun as he did so. As he clambered back to his feet, Alexis twirled with her leg outstretched and slammed her foot against the side of his face. He roared in pain as he fell back again.

"You bitch!" he shouted and rolled quickly toward her. When Alexis jumped backward, she began losing her balance and reached behind for the stair railing to steady herself. This was enough time for the attacker to scramble to his feet and lunge toward her, catching her around the waist. As she felt his arms pulling her toward him, Alexis twisted around so her back was to him. Feeling those tightening arms like vices, she used all the strength she could muster to lean forward to put space between them. She kicked backwards forcefully and he screamed in pain and fury as her foot connected with his knee. His arms dropped away and as she turned to face him she heard a shout and a shot rang out.

The assailant dove and rolled under the plane. Alexis turned toward the shouts and saw Mac's dear face approaching at a dead run.

He was there in seconds, crushing her in his arms. "Are you all right, Lexi!"

Alexis pulled back and encouraged, "Go get him, Mac, I'm fine!"

The words were barely out of her mouth as Mac disappeared under the plane and was gone.

Alexis ran to where Carlony lay bleeding and dropped to his side. As she pulled back his blood stained coat, she heard men yelling and coming toward her. They were airport security and men with orange flight deck vests on. They arrived at her location within seconds and began dealing with the two injured men. Alexis sat on her rear and scooted back out of the way from their ministrations. Several minutes later Quinn was assisted up on his feet and came over to her. He sat down beside her and put his bleeding head in his hands.

"Are you okay, Saunders?" His voice was husky.

"Yeah. I'm fine." As she assured him, she placed a hand on his knee. "What about you?"

"I'll be okay. I'm telling you, though. I owe you big time. You probably saved us all." Admiration was in Quinn's voice. "Where did you learn moves like that?"

"Well, I traveled a lot with my dad. China, Korea, etc." she replied then giggled. "I've studied Zen, Karate, Tae Kwon Do and even Kung Fu since I was three years old."

"Holy shit!" Quinn's esteem for her rose even higher. "What all did you study in those arts?"

"The different styles like ground fighting, throwing styles. Uh…stand up styles like punching, kicking and blocking," Alexis elaborated.

"Jesus! I'm going to try talking you into joining the FBI. We could use you!" Quinn's eyes searched her face as Mac suddenly appeared and knelt down beside them.

"Did you get the guy?"

"No, unfortunately he was able to get away," Mac responded and placed a hand under Alexis' face and tilted it upward. "Are you sure you're not hurt?"

Before she could respond, Quinn answered, "Hell, man! Did you see this lady take on that guy? He's the one that got hurt!"

At that moment police cars pulled nearby with sirens blaring. Eight officers jumped out of their cars, weapons drawn. Mac stood and flashing his badge, headed toward them saying over his shoulder, "I'll be back in a minute, Darlin`."

As the ambulance pulled up near the plane, several men with Carlony assisted the medics in placing Carlony on a cart. As they began assessing his condition and starting an intravenous, the first men on the scene came over to Quinn to assist him to his feet and guide him toward the ambulance. Alexis remained sitting on the tarmac, waiting for Mac's return. Minutes later, Alexis started rising as Mac came toward her. He quickened his pace and got there in time to pull her the rest of the way upright. He pulled her into his arms and just held her tight.

"Let's go. The cops here are handling everything. I told them what I'd seen and that you'd be in tomorrow to make a statement as well." Mac guided her toward a security door into the airport.

Mac and Alexis walked through the airport arm in arm. They headed to his car parked in security parking and headed to his apartment. It was closer, he told her. After opening his door, he pulled her inside and over to the coach.

"You have no idea how worried I was yesterday. I thought my heart would stop beating when I found you were missing." He held her hands and pressed kisses on them. "When Ben told me where you were I was relieved but furious."

"But I..." Alexis objected.

Mac stopped her with a gentle kiss on the lips. "Don't interrupt. I got over that real fast when it dawned on me you were safe. So I waited for Ben's call to tell me when you'd be home. I've been waiting anxiously at the airport ever since."

Mac's fingers traced her lips in a gentle caress. "I was watching the plane land...I had been able to get security to tell me where...then you were all getting off the plane. When I realized that man was shooting at you I flew through the security door where I was standing. I thought I'd be too late to save you and I couldn't seem to breathe as I ran. Oh, Lexi, I thought I'd die on the spot, watching you fight so valiantly against that man."

Mac gathered her in his arms and held her. "Please don't ever let anything like that happen again."

"I had to do something, Mac," she whispered. "But I *was* terrified."

"I know you had to. But I couldn't take it if you were hurt or killed." Mac kissed her eyes and trailed kissed down her face and neck.

"I want you Mac," Alexis stated simply.

Alexis arched upward towards his caresses and moaned lustily. Mac needed no further encouragement as his lips targeted hers. Tongues meshed and hands grappled with clothes. Buttons popped and flew in all directions. The foreplay was frantic and physical. Alexis moaned in entreaty and Mac pulled his head back.

"Do you want me, sweetheart? Lexi, do you really want me?" he begged.

"Yes, Mac. Please…let's make love." Alexis wanted him with such desperation.

Needing no further encouragement, Mac lifted away and began pulling her upright to the bedroom.

"Mac, I love you." she cried out, relieved at last to have expressed her true feelings as they scurried down the hallway.

"God, Alexis! I love you too!" Mac's voice caressed her as he pulled her through the door and led her to the bed, knowing their lives would be forever intertwined.

"Don't you dare move, mister," Alexis admonished him later in bed.

Mac beamed down at her. "I couldn't if I wanted to."

They had laughed and talked and made love throughout the remainder of the day and evening hours. At one point, they also talked of the day's happenings.

"I want you to know how very proud of you I was today when you took on that attacker." Mac hugged her as they lay munching treats on the floor before the fireplace. "My heart stopped beating, I think, but the pride as you kept striking him was so strong. Did you get a good look at him?"

"I did," Alexis nodded. "It was the same guy we saw at the DNC art show talking to Bachman. He was a couple inches taller than me. Dark, greasy hair, but only at the back and a few strands at the sides. He was bald elsewhere. A scar marked the left cheek from the eyebrow down near his ear. It was puckered and really red so I think it was fairly new. He had scars from acne too. Oh, and I think he had a top of a finger on his right hand missing."

"So you can identify him if you see him again." With her nod he continued. "I'll see what the sketch artist has come up with working with Terrie D'Angelo. Maybe you can fine tune the image."

The next day, they headed to the precinct in Mac's car. Hers was still in the garage at work from two days before. Mac introduced her to another detective, Johnny Newsome, working on the shooting at the airport and they went into an interrogation room to talk.

"Tell me first how Quinn and Carlony are?" Alexis pleaded.

"Quinn had some stitches to close his head wound but he was treated and released." Newsome replied. "Carlony had to go to surgery in order to have a bullet removed from his shoulder. He was a lucky man. The bullet missed his lung and a major artery. He's being held for a couple of days in the hospital. They're mighty grateful for what you did. I think Quinn called you amazing."

"Thanks," she smiled. "Now what would you like to know?"

As she explained the happenings of yesterday she was aware of Mac's attention to her details. He even asked a few questions himself. During the discussions, a man from CSI came in with a paper and handed it to Newsome.

"Well this is good news," Newsome reported. "The gun the man dropped at the scene when you apparently kicked him did have a fingerprint on it. The bad news is we have no match as yet."

Mac held out his hand for the paper. At his scrutiny, he came to a conclusion. "I'm taking this with me, Newsome. I am wondering if this is an ex-military man. I'm going to personally call in some favors at the Pentagon and with the Secretary of Defense. This guy has to be on file somewhere. I'll take Lexi to the sketch artist and see what the two of them can come up with."

Several hours later, Mac entered the room where Alexis was busy with the police sketch artist. Mac sat down in a chair and waited patiently until they were finished. When the portrait was completed, Mac looked over Alexis' shoulder to the completed product. Indeed, the likeness was that of the man they had seen talking to Bachman at the art show, just as he had expected it would be. And if he was right, it was the same man who had been doing the raping and murdering of prostitutes throughout Florida and Miami proper.

"Let's go now. I'm taking you to get your car at the court-house garage." Mac navigated through the precinct with his hand resting on her lower back. "Ben wants to talk with you as well."

As they strode through the police station, many of the men and women congratulated her on her heroism. Several of the men joked about her agility in the martial arts and the likelihood that she may need these talents in the future if she was taking on Mac as her husband. Mac smiled at the teasing comments and laughed at some of the brazen and rude jokes. Alexis flushed in embarrassment but took the ribbing good naturedly.

When they were seated in his car, she questioned Mac, "How did they know about the two of us? I mean, they even know about an engagement?"

"Word travels fast in a place like this. The other cops have teased me for years about my obsession with you. It was apparent that I was mooning over you. I'm surprised that you hadn't noticed." Mac took his hand off the wheel and placed it on her knee.

"Well, Ben has teased me before about the sparks flying between the two of us," she confessed. "He once told me that you and I were the only two in our buildings that didn't realize we had the hots for each other."

Mac laughed outright at that as they pulled into the parking garage. He went around to the other side and helped her out. They walked hand in hand to the elevator and ascended to her floor.

George greeted her enthusiastically and explained how worried he was about her when she left with two men. Alexis assured him that he did a fine job in checking it out that day but from now on, they would have to make up a secret code to let him know if she was in trouble.

Mac growled, "This won't happen again. I'm personally going to be taking on her protection."

George laughed and shook his hand. "Congratulations and good luck with this one. She's pretty independent."

"Don't I know it." Mac winked at George and they proceeded down the hallway. Many of the secretaries and prosecutors came out of their offices to hug Alexis and congratulate her on her efforts in taking on the assailant. Ben even came up at his office and teased her about her hidden martial arts talents.

"Yeah," Mac returned with a laugh. "She has a lot of hidden talents."

Ben ushered them into his office and joked, "I'll bet you've found every one of them, Mac."

"Okay you two. Enough." Alexis blushed furiously. "Let's get down to business."

Without explaining to Mac where she had been taken by the two Bureau men, she told a brief synopsis of Santana Regas' story. Then she pulled out the tape recorder from her purse and played it.

"That's it!" Ben exclaimed. "We've got Lager for murder. I'll take this to a judge and get a warrant to search his premises and business as well as his automobiles. I'll get an indictment by tomorrow on charges of murder in the first-degree. Congratulations, Alexis. You've done us proud! Now let's make arrangements for a legal deposition at whatever location the feds want to arrange."

Chapter 12

Alexis and Mac were both swamped with work the next several days. Yet they were anxious to see each other at night. They settled into a comfortable routine at home. They returned home from work exhausted but were never too tired to talk over their day or make love before going to bed. They found themselves joking and laughing and playing pranks on each other. Both became so at ease with each other's nudity they could get up out of bed and walk naked around the condo or soak in the bathtub together and even tease each other as they prepared meals naked in the kitchen.

Over the weekend, they took in a concert and had a romantic dinner at a five star restaurant. They strolled along the beach and cooked marshmallows over an open fire that a neighbor had left smoldering several condos down from hers. Alexis felt so alive and so loved, cherishing the looks and caresses that Mac bestowed upon her.

Monday Mac followed Alexis to work and blew her a kiss through an open driver's window as she entered the parking garage. She exchanged words with Jimmy as he thanked her for diapers and some baby clothes she had sent to their home. Alexis continued to the elevators and rode up with Betty who arrived at the same time.

"You look awfully cheerful today," Betty remarked. "There's a bloom on those cheeks. Is there any news you want to tell me?"

"Just loving life, Betty," Alexis replied and laughed openly.

They had arrived on their floor and the door opened. Both greeted George then headed to their own offices. Seated at her own desk, she began looking over briefs. It was after ten that morning when Gérard returned her call from earlier the previous week.

"Alexis, you have no idea of what kind of week I've put in. I've been visiting some hell holes in New York trying to get in touch with Sirini's cousin, Manny Contini. I finally found him and got some information we can use. He told me that Sirini's office was in Cooper City on 130th Street. I'm in Miami now and have gotten in touch with Mac. We're headed there in a little while. He gave me the location of a key that's hidden there with information we might use." Gérard sounded tired.

"Is he willing to come here and testify?" Alexis crossed her fingers and held her breath.

"Reluctantly, yes," Gérard responded to her question. "But we'll have to guarantee protection. Contini really doesn't think he can add anything to our case."

"Well, maybe he can't but we won't know until we question him if anything he knows is vital to our case against Lager or any of the others. I want to depose him so offer him the protection. I don't just want to take down notes as we talk," Alexis said thoughtfully. "Good luck today in finding something."

After hanging up, Alexis returned to her papers. Some time had passed before Mary, the receptionist knocked on her door and entered her office. There was the usual sullen look on her face but her eyes were downcast as she stepped closer to Alexis' desk.

"How can I help you, Mary." Alexis leaned back in her chair. She was puzzled. Mary had never before approached her or anyone else in the D.A.'s office. "Sit down if you'd like."

"I had to talk with you. I've got this problem." She worried her fingers. "I was told by Mr. Griffin that I had to, I think he said, `clean up my act'. He said I'm too unfriendly and nobody likes me. He said my desk was a mess and it needed to be cleaned up too. You know, because it's the first thing you see in coming off the elevator."

As Mary paused, Alexis said softly, "That's fine Mary. I would like for us to have a better relationship. So don't worry about me. I have never reported anything to Mr. Griffin."

"Yeah, I figured you hadn't. You're always nice to me and speak to me." She smiled slightly.

"So go back to work and don't worry about a thing," Alexis consoled her.

"But you don't understand." Mary stood and paced the floor. "I'm worried I might loose my job. You see, I got busy and began cleaning my desk. You know how it's set behind that tall wall with the large open window. Well, I got busy cleaning all around my desk too and when I pulled the desk out, there was mail and stuff behind it. Even food wrappers."

"So what does this have to do with me?" Alexis was curious.

"Well, I think some of the envelopes are checks and important papers and other stuff," she wailed. "What will I do if Mr. Griffin finds out? I need my job and don't want to be fired."

"It's a natural mistake for things to slip down," Alexis reassured her. "The way your desk is butted up like that to the wall, it's not surprising that this has happened. I bet that when Mr. Griffin finds out he'll address the issue by having someone come in and attach a shelf or the desk to the wall so that this doesn't happen again. Just let him know what has happened."

"I was wondering," Mary hesitated. "Would you go into his office with me? You have been kind to me. Would you go with me to tell him?"

"Sure, Mary," Alexis agreed. "Let's go see if he's there now. Then you can see to the mail that's been missing."

The two journeyed down the hallway together. Upon finding Ben's door open, they entered and found him bending over a cabinet looking for something.

Alexis stated tentatively, "Mr. Griffin, Mary has asked me to come here with her to explain a problem she just found at her desk."

As she approached Ben, Mary twisted her hands together and began her story. Ben listened and refrained from taking her to task. When Mary was finished, Alexis was proud of the way he handled the situation. He did not blame Mary directly, instead, blaming the physical problem of the juncture of the desk and wall. He told her he would get the problem fixed and to bring anything she had found to his office immediately. He did ask her to be more conscientious, then let her leave.

"Bravo. You handled that with great aplomb and discretion. You'll make Mary a big fan of yours yet." Alexis grinned widely.

"Cut out the wisecracks. This could be a real problem for the office. We don't know yet how long this mail has been building up." Ben looked concerned.

The conversation stopped as Mary came into the office with letters and several thick envelopes in her hands. Without a word, she laid the material on Ben's desk and discretely left the room, closing the door behind her.

Alexis decided to leave Ben to the task of sorting through the letters so she excused herself. As she walked to the door, Ben stopped her.

"Wait Alexis, there's two envelopes and a letter her for you. I'll let you go through them and let me know what's been missing."

"Thanks boss," Alexis retrieved the mail and returned to her office. She decided to go through it immediately and opened the letter first. It had been postmarked six months earlier and held a letter from an attorney representing a well-to-do client involved in purchasing marihuana for personal use. The attorney was requesting a stay in the trial until he could become more fully acquainted with the facts of the case.

Well, Alexis thought, that's already been taken care of because he had gone ahead without his attorney's recommendation and pleaded guilty to avoid a trial and further embarrassment to his family.

Alexis opened the large manila envelope which contained pictures of men soliciting prostitution from women on Miami streets. This envelope had a postmark of a month and a half ago and involved upcoming trials that she had passed on to another assistant D.A.

Alexis then opened the third smaller manila envelope which just had her name on it and a small cassette dropped out. A note was attached which held only one word...`Alfonse`. Alexis scrambled out of her chair and rushed to the bookshelves where she retrieved a cassette player and took it to her desk. Placing the cassette inside she turned it on and waited in anticipation for a voice to be heard.

The voices were quiet but distinct.

"Yeah, I know we have a problem. Sirini's dropped out of sight and has taken his accounting records with him, all of his clients' accounting ledgers. I've hired people to look for him but so far we've come up empty." The voice sounded familiar to Alexis but she believed it to be Bob Lager.

A second voice replied, "There's a lot of well known people going to go down if we don't find those records. Some of those people know a lot about your crystal Meth operation and could turn states' evidence in order to protect their own hides."

An angry familiar voice…? Lager … came back. "Do you think I'm stupid? He knows about us filling coffee containers with crystal Meth and selling it worldwide. He fixed the books to cover the millions I've made."

"Christ, Lager, what are we going to do?" The second voice was urgent.

"I don't know yet, Greg, but I'll keep trying to locate those books from Sirini. I have to keep watch over everything. I can't trust anyone at the two plants. I know the D.A. is after me now and I have to be careful. And I want you to keep a low profile and put off any transactions overseas. Do you think you can handle that one small task? I don't want you coming here to my office again. I'll take care of contacting you like I always do, through prepaid cell phones," Lager retorted.

"I'll take care of my part, Bob, but you get busy on your end and take care of Sirini."

"Leave now before anyone sees you," Lager hissed as the door closed and the tape was silent. Alexis listened for several more minutes to a blank tape before she clicked it off.

Alexis grabbed the recorder and headed to Ben's office and rushed past Betty to hurry through his door.

Ben looked up surprised from what he was doing. "What's up Alexis?"

"The icing on the cake, Ben," she said smugly. "You're never going to believe what I have here. A tape from Alfonse about

Lager. In the tape Lager admits to his crystal Meth operations and even that Sirini apparently fixed his books. Listen."

Alexis replayed the tape and when it was finished, they both laughed out loud.

"Well, I think we can safely say that Lager is going to jail. I want you to get a voice analyses from the FBI just to make sure we can connect the tape to Lager," Ben instructed Alexis.

"Of course." Alexis gazed at Ben seriously, "I want you to know I'm making no deals with him, Ben. I want him on all charges, and then will go after him for the first degree murder with death specifications of José Alfonse."

"I agree, Alexis but let's also see who else we can nail with him. Maybe he'll give someone else up." Ben agreed then suggested.

Alexis nodded then left to see Betty to place the tape in the vault for security. Afterwards, she returned to her office to complete more work, all-the-while wondering what Mac and Gérard had found at Sirini's office.

Mac and Jim Gérard headed to Cooper City in search of Sirini's office, conversing about Jim's recent trip to New York and his finding Manny Contini. They arrived at what appeared to be a well-to-do area of the city housing businesses. They parked and approached a three story building which apparently held the office of Charles Sirini. Inside the entry, they peered at the board listing office spaces. Sirini's office was listed as on the second floor so they headed up the stairs. Approaching the office, Mac noted the darkness inside through a small narrow window in the door. He also noticed a metal closed sign at the side.

"Doesn't look like anyone's here," Mac stated the obvious. "Look at the floor beneath the mail slot. It's been a long time since anyone's picked up mail."

"Yeah," Gérard confirmed as he looked through the window and jiggled the knob.

"What say we take a look inside?" Mac began to take out a locksmith tool and picked the lock quickly. They entered and shut the door, fumbling along the wall until they found a light switch. "Looks like somebody's been here already."

As Mac and Gérard surveyed the room, they saw an office in disarray. Papers were strewn about and filing cabinets were open with folders flung everywhere.

Gérard began walking through the mess. "I don't think we'll be finding anything here to help us. Somebody's done a good job of searching through this place. Contini did tell me that Sirini mentioned something about an `owl`. We need to look for an owl."

Mac agree but decided to search anyway. "Well let's do a search, then we'll figure out what to do."

The two spent until mid-afternoon probing stacks of papers. They found nothing in the accounts that was pertinent to their cases. Searching the desk, a whole wall of book shelves, and ledgers lying about in the office, they still found nothing.

"I don't get it." Mac was puzzled. "You say Sirini's cousin said to look for an `owl`. There are no ceramic owls, no pictures with owls, no sculptures, no owls."

"Yeah, I don't see any photos of him with owls either," Gérard concurred.

"What exactly did Contini say? Think. We need the precise words," Mac insisted.

Gérard pondered for several minutes, sitting down while he did so. Mac paced the floor.

"He told me `Chuck said to look for `owl`," Gérard finally stated.

"Whoa!" Mac exclaimed, "maybe he meant `Al` not an `owl`. And we're to look here in his office?"

Gérard nodded and both men looked steadily at each other. Minutes passed.

Mac headed toward the bookshelves ladened with novels and accounting texts. Gérard jumped up and headed to the shelves as well. They perused the titles as the clock on the wall ticked loudly. Mac shouted with glee as he pulled out a book.

"Look Jim," his voice was tense with excitement. "`Al` by Tim Gantry. With that, he opened the book and found a cutout section in the middle in which a key and tag was attached. "Bingo!"

Gérard looked over his shoulder and read the tag, "`Montry Storage`. What now Mac?"

Mac closed the book and walked over to the desk and dialed the phone, "I'm calling a detective I know on the police force here, Mike VanHues. I've got to tell him what we've found and to come here now."

For the next several minutes Mac explained to Detective VanHues why he was here breaking into the office and what he had found. Gérard could tell by the irritation in his voice that VanHues was really pissed off at Mac. Mac hung up the phone and stated glumly, "That did not go so well."

Mac and Gérard strode about the room until, within a short period of time, they could hear sirens approaching.

"We going to be arrested, Boss man?" Gérard smirked.

"God, I hope not." But Mac returned a slight smile as the door was opened and in marched VanHues and two other cops.

"Okay, spill it Mac before I have these guys cuff you two and take you directly to jail," VanHues barked angrily. "This is breaking and entering."

"Well, technically it's not." Mac held up his hand to stop any words. "This is the late Charles Sirini's office. He was murdered in Miami. His only living relative, Manny Contini, sent us here to find something that would help us find the culprit. He didn't have a key to give us yet as he hasn't got his inheritance yet through the court."

"You can substantiate this?" VanHues was skeptical.

"Yep, now this is what has happened since we got here." Mac then proceeded to tell the cops step by step what had transpired. He pointed to the book on the desk. "Pick up this book now and look inside. Everything is exactly how we found it...the key still taped in the book. We should be able to get prints off the page and key or tag. I need this from your CSI ASAP. Then I need for you to come with Gérard and me to this `Montry Storage`."

VanHues looked to his two police officers and nodded at them. "Seal this place off and get the mobile CSI to come here and work the rooms. Wait for the call that we've obtained a search warrant. Let's go Mac."

Mac and Gérard rode with VanHues to the police lab adjacent to the station. While Mac and Gérard headed to VanHues office as instructed, Mike headed to the lab. He returned shortly to sit down with the two and discuss everything the knew. They called the police chief and asked him to get a search warrant and it was obtained in an hour. CSI called to the office and established the prints to be that of Sirini on the key after they were sent for confirmation to the Miami CSI.

"Let's go. Jim and I will wait at your car while you get the key. Then we need to go to the storage facility." Mac headed to the door without Mike objecting.

The three met up in the parking lot and headed out to Montry Storage. The ten minute drive was tense with expectation. The three climbed out of the car simultaneously and went over to the door marked on the key. They slid the door open to find boxes stacked six feet high throughout.

With gloves on they began to open some lids.

"Whew, look at this," Gérard's voice lifted in excitement. "These are accounting ledger's of Thompson's. Also someone named Tilson."

Mac responded as he opened several more cartons, "Tilson is a crony of Bachman. Does building projects with him. Look here, I found Lager's accounts. Bet you they don't match his audited books for the IRS. I need to take these with me, Mike. Can you get me a bag to put them in or even come with me to Miami to substantiate they haven't been tampered with?"

VanHues paused then agreed. "Let me call a cruiser to seal this off. It's going to take a while to process all of these cartons even though they're apparently somewhat alphabetical. As soon as the cops get here I'll call into the chief and tell him where I'm going. You know I've got a lot of explaining to do to him."

It took about a half an hour before VanHues was ready to leave the scene. They headed to Miami, discussing all the possible cases that might have evidence in those boxes. Upon arriving at the precinct, Mac and VanHues headed to CSI while Gérard headed home. Once the material was handed over, Mac suggested a quick dinner in the cafeteria. They ate hungrily and soon parted.

Mac scurried up the annex stairwell, anxious to get to Alexis and tell her his news. He arrived on the floor and hurried to her office only to find it empty. He searched and only found Betty at her desk.

"Where's Alexis?" Mac's voice was nervous.

"She left about an hour ago. She was going straight home."

"Thanks, Betty." As Mac headed down the elevator, he realized he didn't have a car. He would have to drive in the morning to Cooper City. He ran the block to the precinct and asked Sergeant Collier at the desk to borrow his car.

"It's an emergency, Collier," Mac assured the cop.

Collier tossed him the keys. "Don't wreck it, Mac. I'll have two of the cops on patrol stop over and pick it up. Just call me when you get wherever you're going."

As Mac darted out Collier yelled, "You owe me big time buddy!"

Mac pulled out all the stops in racing to the condo. He kept reciting a mantra, `Alexis is fine, Alexis is fine. She got home alright.`

The drive seemed endless. The darkened sky and slight fog gave the night an element of eeriness. He passed cars at record pace as he zoomed in and out of traffic, all-the-while trying to call Alexis from his cell phone. Horns honked as he barely kept from hitting bumpers as his car zigzagged. In the back of Mac's mind, he was waiting for flashing lights to appear in his rear view mirror. Finally, he arrived at Alexis' condo, pulling in front on the street and jumping out of the car. He slammed the door and keeping his hand steadily on his gun in his shoulder holster, he ran up the sidewalk. Digging out the key Alexis had given him, he inserted it and opened the door calling out, "Alexis! Are you here?"

Mac's breathing faltered as he waited for what seemed like ages. He stood stock still.

Suddenly, Alexis appeared in the hallway, "Mac, what's wrong? Are you okay?"

She ran to him and grabbed him by his arms as he suddenly came to life. Mac took her in his arms and swung her around.

"God, am I glad to see you. I was worried sick about you driving home all by yourself." Mac lowered his lips in a brutally hard kiss.

Alexis pulled away and protested. "Mac, you're hurting me."

Mac suddenly realized how hard he had kissed her as he stared at her reddened mouth. "I am so sorry, love. I didn't mean to hurt you. I was just felt so relieved when I saw you."

"Wellllllll," she slurred slyly, "You could kiss it and make it feel better."

"Gladly Darlin'," and with that, he closed the front door and began to caress her lips with his own.

"Do you know how much I love your smell…like fresh spring flowers in a field," Mac inhaled deeply. Alexis shuddered with longing as his husky voice caressed her ear. Alexis hands glided over his six-pack stomach and roamed back up to his brawny chest.

"I want us to be together. I love you. Marry me," Mac's voice was suddenly low and vibrant.

Alexis grasped the top of his shoulders as tenderness and love filled her. "I love you too, Mac. Do you think…?"

Mac enthusiastically devoured her mouth and pressed kisses down her neck.

"Yes, I think we should get married. This weekend. Now!" He stopped talking and pressed a hard kiss to her lips.

"Mac, stop. We have to talk about this," Alexis objected.

"Nothing to talk about. I'll call your parents and ask them to come and help set up the details. My mom will help as well. They'll be thrilled. Hell, I'm thrilled!" Mac began to laugh and hugged her.

"Okay, we'll get married but not this weekend." Alexis joined in with a giggle. "A couple of weeks from now…"

Mac kissed her solidly then growled. "No. Not negotiable. ASAP. This weekend or next. No later. Do I have to persuade you?"

Alexis eyes narrowed and she whispered slyly, "Well, I think I could be persuaded…" and she giggled as Mac did just that.

Chapter 13

Mac was true to his word. Together they called her parents and explained they wanted to get married in a week and a half. Dee and Michael were surprised but ecstatic and they promised to begin with arrangements in the morning. Mac's parents were just as enthusiastic and said they would call Dee and Michael as soon as they got off the line.

That evening Alexis and Mac talked about the events of the day. Both were exultant about what had been revealed. It was well past midnight before the two fell into each other's arms in a deep sleep.

It was only six in the morning when both awakened to hurriedly get dressed and head to Cooper City in order that Mac could pick up his car. They had agreed upon this the night before but hadn't counted on the ride back being so lonely for them both. Frequent calls to each other on their cell phones kept them conversing and laughing until they reached the courthouse. Alexis proceeded into the parking garage while Mac headed to the precinct.

Alexis felt as if she was walking on air. Happiness filled her and her face showed her jubilation. When she approached Betty's desk where the secretary and her boss, Ben were chatting, the twosome stopped and gaped at her in amazement.

"Hey lady, did you take a happy pill or what?" Betty asked in amusement.

"What's going on, Alexis?" Ben questioned. "You look like you swallowed the proverbial `canary'."

Alexis grinned widely. "I kind of feel like that too. I came to ask the two of you to a wedding next weekend."

Alexis waited for the response which came quickly as both Ben and Betty grabbed and hugged her.

"Oh my God! I'm so thrilled for you." Betty kissed her on both cheeks as she held Alexis' face between her hands.

Ben bent over to kiss her after noting, "It's about time you two make it legal. Maybe I'll win the office betting pool after all."

"You guys have been placing bets on me marrying?" Alexis was appalled.

Betty tried to soothe her. "Now honey, there's about twenty of us in the annex that bet on you and Mac tying the knot. And this was started about three years ago. All of us could see you two had the hots for each other. All but you two, that is."

With that, Betty and Ben sniggered.

"Boy am I ever embarrassed." Alexis gave another wide grin that dispelled any doubt that she was. "So I'm a little slow in the love department."

"You are at that." Ben agreed. "Now, you know we'll both be at the wedding. So let's get on with other business. The court recorder called to say Judge Masters is back in town. Masters has scheduled the court case for Lager to resume on Monday. We need to get any more evidence we've received over to the defense team for disclosure. We don't want to loose the ability to use it because we didn't share it with the defense."

"Gotcha, boss." Alexis saluted him smartly. "Let's go into your office so I can tell you what Mac and Gérard found at Sirini's office yesterday."

Alexis filled out the remainder of the day preparing for Bob Lager's final days in court. Mac called and told her he would be over to the annex before four in order to enlighten her on new information.

Four o'clock on the nose, Mac marched into her office, an unyielding look upon his features. Alexis knew better than to tease him in this mood. She waited for him to begin but was surprised when he went around her desk and tilted her face for a sweet kiss.

"That was the number one thing on my mind." Mac still looked grim as he slid a picture before her on the desk. "The number two is this...we've matched the fingerprint on that gun you kicked away at the airport. It belongs to a man named Todd Butler. He's ex-marine that was dishonorably discharged six years ago. He was a soldier of fortune for various countries in the Middle East and Europe as a hit man from the time of discharge until two years ago when he disappeared. I guess he couldn't get any more contracts with the U.S so prevalent in the Middle East and with Europe being so cautious since 9/11. He is a *very bad man*, Alexis."

Alexis was mesmerized by the picture. "This is the man that attacked me, Mac. I'm sure of that. How are we going to find him?"

Mac viewed her intently and swore, "We'll get him, honey. He's in the area and got paid for a hit so he won't just go away. He can't hide from us forever."

"At least not until he accomplishes his task," Alexis appeared so forlorn that Mac took her gently in his arms and just held her.

As his hold loosened, Mac added, "We also have the word from forensics. Those Lager accounting ledgers were indeed done by Sirini. His fingerprints match as does the handwriting analysis. You're going to be able to add them as evidence in your current trial. We have all the boxes from storage and I've got someone looking through them and listing who Sirini's clients were. With the real accounts being rescued from storage to compare to the fixed books that Lager has on file legally, you should be able to nail his ass for IRS fraud and other crimes."

"That's great news Mac. The trial resumes on Monday so I'll have to offer that up to the defense tomorrow." Alexis still looked beat.

"Come on, I'm taking you home. We'll leave your car." Mac plucked Alexis' purse from her drawer and guided her out of the office.

"I'll willingly go but first I want to see Betty for a moment," Alexis headed toward Ben's office. Upon arriving at Betty's desk, she found her filing.

"Betty, I want you to contact Judge Zeller to make out search warrants for Eric Thompson, Daniel Bachman and Carson Klein's homes, offices, and vehicles. I have the paperwork all done. I have a tape on my desk that lists what evidence we have against the men so far. It should be enough to get those warrants. I don't want them served however until after noon. I'm going to have Mac pick Thompson and Bachman up in the morning and take them to the station and have the Fort Lauderdale police do the same for Klein for questioning." Alexis looked directly at Mac. "Tell them to bring their attorneys. We're going to see who we can break first to role over on the other."

"Gotcha, sweetie," Betty turned to Mac and gave him a enormous hug and smacking kiss on his cheek. "By the way, handsome, I want to offer my congratulations on your upcoming wedding date. I'll be there with bells on."

Mac grinned broadly as he finally extracted himself from Betty's arms. "You know that when I have a wife we're going to have to give up these tender moments."

"I know, honey, and if it was any other woman than Alexis marrying you I'd go down fighting," Betty teased back. "I guess the wedding will be the last time I can give you a kiss without drawing the wrath of God from your wife."

"I don't know about that," Alexis purred and then hinted, "Isn't `variety the spice of life`...and then for me...`what's good for the goose...?"

"Whoa, just one damn minute," Mac protested with a laugh. "You don't get any kisses from anyone but me!"

Betty laughed with Mac and Alexis. "Just like a man to exert his own rules. I don't think you're going to have to worry, Alexis. It's only *your* kisses he wants. All the hot women in the these two buildings have practically thrown themselves at him over the years and he failed to respond. He only had eyes for you. You lucky woman."

"God, Betty, you're making me blush." Mac tugged on Alexis's arm, "Come on, Lexi, we've got business at home."

As they turned to leave Betty's laughter rang out, "Right. Monkey business."

The two enjoyed a pleasant dinner at a Japanese steakhouse on the way home. Both expressed amusement at each others attempts at catching shrimp with their mouths as it was tossed in the air by the chef. Alexis fought down her giggles as Mac showed his ineptitude at using chop sticks on his food. Those big strong masculine hands that caressed her so tenderly welded the chop sticks like greased uncooked spaghetti noodles. Upon returning to the condo later that evening, Mac and Alexis sat down and wrote out questions Alexis needed to ask the three men getting subpoenas in the morning. They sipped wine before the fireplace and lounged back on pillows stacked high on the floors as they wrangled about what to ask each man. It was well past one in the morning again when the two fell asleep by the fire. Mac was able at one point during the remainder of the short night to cover them both with a blanket and take Alexis in his arms.

The precinct was bustling when Mac and Alexis arrived at 9:30 that morning. They had first stopped at the annex at seven to pick up some papers needed for the questioning then headed to CSI to get the accounting books of Sirini's. They only had Thompson's and Klein's audited and still had Bachman's to do since his was just recently found in all those storage boxes. Mac had detectives pick up the two men in Miami at 9:30 and was going to have Klein picked up by FLPD after noon.

It was 10:20 before Thompson arrived and was taken into interrogation room seven where Mac and Alexis waited. Thompson sat down with a thump in the wood chair.

"I don't know what the hell you think you are doing. Am I under arrest for something because if not I'm walking out of here?" he rasped.

"Now Thompson, don't get all huffy," Mac consoled him with tongue-in-cheek. "You aren't going anywhere until your attorney is here and we've questioned you. You were instructed to call him when the detectives picked you up. I assume you did just that."

"You're damn right I did," Thompson was breathing fire. "I'll have you know that my..."

The door whipped open and Attorney Brett Kaiser strolled into the room and placed a hand on Eric Thompson's shoulder.

"Shush, Eric. I'll do your talking. Now what is this all about, Saunders." Kaiser ignored Mac in the room.

"Mr. Kaiser, you're client, Eric Thompson is here for questioning on various cases I'm involved in." Alexis was in her most professional mode. "I'm going to have MacDonald read him his rights and then, while being taped, question him about involvement in theft and corruption in office, paybacks as well as ethics charges involving Daniel Bachman and Carson Kline."

When Thompson jumped up in rage both Kaiser and Mac shoved him back into his chair.

Mac read him his rights, "Eric Thompson, you have the right to remain silent…"

Thompson sat there stiffly as his eyes drilled holes into Alexis' being. She refused to be intimidated. When Mac was done both Kaiser and Thompson awaited questioning.

"Before I begin, I will inform you that at this time detectives are bringing in Daniel Bachman and Carson Klein for questioning. We also have subpoenas for police to go through your homes, offices and vehicles. I'm telling you this so we can have an understanding, Mr. Thompson." Alexis stared purposefully then bent over and placed the large file containing Sirini's fixed books belonging to Thompson on the table and flipped open the folder. Thompson paled as she paused and he perused the top paper. "One of you guys are going to roll on the others. Whomever does it first will get the best deal from the DAs office. As you can see, we have your real accounting books from Charles Sirini. We will be obtaining your doctored books that you show the IRS and use for tax purposes when we go through your office and home. We have your girlfriend's statements as to your shady dealings and with whom those are. By the way, she is in protective custody starting today."

Brett Kaiser leaned over and whispered into his client's ear but Thompson remained silent. Alexis sipped water from a glass then continued. "This is what we know. You made a lot of money through your dealings with Daniel Bachman since you were the state representative on the acquisition and spending committees. We know you were the first to know about state and local projections and special projects throughout Florida and those in particular that Daniel Bachman brought to committee. We have his and Klein's ledgers showing the hundreds of millions of dollars Bachman made by skimming and doing substandard work on various constructions over the years. We also know that you profit by getting a percentage of what you are able to bring to Bachman as business or push through committee and through inspections payoffs. We know you have had regular meetings in the McMillan Pretorious building with Bachman, Klein and another man unidentified as yet."

Mac stood still leaning against the wall watching the color fade then return to Thompson's face. He was loving every minute of this and he gave a big grin toward Alexis which she tried to pretend she did not see. As she drank some more water Thompson's attorney whispered again at length into Thompson's ear. He still remained silent as Kaiser pulled away and sat back.

Alexis resumed her speech. "Before I begin questioning you I will also give notice that I have a witness that says you know our `Whisperer` AKA Todd Butler and that you have met with him. We're currently searching for him for attempted murder charges."

Alexis got the reaction she was waiting for. Thompson's face turned ruddy and he pushed out of his chair, darting toward the door. Trying to open the locked door was futile as Mac and both attorneys knew. Mac stood close to Thompson to see what his next move would be, hands ready to take him down. Eric swung about and stared widely as his attorney asked, "Can we have a few minutes while I talk with my client?"

Alexis nodded her assent and she and Mac signaled the cop outside the door to let them out. They turned to high-five each other.

Mac said quietly, "I think he's going to crumble. How about you?"

"God, I hope so." Sergeant Collier came into the hallway and informed them that Bachman was in interrogation room two. "I'm counting on him helping in a case against Bachman. He's the big fish I want to fry."

Their conversation was nixed as a knock on the door signaled that Kaiser wanted them to return.

Alexis faced Thompson at the desk standing. "Well, what's the verdict? I want to remind you that along with those charges I mentioned, we might be able to add attempted murder and maybe even tie you into the prostitutes' murders and rapes since you have met with Butler."

Thompson's face was beet red in anger. "Now wait a minute. You're not getting me for attempted murder. I had nothing to do with Butler. All I did was give his name to someone."

Kaiser placed his hand on Thompson's arm to hush him. "What do you want from Mr. Thompson, Ms. Saunders? And what's the deal?"

"We'll start with taking care of the charges against Thompson. I outlined to you earlier as to what we believe went down with Bachman. We also want a list of as many people he can think of whom he pulled into these dealings with Bachman. For your offenses that I currently am filing charges on I'll offer fifteen to twenty-five years with the possibility of parole after seven. If you're truly not involved with Butler then I'll try to absorb any other crimes into that sentence. Now, did you help Bachman's projects get through special committees and take payoffs from him? Did you assist in getting inspections passed even though deficient and substandard work was done? Remember before you answer, your ass is on the line."

Kaiser conferred with Thompson in a whisper, then turned back to Alexis. "Well take the deal. You can answer the questions now, Eric."

"Yeah. Yeah. I did that. I'll admit to it," Thompson's voice was shaky.

Alexis could barely control her glee. "Fine, it's a deal. Now, what do you know about Butler?"

Thompson paled, "Honestly, I knew nothing about what he was going to do here. I have a brother that lives in New York, and went to high school with Butler. He knew about his problems in the service and what he did afterwards. My brother has always been afraid of him but was fearful to break off any contact. When I was asked if I knew any hit men, I thought of Butler because my brother gave me the impression that he was doing jobs. I gave the name to the guy."

"So you had no knowledge about what was being planned?" With Thompson's shake of the head, Alexis continued. "So who did you give the name to?"

"Uh...I...do I really have to tell?" Thompson's hands were shaking.

"You do if you don't want to be charged with attempted murder by hiring Butler," Alexis waited with baited breath.

"Okay. Bachman asked me for the name, but I didn't know what he wanted it for. Until I heard about your accident, I had no idea what his intention was. I thought maybe Bachman wanted him to scare somebody," Thompson implored.

"Do you know the unidentified man you met with at the McMillan and Pretorious building?" she persisted.

"No, I had never been given his name," Thompson said stiffly.

Alexis placed her pen upon the desk top. "All right, I think that's enough for right now. I have to talk with Klein and Bachman. The Fort Lauderdale police are bringing Klein down as we speak to Miami. From what Klein has already told us, I believe your testimony will be corroborated. I want you to stay here and I'll order you some lunch. After I've talked with Klein, and Bachman, I want to depose you. Mr. Kaiser, if you want to leave for a while, we'll notify you when were ready to talk again with your client. I am not allowing Thompson to leave this this room except under guard and he will not be in contact with either Klein or Bachman. I want no collusion in their testimonies."

"I understand, Ms. Saunders. I will be back when they call, Eric. Thank you so much." With that Brett Kaiser took his leave.

After leaving Thompson with pad and paper to begin writing list of names involved in the schemes, Alexis and Mac returned to the hallway to discuss the next step.

"You want to see Klein next before Bachman, don't you?" Mac inquired.

"Yes, let's go see if the FLPD has brought him in yet," they both moved down the corridor peering into the various interrogation rooms. Mac stopped in front of room one and halted Alexis by grabbing her arm.

"Klein is sitting in here with someone I don't know," Mac lowered his voice as Klein got up and paced the room. "Are you ready?"

With a quick nod, Alexis entered the stark room and seated herself at the desk while signaling Carson Klein to take a seat. "My name is Alexis Saunders, I'm an assistant DA. MacDonald here tells me you are Carson Klein and this man with you must be your attorney."

Klein nervously twisted his fingers and bit his lip. "Ye...Yes that's me. My attorney is Rupert Freeman."

Alexis shook hands with both men and began, "I believe you know why you are here today, Mr. Klein. You have already talked with MacDonald's men and Mr. Gerard and told them of your involvement with Daniel Bachman. You have previously been too afraid to testify. From this point on you will have little options. First of all, I want you to know that I have some leeway in what I charge you with in your shady dealings in ripping off land and construction deals with Bachman. But you will be given only one opportunity to take the deal. I will tell you I currently have both Eric Thompson and Bachman in interrogation rooms."

With that news Klein looked about ready to vomit as he slid forward in his seat and placed his head in his hands. Alexis continued while Mac smirked as he leaned against the doorway. "We also have your accounting ledgers from Charles Sirini and we are currently searching your home, office, and vehicles for your any other incriminating evidence that could be hidden. Of course we do have a warrant for the search. Along with this, we could possibly connect you with the attempted murder on myself after you gave your car to the man who tried to run me off the road."

Klein burst out, "I had nothing to do with that. Please believe me. I only did what Thompson told me to do. I left my car out."

"But that could be construed as aiding and abetting, Mr. Klein." Alexis remained stern. "Now Mr. Freeman, you had better advise your client. I can nail his ass for IRS fraud, taking kickbacks, corruption, and in his case even mail fraud because some of his schemes involved the U.S. Postal Service. He could get 20 to 28 years for just those charges, let alone any others we might come across during the investigation. I am offering no more than 10 to 13 years with the possibility of parole in 5 years for telling me about all of his dealings including those with Bachman and Thompson. He will have to name any others involved in his deals. We will also offer protection for his family until we have Butler, the man who `borrowed` his car, in custody. Would you like to talk with your client alone?"

At Freeman's nod, Mac and Alexis left the room to wait outside.

"Well that was certainly a defeated man. Nice going counselor." Mac took her hand and stroked her ring finger, lingering on the diamond he had placed on her finger. 'I don't think you're going to have any trouble getting him to take the deal. Particularly, since you offered his family protection."

"I hope you're right, Mac. This could really make the case against Bachman and possibly even higher ups in government." Alexis was pensive, "God, just thinking about that makes me exhausted. It's going to be a long couple of years to get all of these guys in court."

"Well, honey, you can't do it all by yourself," Mac was insistent. "You have to get some others to do the prosecuting. Maybe Ben will even do a case."

"I know you're right, Mac. It's just that I'd personally like to be the one to put them all in jail."

A knock from inside the room brought them to attention. They entered the room and waited for Freeman's reply.

"My client has decided to accept your offer, Ms. Saunders. He just wants out of this mess he's in but at the same time he wants his family to be protected. By the way, he also has some tapes to turn over to you. I hope you understand his reluctance to testify after he talked with Mr. MacDonald's men originally."

Alexis gave no quarter. "Unfortunately, I *don't* understand how anyone could cheat and steal to begin with then protect those who are involved in corruption and possibly murder. You should have been willing to bear witness from the time you were found to be involved. But, that is beside the point. If you are accepting the DAs offer then I'm going to have you wait awhile before I depose you. You will have to wait in here but if you would like some food...?"

"No...I couldn't eat a thing. Maybe some water please," Alexis tried not to feel sorry for Klein who sat there so forlorn. She left the room with Mac trailing her.

"Well, on to Bachman," Alexis was most nervous at confronting this man. They opened the door to the interrogation room two and stepped inside.

Bachman came nose to nose at Alexis as soon as she entered. Before he could say a word, Mac growled, "*Back off!*"

Daniel Bachman took a hesitant step backward then blustered, "Who the hell do you think you are? Why have you brought me here, you bitch!"

Mac intervened again as he seized hold of Bachman's arm and pulled him backward to a chair where he forcefully made him sit. "Shut up and don't you ever call this lady a bitch! You hear me?"

Mac brokered no arguments. Bachman clammed up as his attorney, Larry Jones, offered, "What's this about Ms. Saunders?"

"I have found evidence enough to prosecute Mr. Bachman. He has abused his office and taken bribes and kickbacks. He has offered up illegal deals through the mail. He solicits contributions for candidates who best see his way into viable developments, thus bypassing committees and regulations. He has given payoffs to those who turn a blind eye. We know he not only profits by skimming and doing substandard work but then apparently he's able to get big contributions for the DNC and then has the money laundered."

"What proof do you have?" Bachman was furious.

"Shut up, Daniel." Larry Jones was adamant.

"Proof." Alexis placed her hands on the table and leaned toward Bachman. "Well now, let me see. MacDonald here has cops going all over your homes, vehicles and offices looking for further evidence above what we already have."

Bachman leered, "And what might that be?"

Alexis grinned into his face. "We have your *real* accounting books that Sirini had hidden. The IRS will be interested in comparing those against the ones you turn in. We also have two of your cohorts in crime that are willing to testify against you."

Mac pushed down on Bachman's shoulders as he tried to jump upright. "And who might that be?

Alexis returned smartly, "Well, *that might be* Carson Klein and Eric Thompson in rooms one and seven. They are not only willing to testify against you but to give me names of others involved. And I'm sure we can work out a deal with those characters to testify also."

"You know nothing. You're just trying to bring me down for some personal reason," he barked.

"You're right, I do have a personal reason. I hate corrupt politicians who say they are working for the people...instead they are stealing them blind and denying them the funds necessary to assist them in health care, heating, jobs and even food," Alexis agreed.

Freeman interjected before Bachman could reply. "I think it's better if I talk to my client alone before we go any further, Ms. Saunders."

"Go right ahead, Mr. Freeman." Alexis stood and ambled to the door. "I would like to enlighten you on one other thing. We can also add `attempted murder` to the charges as he hired Todd Butler to make a hit on me. We can substantiate that through Thompson and Klein. So talk all you want with Mr. Bachman. He'll come out better if he cooperates with us and tells all. I might be able to offer a *little* better deal in the end."

"I did not hire Butler. I swear!" Bachman yelled as Alexis and Mac left the room.

Alexis continued to walk out and took a few steps before collapsing on a bench in the hallway. Mac plunked down beside her and placed an arm across her shoulders. He teased her ear with a whisper of a kiss.

"I love you, darling Lexi," he crooned. "I adore you when you go all masterful and mean. You were phenomenal in there with all those guys."

"Thanks Mac. I needed that encouragement." She kissed him on the tip of his nose, took a deep cleansing breath and energized, she stood and marched down the corridor.

"Where are you going?" Mac's imperative voice questioned.

"Why darlin'," she cooed. "I have work to do. I'm going to enlist the aid of a court stenographer and depose those two willing men before they change their minds. You need to get busy and dig up more evidence. I can use as much as you can get me."

Mac watched they sway of those lovely curvaceous hips in that tight navy skirt and high heels as they moved down the hall. He licked his lips then whistled loudly and headed the other way as Alexis' laughter filtered back to him.

Chapter 14

It was well after nine at night when Alexis was finished with questioning Carson Klein and Eric Thompson. They gave her invaluable concise information about the grafts taken and schemes put together by Daniel Bachman that resulted in tens of millions of dollars profit by the DNC chairman, his cronies and themselves. Alexis was appalled by the scope of the corruption, knowing that she would have to pull in federal prosecutors to aid in the prosecution of all the high ranking government officials and elite businessmen. She had notified Ben Griffin before she began questioning the two men and he stayed throughout the process, intervening several times with his own inquiries. The sessions were long, but in the end, Alexis had the necessary information to put both behind bars as well as indict Daniel Bachman. While in the interrogation rooms, Griffin was able to secure arrest warrants for all three men so they would be spending the night in jail because it was too late in the evening to hold court and enable a judge to set bond. Alexis could see the relief in Klein's face and knew without a doubt that he would not post bond no matter how insignificant it was because he feared for his safety. Thompson appeared disgruntled about the whole process yet Alexis was ambivalent as to whether he would secure his temporary freedom with bond or stay safely tucked away in jail.

Daniel Bachman was another matter all together. He apparently felt he could beat any charges even though the prosecution had witness statements and account ledgers. Bachman remained stubbornly silent with a fierce look on his face that belied his steady calm. Alexis, fed up with dealing with this monster finally left the interrogation room, ordering Bachman to be taken to a jail cell. She returned to the annex where she worked to get her papers and notes in order. Mac arrived shortly afterwards and without exchanging a word, they left the building for home and fell exhausted into bed without eating a thing.

The next morning, both arose to bright sunshine and expected temperatures of 80 degrees. As they individually got ready for work, they grabbed a piece of toast and some fruit.

Alexis strolled to the answering machine where three messages were showing. She pressed the button to hear them.

(Beep: message 1) Alexis. This is your mom. Give me a call on my cell. Your dad and sister and I are in Miami. We need to get your wedding dress and your sister's picked out. Call me so we can set this up. I've already talked with Mac's mom and we have some details we would like to go over about location, etc. We're at the *Hilton*.

(Beep: message 2) Alexis dear, Mac...I have found the most gorgeous place for your wedding on the outskirts of Miami. I need your approval to secure the place. Call me. Oh, this is Nora.

(Beep: message 3) Hi Alexis. This is your sister, we're in Miami and waiting to hear from you. Nora MacDonald and Mac's sister are going with us to look for a wedding dress. Give mom or me a call on our cells.

"Well," Mac crossed his arms over his broad chest. "Looks like you are going to be pretty busy the next few days."

"Oh God, Mac, how am I going to do everything between now and next weekend?" she wailed and lowered her head into her hands.

"It'll be okay, honey. We'll both concentrate on the wedding plans this weekend and get as much as we can done. We'll leave the rest to our moms and sisters to do." Mac appeared calm.

"I guess that'll have to work because I have to be in court next week for Lager's trial." Alexis gathered her wits together and smiled. "I *can* do this."

"You know you can, darlin'. Besides, my mom is great at organizing and I'll bet the way your folks entertain, your mom is good at it too."

Alexis shook her head in the affirmative, "You're right about that. Okay, let's go and I'll call everyone on the way to work."

Details were worked out with the parents for later in the day. Alexis was going to leave work early so the women could look for dresses in several private boutiques. Mac was leaving his car with Alexis in order that they could use it for shopping. Mac revealed he would meet up with them later when Alexis called. Alexis resumed another hard day at work. As she had expected, Carson Klein did not put up bail when they were all presented to the court for bond hearings. However, Thompson and Bachman did while refraining from looking at each other in the courtroom. Mac was in the back of the room as the men were escorted out by their attorneys, Thompson hurrying ahead with his head down and Bachman lagging behind to cast evil looks at the prosecution's table. Mac followed the men out and went down the second elevator with Bachman. There was little conversation by the man as the lift descended. Bachman strolled to a drinking fountain disregarding Thomson's hurried exit to the doors and through the crowd. Mac's hair at the back of his neck stood up as suspicion lingered in his mind.

What the hell was going on? Mac pondered. Why was he just standing there where the crowd of reporters could see him through the doors anticipating his exit. Mac suddenly made for the doors at a run and was through them in a matter of seconds. His eyes perused the crowd as he pushed through it and noted Thompson close to the street being pushed by his attorney toward a black Mercedes. They reached the door as Mac pushed back his coat and unsnapped his shoulder holster, running down the stairs. Eyes scanning as he rapidly approached the car, a white Dodge van with no license plates pulled to a stop right in traffic to the rear of the Mercedes. A gun barrel poked through the cracked window as Mac pulled his gun out and began yelling.

"Get down! Get down! Get down!"

Individuals began running and dropping toward the ground in panic. Screams blasted the air. Mac lunged for Thompson and his attorney as gunshots rang out. He tackled them to the ground and rolled, coming to a crouched shooting position as the van began to move. As more shots were fired from the van, Mac clutched his gun with both hands and fired repeatedly as the van sidled the Mercedes. His aim was apparently dead on as no more bullets rained from the white vehicle. Mac continued to fire at the driver window and suddenly the van was careening off to the left into traffic. It rolled erratically toward the buildings further up the street and as Mac ran toward it, the van crashed into an electric pole. As Mac inched toward the passenger window policemen pounded the pavement behind him, guns drawn. He peeked his head around the edge of the window and saw blood everywhere and two men slumped forward. Their faces appeared indistinguishable. He placed fingers to the carotid pulse on the passenger and found it missing as another cop did the same to the driver.

"Dead." Both Mac and the cop recited simultaneously. Mac pulled the passenger backward and noted long straggly blood filled dark hair. He peered at the face but couldn't quite discern if there was a one inch scar on the right cheek because of the bloodied face. Mac felt confident, however, that this was Todd Butler, the `Whisperer'. An autopsy would determine the identity. Mac glanced back at the courthouse and noted the police force holding back crowds of people and reporters. He looked over to where Thompson lay, bleeding profusely on the ground and surrounded by policemen trying to assist the dying man. As he scanned the courthouse stairs, he finally set eyes on Alexis, leaning against the bricks, arms crossed and clutched tightly. Mac holstered his gun, pushed through the throng and took two stairs at a time until he reached her. She was pale and immobile, like a statue. He gently folded her in his arms and muttered inconsequential words. Finally Alexis moved and buried her face in Mac's neck.

"Oh Mac, I was so worried when I heard what was happening! If something had happened..." Alexis' words drifted away.

"Nothing did, love. Nothing did," he soothed her. "Let's get you back inside and then I have to return here."

"No, I'll be all right now. Honestly." Alexis gave a small but telling smile. She had been afraid but now, having him in her arms unharmed, she felt safe and reassured. "Really. Go back to the scene, Mac. I feel I can get some work done. And I'll be leaving shortly anyways to go shopping. Remember?"

"How can I forget," Mac grinned and released her. "Go find yourself something beautiful for the wedding. Enjoy your time with the women. Everything here is fine now."

Mac pressed a quick kiss on her open lips and ran back down through the mass of people. Alexis returned to the annex and tried to concentrate on her upcoming court case.

It was after two in the afternoon when four excited women barged through her office door. Alexis stood to greet all with a hug and a kiss. She still felt apprehensive because of the shoot out earlier in the day and sorrowful as Eric Thompson did not survive. Yet she felt a decided sense of relief that Todd Butler was dead. Mac had called awhile ago to let her know the assailants identity and she breathed a sigh of relief that that part of her life, one in which she was a possible target, was over.

"Okay. Lex, we're out of here. We're driving Nora's car since yours is too small for all of us." Jasmine was jubilant with thoughts of the upcoming wedding. "Meredith and Nora have three wedding boutiques for us to go to. We've got a lot to do. Let's go."

The foursome headed up 2nd Street until they arrived at `Wedding Cache`, an elegant looking place with heavy satin drapes covering the windows. Inside they found dark green plush carpet dotted with lavender and green damask chairs. These chairs surrounded several platforms of various heights with three paneled mirrors behind them.

"This is our bride, Alexis, and we need wedding attire for next Friday." Jasmine was always the outspoken one.

The thirty-something salesperson questioned, "I'm Mae. Do you have any idea what you would like in a wedding dress?"

Alexis spoke out, "I think something simple. White or candlelight. Probably strapless or with the chiffon slip of a sleeve that covers just the top of the shoulder. Size 6 or 8."

Mae left the room and the women continued to chat.

Dee kissed her daughter's cheek, "You know price is no object, darling, so get what you truly want to walk down the aisle in."

Alexis protested, "Mom, I can take care of my own wedding. I don't feel you need…"

Dee interrupted, "You're dad insists that he's paying for everything. Now don't argue."

Nora protested as well, "We are planning on helping with the wedding, Dee."

Dee held up her hand with a smile. "Stop. This is my daughter's wedding and it's our right to give her what she wants. If you wish to buy her flowers that's fine, but the rest we'll take care of."

Mae returned with four gowns and led Alexis to a changing room behind the mirrors. She sorted through the apparel and pulled out the designer gown she thought she liked the best. As Alexis slipped the first gown on, she gasped in amazement at her reflection. Mae responded with a sigh of approval as she laced the back of the white chiffon and lace gown upward. The bodice was straight across and had a beaded and crystal epaulet. Beads and crystals also transversed the princess line gown in vine-like patterns. A chapel-length train held the same design. Slipping her feet into lovely crystal and satin heels Mae had brought in, Alexis stepped out to the `aahs' of the other women.

"You look stunning, Lex," her sister said in awe.

"Absolutely gorgeous, honey," her mom assured her.

Nora quipped, "I think that's your gown Alexis."

Meredith couldn't speak at first then interjected. "This dress was made for you. You look like someone out of a fairytale. Mac is going to cry his eyes out when he sees you."

Alexis swayed back and forth and turned several times before Mae interrupted. "Would you like to try on the other dresses now for comparison?"

Before others could speak, Alexis replied firmly. "No. This is the dress I've always thought about in my dreams. I glanced at the others but chose this to try on first because I liked it best. No, I want this one."

"A veil then?" Mae questioned.

"Of course," Alexis felt singing. This dress made her feel so special.

It did not take long to pick out a satin trimmed veil that would fall to her waist but still did not disguise the intricate lacing down to the swell of her buttock.

"I have that two strand diamond tiara that I wore to the Oscars one year. If you would like, darling, we can have the veil attached to it." her mom suggested.

Jasmine trilled, "You lucky girl. That will look just beautiful on you. It'll work perfect."

Alexis grabbed Jasmine's hand, "You'll have it for your wedding too, Jas."

Jasmine and Alexis hugged each other as Mae chimed in. "How about accessories? And the attendant's gowns?"

They spent the next hour finishing off the accessories, lacy underwear and hose. They even found a lovely two piece navy blue bridesmaid dress that was A-line with an asymmetrical front drape and crystals across the strapless bodice and along the drape. It came with a bolero jacket. It was while Jasmine was trying on the dress that Alexis turned to Meredith and asked, "I would love to have someone from your side of the family to be in my wedding. Would you do me the honor of being my attendant?"

Meredith squealed with surprise and hugged Alexis.

"I would absolutely love to. Get me a dress to try on," she ordered Mae with a laugh.

They for headed out of the store complete with purchases that didn't need altered. Both mothers decided to wait and shop together during the week for their dresses. They strolled next door to the attached tuxedo store, `Tux on Demand` and picked out what the men were to wear. This accomplished, they headed to the private country club, Grecian Palace, on the outskirts of Miami.

Upon seeing the facility, Alexis was thrilled to say the least. The white Greek architecture was surrounded by opulent colorful vegetation of all kinds. The abundant palms dotted the grounds and were placed strategically along flagstone pathways leading toward more floral gardens and water cascades culminating in a large pond. The building had massive Greek fluted columns topped by inverted double scrolls and was supported by a horizontal superstructure called an entablature that surrounded the building and the twenty foot walkway. Massive wood and gold edged doors swung open to a vast atrium in marble and stone. Grecian statues fashioned after those seen in Europe lined windows embedded in the stone and two enormous marble stairways curved upward on either side of the entranceway. As they ascended the stairs, they came level with a simply beautiful ballroom with ten chandeliers hanging from the thirty-foot ceilings and windows from floor to ceiling along the back curved wall. Earth tone granite tables on heavy metal frames were scattered about and a bar of stone, white marble and the same granite took up no less than forty feet along one wall. Walking back to the windows, Alexis sighed with pleasure at the view. It was surreal.

"This place is beautiful, Nora, mom. It's perfect." Alexis turned to them. "I would love to have the wedding outside if possible and the reception in here."

Everyone embraced and laughed and all talked at once as a manager walked up to them.

"May I be of service?' the male requested. And they all began to talk at once.

It took two more hours before details of the wedding were completed. Food, appetizers, wedding cake, flowers and decorations were all chosen. Alexis decided on crystal and china patterns, picking a white edged in silver and embossed in dark blue Egyptian symbols to adorn the tables. This full service facility even offered various guest gifts. Alexis chose silver and crystal bells to be set at each place.

It was after seven before the group was ready to leave, making cell phone calls to their respective mates. They were all to meet at Stevro's Steakhouse, an upbeat pricey Miami restaurant which often sported celebrities and whose owners were friends of the MacDonald's. The restaurant's motif was futuristic looking with its outlandish mismatched chrome and leather tables and chairs and partitions that separated dining areas holding sculptures and objects of similar bizarre shapes. The manager escorted Alexis and her entourage to an alcove where Mac, Steve MacDonald and Michael Saunders were waiting. The men rose simultaneously and held the chairs for the ladies. This spirited group began talking all at once until Mac chimed in.

"Whoa, we can't understand what's being said. Slow down. I guess your day went well."

Nora preened with pride. "We got everything in place for the wedding. The place, dresses, meals. Everything.."

Dee broke in, "All you guys have to do is get measured for your tux. Mac, you and Alexis need to choose wedding rings and perhaps you can use tomorrow to register at several places for gifts."

Mac turned to Alexis and picked up her hand to caress it. "Are you happy with everything, sweetheart? Did you find what you wanted?"

"My gown is fabulous, the first one I tried on. The reception is going to be beautiful and the wedding, hopefully, will be outdoors there. You need to choose a best man and groomsmen. I'm having both your sister and mine. Everything else is done but the invites and the club, Grecian Palace, will send them out Monday but we have to get the guest list to them by Sunday afternoon. Mom and Nora have already compiled their own lists so it's up to you and me now," Alexis prattled on enthusiastically.

"In that case, let's order food. I'm starved." Steve Saunders stomach growled loudly just at that moment. Everyone laughed and began chatting as orders were taken.

Later that night in bed, Alexis and Mac lay in each others arms talking. They had a busy schedule to complete the next two days but it was a relief to have the wedding plans out of the way.

"I told you our two moms could get this wedding planned in short order," Mac said smugly.

"You were right. Everything is going to be perfect. I just didn't think it could be done so quickly." Alexis ran her finger across Mac's naked chest and circled a nipple. He responded with a growl and pulled her tightly against him.

"Will you be ready for the resumption of the Lager trial on Monday or do you have more work to do over the weekend?" Mac nosed her cheek and planted a light kiss behind her ear. She shuddered.

"I'm ready to begin again," she replied. "Ben thinks that since we now have his account ledgers we might have him trying to make a last minute deal. I don't want to do that though."

"But it would surely make your job a lot easier."

"Yes, but I'm not going to give him much of a break for pleading guilty. After all, he has polluted our streets all over this country and world, for that matter, with drugs and killed countless kids and adults who have misused the drugs," Alexis tone was unyielding.

Mac kissed her lips gently, "I agree with you on that. Prosecutors do cut too many deals as far as I'm concerned."

"You and I are hard people, Mac," Alexis folded her hands primly and lowered her gaze, giggling as she remarked, "You're very hard."

"Naughty, naughty girl." Mac plundered her mouth and their lovemaking began.

Chapter 15

The courthouse was packed today with reporters and spectators as Alexis strode confidently in on Monday. The weekend had been filled with fun dinners with relatives and trips to the various stores and malls to register for needed as well as extravagant items. Alexis' parents and sister were staying until the wedding on Friday. Her brother Cal and other relatives were coming in on Thursday. Alexis found out that Mac had already talked with Judge Masters about adjourning court on Thursday and being off until Tuesday. Surprisingly, the judge had agreed.

As Alexis approached her desk in the courtroom, Bob Lager's defense attorney motioned to her to come over to his desk.

"We need to talk. I've asked Judge Masters for a sidebar in her office and she has agreed." Ron Handler appeared nervous.

"Is this about a deal, Handler?" she questioned.

"Let's go into the judge's chambers and have Bob brought in there to discuss this." Handler was vague.

Alexis nodded and headed toward the appropriate door with Handler following. A few minutes later Lager was brought in looking disgruntled and with his hands cuffed behind his back. The policemen stood at attention by the door but kept careful watch over the prisoner.

"So what's this about?" Alexis queried.

"Uh, Ms. Saunders. We received the various items you have put into evidence. The ledgers. The tape. The personal witness,

Santana Regas," his voice faltered and he coughed. "We are willing to cop to all charges in relation to the crystal Meth. However, because Mr. Lager is now indicted for aggravated murder with death specifications, we would like to bargain for those charges to be reduced. This was a crime of passion as José Alfonse took his love away from him and was beating her to a pulp. This isn't aggravated murder."

Alexis looked both men squarely in the eyes. "Mr. Handler. Your client's crime was not one of passion but greed. He planned and executed the killing of José Alfonse in order to protect his financial empire from taking a tumble. I will go for the aggravated murder charge and the death penalty as well."

Lager sputtered angrily, "I knew she wouldn't…"

Ron Handler interrupted his client. "Shut up, Bob. Uh, Ms. Saunders, this trial we are currently in can go on much longer as I try to refute your witnesses. And then the various appeals we shall make will add much expense to your budget. Then, of course, there will be the murder trial and all those appeals…" his voice dragged to a stop.

"What deal do you want?"

"Second degree murder charges, 15 to 20 years with a chance of parole. Then he'll plead to all of the crystal Meth charges," Handler tried to negotiate.

"No way," Alexis took a deep breath and went on. "If he pleads *now* to all drug charges and aggravated murder, then he can have this one time offer to avoid a murder trial where I'll be going for the death penalty. I'll take the death penalty off the table and offer life instead with no chance of parole. He'll get 20 to 25 years in prison for the drug charges which will run consecutively. Take it or leave it."

Lager turned away and stalked over to the window. His attorney followed and conversed quietly with heads bowed.

Minutes ticked by as they appeared to be arguing. The door opened and Judge Masters walked in. She went to a closet and took out her robe without acknowledging anyone in the room. The judge then took her place behind her desk but did not take a seat. She finally broke the silence.

"Mr. Handler, I was under the impression that you were meeting with the prosecution in order to work out a deal. Has this been accomplished or do we resume the trial in fifteen minutes?"

"Just one moment, Your Honor." With that, Handler turned back to Bob Lager and whispered a few more words.

Angry and defiant, Lager glared first at Alexis then at the judge. "I'm taking her deal."

Judge Masters was surprised at the accused change of mind, "What's the deal, Ms. Saunders?"

"In exchange for pleading to all the current charges of producing, packaging, shipping and distributing crystal Meth; engaging in a criminal activity by being the principal owner of this enterprise; and a money laundering scheme; we're offering 20 to 25 years in prison which will run consecutively with life and no chance of parole for the aggravated murder of José Alfonse. I'll not charge him with first degree murder with death specifications in order to avoid a lengthy trial and appeals as well costly expenses." Alexis stood stiffly before the judge and recited the charges in a prim and constant voice.

Judge Masters nodded to Alexis and gazed steadily at Lager. "Are you agreeable, Mr. Lager to what the prosecution has just stated?"

Lager lowered his head but gruffly added, "Yes, Your Honor."

Judge Masters immediately responded. "Very well, we shall return to the courtroom and I shall advise the jury that a settlement has been reached. I shall have the court recorder read the exact charges for this case and you shall have to state in court that you agree to the resolution. After which, I shall then dismiss the jury and you shall be taken back to jail until transport to prison is arranged. Is this understood, Mr. Lager?"

"Yes," Lager acknowledged succinctly.

Judge Masters had the policeman escort Lager into the courtroom followed by Alexis and Handler. Everyone took their seats at appropriate places and waited several minutes for the bailiff to call the court to order. Judge Masters entered and within an hour the case was over and the jury dismissed.

Alexis gathered up papers and headed for the annex. After placing them on her desk, she went in search for Ben. She found him coming out of the legal library.

Ben was puzzled at her early return, "What's going on? I thought you were in court."

"I was," Alexis gave a rueful grin, "and you'll be glad to know I bent a little and made a deal with Lager. I didn't press the issue and insist on taking him all the way through the court system."

"Well, well." Ben smiled. "So my little protégée finally has grown up a little."

"I don't know about growing up. I just figured that the money I saved you in prosecuting these two big cases could be used to increase my salary," Alexis joked.

Ben laughed heartily. "You thought wrong, my dear lady. That money is going to be needed to prosecute all the new cases you are bringing forth. My God, Alexis, you've indicted Klein and now even the illustrious Dan Bachman. We'll be lucky to get pleas out of them. And the Bachman trial is going to be a long one. He'll never cop a plea."

"I know," Alexis sighed. "Plus we're getting more names from Klein of men involved in the criminal schemes with Bachman. It's going to be a couple of years to wrap this mess up."

"Well, finish your notes for the day and go home. You deserve a rest. Take the remainder of the week off and get what you need done for the wedding. Since there's no longer a trial you have to be here for you get the next week off for a honeymoon. Let Mac know. I'm sure he'll be able to take some time off as well."

Alexis suddenly hugged Ben and kissed his cheek. "What a doll! I think I love you."

As several people looked perplexed at the two of them in the hallway embracing, they both burst out laughing.

Alexis finished her work by two and left a message for Mac that she was out of court and was off for the next two weeks.

Alexis headed home where she found several messages on her answering machine. She returned the first one to Nora who informed her that she had talked with Dee and they were going to put an engagement announcement in the newspaper the following morning. Alexis was to check her e-mail for a copy of what the two had composed and if there were to be any corrections, she needed to call the *Miami Herald*. Nora had even used a picture taken at the family gathering to celebrate their engagement to put with the announcement. Alexis hung up and immediately opened her computer and found the e-mail. The article sounded fine as far as she was concerned but she didn't know about Mac. She found it was somewhat exhilarating to find out more information about the man she was to marry. He had impressive credentials from college and the service. Some of the information had to be left out due to the covertness of his missions.

Mac returned home tired but smiling as he came through the door. He grabbed her around the waist and spun her in circles.

"Hold on," she laughingly protested. "What has gotten into you?"

"I just want to celebrate your court victory. Quite a win for you, darlin'. I was really impressed that you got Lager to fold."

Alexis smiled into his eyes as he held her on level with his massive frame. "Well, the evidence you guys compiled for me certainly helped the situation."

"I'm very proud of the way you conduct yourself, counselor. In the court *and*…in the bedroom," Mac's lowered voice was sexy and exciting as usual for Alexis.

"Have you no shame, sir?" Alexis got no further before Mac's scrumptious mouth pillaged hers.

After several moments Mac's husky voice questioned, "Do you want to go out to eat tonight?"

"No. I'd rather stay in. We'll be eating out on Thursday and the remainder of the week. Speaking of which…did you receive my message about having the rest of this week and next off?" Alexis was delighted at the thought.

"Yes, but Ben had called me prior to your message so I could finagle to have the time off. So where would you like to go on your honeymoon?" Mac let her drop to her feet but continued to nibble her neck.

"We don't have to go anywhere if you don't want to," she placated.

"Oh, I think we should go somewhere. With all your upcoming cases, we might not get away for awhile. I'll surprise you on our wedding day with the venue." Mac pulled away and tugged her toward the kitchen. "Come on, sweetie, I'm starved."

As they worked together preparing a meal of salad, they talked of their upcoming wedding. Mac, Steve, and her father were going to get fitted for their tuxes the next day. The remainder of the wedding party were going at their convenience. His two closest brothers in age, Mark and Jason, were groomsmen and his remaining brothers and hers, Cal, were ushers.

Late evening, Mac had some calls to make to tie up loose ends on a few cases. Alexis chose to search through clothes for items to take on the honeymoon. She made a quick decision to do some shopping on Thursday for some bedtime finery and several new outfits because much of her clothing were either gowns or suits. That conclusion made, she peered through her underwear drawer and decided only a few new items would be needed since she had a hefty amount of silky, lace-trimmed stock already on hand. Mac came in midway through the hunt for clothes and seemed fascinated by the skimpy undergarments laying about.

"You don't really think you're going to need all of these, do you?" With that, he picked up a thong by the thin band and twirled it around on a finger.

"Give me that, you dog," Alexis chuckled as she leapt toward Mac who held the item high above her head. "Come on, Mac, I'm trying to get some things organized."

"Well I can guarantee you won't be wearing these much." Alexis jumped upward as his hand began a downward descent. She was able to swipe it from him and turned to walk away.

"And, yes, I will be wearing these." But as she got a few feet from him, Alexis twirled suddenly and used the thong as a slingshot that ended up hitting Mac squarely in the face.

Before she could move an inch, Mac was scooping her up in his powerfully built arms and flinging her on the bed as his body covered hers. Alexis tried to protest but was unable to as Mac ground his mouth on hers. She responded just as fiercely and soon they were naked and straining toward completion. They fell asleep shortly afterwards with legs still entangled.

Both rose early the next day invigorated, knowing that they would have over a week and a half off. Mac picked up the paper in front of their door and took it into the kitchen. Alexis stopped scrambling the eggs long enough to glance over his naked shoulder as he sat at the table. She flipped it to the society and viewed their engagement picture and article. The picture looked pretty decent, she thought.

"Who took that picture, Mac?" She was curious because she really didn't remember anyone taking them.

"That was my brother, Jason," he informed her. "We make a striking couple, counselor. We'll have great looking kids too, don't you think?"

"My, aren't we vain?" she purred as he snatched the paper out of her hands.

"Your eggs are burning, dear," Mac reminded her smiling and continued to read.

Mac left later that morning and Alexis called in two times to remind Betty of several issues that needed to be dealt with while she was away. During the second call, Betty advised her of a phone call from her previous employers, McMillan and Pretorious. They asked if she would call in to their number ASAP. Not knowing what this could involve, Alexis phoned immediately to the number Betty had given her. A girl by the name of Lenore answered and asked if she could come to the building at 12:30. Alexis questioned as to what this was in regards to but the girl did not know. Realizing she had some errands that would take her close to the office, she assented and began to get ready.

Wearing jeans and a casual sea green off-the-shoulder top, Alexis headed to McMillan and Pretorious in her vehicle. She had written a quick note to Mac telling him she had to stop at her former employers building but wouldn't be long and would meet him at 1:30 p.m. at her office. He could call her on her cell if he needed anything. She parked on the street upon arrival and headed into the stately red brick, seven story building that took up half of the block. She entered one of the six paneled glass doors and started toward the elevator. Her name rang out and she twisted to see where it had come from. Walking sedately toward her in a blue suit with a gold tie was Len Pretorius, coming from an alcove to the right of her that housed several leather chairs and large ferns and a table. Alexis didn't feel like confronting him but stood still until he reached her.

He grasped her hand and in his overly pleasant voice he remarked, "I see congratulations are in order. I just read the newspaper. I can't personally see you being happy with a man like that but I guess time will tell."

"And I don't particularly care what you think, Len," Alexis mocked.

"Well, I'm sorry I said anything, Alexis. It's your life." His eyes squinted in displeasure. Len did not look for the most part pleased at her response. "But anyway, I have something of yours in my office that apparently spilled out of your purse on one of our dates."

"I don't remember that happening. What is it?" She was certainly curious.

"A piece of jewelry," Len told her.

"I haven't lost any jewelry that I know of." Alexis was doubtful.

"Well, I'm almost positive that it's yours." Len sounded a little doubtful as well. "Will you come up to my office and look?"

"Of course," she reluctantly agreed. Len then escorted her to the opening elevator and pushed a button. Several people got off on the second floor, leaving them alone. Alexis felt nervous as Len continued to stare silently at her while leaning against the side wall, hands in his pocket. The elevator dinged and the door slid open and Len gestured Alexis to take the lead. She stepped out and took several steps before she realized she was not on his office floor. Turning, she began to speak when her mouth suddenly dried up as she looked into the malicious, angry face of Len Pretorius. Her eyes dropped. In his hand he held a gun. He took several steps toward her as she backed away.

"Move on down the hallway to the fourth door on the right," Len ordered.

"What's this about?" she tried to remain calm and keep her voice steady.

Len rasped out, "I said move it, Alexis," Len began approaching her and she backed further down the hall. "Keep moving to that fourth door."

Alexis moved slowly while assessing her chances of getting out of this. Len was afraid and it showed as his gun hand shook slightly. She had to be really careful that she didn't make any quick moves or the gun would go off, she was sure of that.

"Keep moving and don't think I'm going to get close to you. I'll shoot you first. Remember, I know about all your martial art abilities. So stay back or I'll fire," he reiterated. They reached the doorway and Len ordered, "The door's already unlocked. Open it and walk through it to the middle of the room. Do it *now!*"

Alexis complied and stood at attention while Len closed the door. "Now will you tell me what this is about Len. Is this just because I wouldn't date you?" she asked incredulously.

"Don't be stupid. Of course not," he sneered. "I started dating you just to see what you knew about myself and my friends' dealings."

"What friends?" Alexis still couldn't see his reasoning. Was he a lunatic?

"My friends, Alexis," he shouted with fury. "You've been after all of us. Bachman, Thompson, Klein. We've all been involved in some deals together."

"But you're an importer and exporter, Len..." she began but was interrupted, unable to believe what was happening.

"You know nothing. Yeah, I import and export...steel, drugs, guns. I've had dealings with Bob Lager and his crystal Meth. I knew if he broke and took a deal he'd rat out on me soon. That was bad enough...then I heard about Bachman. Man, you just kept going."

"How were you involved with him?' she questioned, scared to death by the thought of her life ending here with no one to find her.

"I brought in substandard steel from Asia and other products like bolts, etc. that he used in his construction. Things from over there cost just pennies compared to here in the U.S." Len elaborated. "If you were able to nail Bachman, then he'd probably open his mouth and you'd be able to take me down. I had to do something to keep you from getting any real evidence against him and me and Lager. All of us were meant to profit from you not getting each other to talk and the real evidence had to be kept out of your hands."

Alexis was thoughtful for a moment. "The real evidence...meaning the real accounting books that Sirini kept in hiding. Correct?"

"Smart lady," he praised sardonically.

"So if you were trying to get the books out of the picture, who actually hired the hit on Sirini. Bachman?"

"You're not as smart as I thought." God how she hated his sarcasm. "I was the first one to make the move to hire Butler. I got his name from overhearing a conversation. Bachman had this idea to have Sirini murdered but didn't have the balls for it. He had asked Thompson for the name one night after I had stepped out of the room for a minute. Thompson told him about this childhood friend of his brothers. Then Bachman apparently couldn't do it because a year went by and nothing happened. Then your investigation intensified from what I was hearing and I knew it was only a matter of time."

"So you hired the hit," Alexis stated matter-of-factly.

"Yeah. Yeah, first Sirini to get my ledgers back and shut him up. But nothing went right. You happened to be in the seat beside him and I didn't know what he could have told you. Then I figured you might have some written information...maybe even my ledgers. So I got in touch with Butler and he was to take care of you by running you off the road. It was to look like an accident but failed. Bachman and Thompson knew about this because by now they knew I had hired Butler to kill Sirini. They weren't at all happy I had involved them in murder. But they agreed finally that you had to be stopped. By this time your attention was still pretty much diverted to your case with Lager. The other cases weren't in progress yet. But the car incident failed. I had to do something. You had to be dead in order to stall all the cases involving Bachman, me, Kline, and Thompson. To give me time to take care of the others I'm involved with. You've given me headaches, lady. I still needed my ledgers and broke into your house hoping to find them. But you walked in on me."

"My God. You were the one! The fingerprint we didn't have on file. And when Mac and I caught you in my apartment that night..."

"I was looking again," he finished for her. "I was getting desperate since I couldn't get to you personally because of MacDonald. Still nothing. Butler was on my case because I had only paid him half for the attempt on you. So I told him he had to finish the job first. That's when he tried at the airport and failed again. Christ... it was costing me a fortune to have you followed."

"Why still go after me, Len? Why did Butler kill Thompson?" Alexis was pretty sure his conversation, his story, was coming to an end. What was going to happen to her then?

"Thompson and Klein were folding as you kept coming up with evidence. It was only a matter of time before I would be in the picture. They were all going to be dead eventually because I had hired Butler to take out all three. I needed to be in the clear and that was the only way. You were still getting too close, though, and would start piecing together the information that would bring my name into this mess." Len glared at her.

"But I had nothing on you. Thompson and Klein didn't know your name if you were the man that met with them here. We knew Butler had met with a man at a bar who was a `well dressed individual with an arrogant demeanor` but we didn't have a clue that it was you. That's all we knew." Alexis was trying to remain calm, carry on this conversation and try to figure out what to do next.

"A matter of time, I told you. You would have found my papers for LNP in Sirini's storage too."

Alexis practically choked. All that time she and Mac had stared at Sirini's papers in her bedroom that were labeled L & D or P was really LNP. "Your initials, not a company?" she questioned softly.

"Yeah, I thought it better to label them that. Lenard Newton Pretorious. The IRS didn't mind that I had a company name on the forms with a slash and my initials. The real books only had the initials on them." He muttered a foul word. "I didn't want it to end this way, Alexis."

"It doesn't have to, Len. You'll be adding my murder to all the charges the DA will be bringing against you. We do, indeed, have your books and you'll be going to prison for all of those re-lated charges. Don't add murder to it," she pleaded.

"Too late." Len raised the gun and Alexis heard the click of the safety being removed. "They won't connect me now to Thompson's murder with Butler gone and no one but Bachman and you can connect me to Butler. Bachman sure as hell won't admit any connections to Butler with him dead. I think I'll take a chance that they can't associate those accounting books to me. No one has done that so far. So Alexis, this is goodbye. Sorry, darling."

A shot rang out in the stillness.

Mac joined his father and Michael at `Tux on Demand` before some of his other brothers arrived. They joked about cur-rent events and sports topics. A comradery had already been es-tablished between himself and Michael and Mac encouraged Alexis' father to tell private stories about her as a youngster. He laughed at some of her escapades which were tame in comparison to her siblings' but which were still delightful. Brent and Paul came into the store just as Mac and his entourage were ready to leave. The older men decided to wait so everyone there could get an early lunch. They walked across the street to `Madge's Timely Café' and ordered deli sandwiches and fries. Long into the meal and conversation, Mac's cell phone beeped.

"Excuse me. Mac here," he identified himself and listened. Barely a minute went by before he exploded. "Shit, thanks Collier."

"Pay for my lunch…I've got to go!" he abruptly told the men and ran out of the restaurant. Jumping into his car, he pulled out his siren and jammed it on the roof. He floored the car, barely avoiding an accident as he pulled into traffic. Mac flipped open the cell phone and speed dialed the condo. No one answered and he tossed the phone onto the passenger seat.

God, but he hoped Alexis was okay. He had just received word that CSI looked more closely at Sirini's records that had been in Alexis' apartment. They decided upon comparing every page that the company was not L&D or P but L.N.P., a person's initials. It took but a second for Mac to translate the first and last initials as belonging to Len Pretorious. That bastard had better stay away from her, he fumed, as he glanced at his watch...*12:05 p.m.*

The ride to the condo seemed never-ending. He pulled in front and drawing his gun, he stormed inside calling out for his woman. Both hands were on the gun as he quickly searched the place then returned to the kitchen where he noted a piece of paper laying on the counter. `Got a call from Betty and have to make a quick detour at 12:30. Be home after. Love, Alexis' the message stated. Mac picked up the phone and called the DA's office. He let it ring and was ready to hang up when Betty answered.

"This is Mac. What was the message you gave to Alexis this morning?" he practically shouted.

"Uh...let me think. Um...I know. She was to call her former employer for something. They said it was important." Betty wanted to know if everything was alright but was cut off by Mac hanging up.

Mac holstered his gun and headed to his car at a run. He turned the vehicle around with a squeal and lights flashing and siren sounding, headed toward law firm of McMillan and Pretorious. While driving he had dispatch patch him through to the office. A secretary answered and after identifying himself he asked if Alexis Saunders was there.

"No, sir. She hasn't been here," the voice was wobbly. "Is everything okay? I mean, well...I probably could get in trouble for this but..."

"You won't get into trouble. What do you know?" Mac demanded.

"You see, I did this favor for a friend, the nephew of my boss, Mr. Pretorious," she stammered in fright.

"The nephew, Len Pretorious? What did he have you do?" Mac growled.

"Well, he had me call Ms. Saunders' office and ask for her to come here at 12:30. That was all!" she wailed.

"Was she to meet him?"

"I was only to say that *we* wished to see her for an important matter. That's all," she stated firmly.

"Where's Len's office?"

"On the second floor, Room 236," she answered as the phone clicked dead.

Mac drove his car like a maniac through traffic. As he approached the block housing McMillan and Pretorious, he phoned dispatch and asked for backup. Glancing at his watch, he noted the time again...*12:25*. He scurried through the entrance and took the stairs to the second floor, all the while unfastening his gun and drawing it. Mac entered the hallway and rapidly transversed it until he stood in front of Room 236. Bursting into the room, gun drawn, he could see he had terrified the secretary.

Mac barked out, "Miami P.D. Pretorious, where is he?"

The secretary could barely utter, "He's not here. I mean... he's been gone for about 45 minutes."

"Do you know where he went?" All 6 foot 5 inches of him was angry and alert.

"Well, I was taking some letters to be posted in the lobby and I did see him with a woman. They took the elevator," she offered in a small voice.

"But didn't come back here?"

"No," was her short reply.

"Was she reddish blonde hair, sharp looking?"

"Yes, I think she used to work here years ago. She was really friendly," the secretary added.

Mac holstered his weapon and thought for a moment. Where could they be? If they took the elevator together...? Suddenly Mac remembered Klein's testimony about the empty fourth floor. He skyrocketed out of the office and headed up the stairs. Cautiously opening the door, he listened intently. He could hear voices somewhere down the hallway and with gun drawn, he headed toward the voices. Suddenly he was in front of the door where he could hear Pretorious and Alexis. He could see their shadows through bubbled glass, Alexis on the left and the taller Len on the right. He listened.

Pretorious' low voice could be heard saying, "Thompson and Klein were folding as you kept coming up with evidence. It was only a matter of time before I would be in the picture. They were all going to be dead eventually because I had hired Butler to take all three out. I needed to be in the clear and that was the only way. You were still getting too close, though, and would start piecing together the information that would bring my name into this mess."

Mac was ready with his weapon, but continued to listen while Pretorious told his story. His heart ached for Alexis who must be so terribly frightened.

The conversation continued as Mac listened to Pretorious incriminating himself. He could sense by Len's voice that he was getting very agitated. Suddenly the voice became strained and he heard, "They won't connect me now to Thompson's murder with Butler gone and no one but Bachman and you can connect me to Butler. Bachman sure as hell won't admit any connections to Butler with him dead. I think I'll take a chance that they can't associate those accounting books to me. No one has done that so far. So Alexis, this is goodbye. Sorry, darling."

Mac didn't even hesitate to call out for fear that a fraction of a second could mean Alexis' death. He fired through the hazy privacy window toward the taller figure at what he thought was Len's abdomen. Glass shattered and Alexis screamed as Mac watched Len collapse to the floor. Mac reached through the broken window and unlocked the door keeping his gun drawn and ready. He pushed through as he heard police stomping down the corridor. He dropped down beside Pretorious after kicking the man's gun out of the way. He felt for a carotid pulse and was relieved to feel a thready one. Four policemen stormed through the door, guns drawn.

Mac immediately identified himself and stood up. "Miami P.D. Detective MacDonald."

He then turned to Alexis where she stood gallantly alone, eyes wide with fright. "It's okay, darlin'. You're going to be fine now."

Mac took her in his arms as she sighed deeply but didn't respond.

Hours later, Pretorious had been taken to the hospital under guard and Mac and Alexis had related their story of the day's happenings. Both were emotionally drained and headed to the condo in Mac's car. One of the cops drove Alexis car home as his partner followed.

Upon arriving, Alexis headed for the bathroom and some medicine for a migraine. Mac followed.

"Honey, are you going to be okay?" Mac's voice was so sweet and concerned.

"I just want to get rid if this headache and sleep, Mac. Could you just come to bed and hold me?" she implored.

"Gladly," Mac began stripping down to his boxers and crawled into bed waiting for her return from the bathroom. It didn't take long for the exhausted Alexis to fall into a deep sleep. Mac just held her and stared into her dear face, recalling the horrific scene he had witnessed. Hours later, he too fell sound asleep.

The two awakened about five in the morning after an uninterrupted sleep. Alexis appeared solemn but talkative about the wedding. She did not go into yesterday's ordeal. Both ate breakfast and made some calls. Mac phoned Ben about what had happened and Ben wanted Alexis on the phone. Mac could hear her stilted replies but in the end, she laughed at something he said.

Alexis loosened up by the end of the day and even made the first move in making love with Mac. Their love making was slow and tender, almost making her cry. She adored this man and he, she was sure, felt the same passion for her. It was going to be a match made in heaven.

The days passed in a hurry. The rehearsal was a fun event attended by all the relatives. Mac thought Alexis looked particularly scrumptious in a red sundress and strappy sandals..

The wedding day was bright and the skies baby blue with no rain in sight. The evening temperature for the five o'clock wedding was to be in the mid seventies. Dressing at the reception hall with her two attendants, Alexis was surprisingly calm. Her mom and Nora came in in their finery and both looked elegant and thrilled at the prospect of their children being wed. During the preceding week, the four in-laws had established quite a rapport and were already planning trips together and visits to the west coast.

Alexis stared at herself in the mirror. She looked and felt ethereal in her dress and veil. Jasmine stepped behind her helped put on the fabulous pearl and diamond necklace, a gift from Mac the night before. She stepped back and turned, staring at all her loved ones in the room.

"Jasmine, Meredith, you two are gorgeous." She strode over to her mom and Nora. "Ladies, you are just as beautiful as when you were teens."

Her mom kissed her cheek. "Is my daughter insinuating we're old, Nora?"

The two older women laughed heartily as Michael, Alexis' father entered.

"They're all ready. Let's go, sweetie." Michael held out his arm for Alexis as the other women headed out before them. He looked tenderly into her face and continued out with, "Be happy."

"I will," she assured him with a brilliant smile.

Mac couldn't believe the gorgeous creature coming down the stone path was going to be his wife. How had he gotten so lucky to find such a beautiful woman inside and out? Her caring nature, her openness, her integrity all made her the woman of his dreams. His eyes teared as his sister had said they would and Alexis was aware of his emotion as she approached her future husband.

Alexis was finally at his side, the blue cloudless skies, green landscape and flowering arrangements a frame for her loveliness. He was mesmerized but finally was brought to attention by the minister clearing his throat to get Mac's attention. Everyone chuckled, including Alexis and himself. The ceremony began.

"You may now kiss your bride." The minister concluded the service. Mac drew Alexis into his arms and cradled her head as his lips gently touched hers. His wife at last.

After a lengthy and crowd pleasing kiss they were declared `Alexis and Mac MacDonald.`

Alexis had been surprised to find his real name was James Douglas during the ceremony. Mac had almost laughed out loud when he noted her widened eyes when his name was revealed but only grinned instead. She had returned the look.

The reception went on in grandeur. The food was terrific, the band was infectious, and all, including the bride and groom, danced well into the night. The standard wedding practices, …bouquet toss and garter throw…were accomplished with much hilarity. It was after one o'clock in the morning when Mac asked Alexis if she was ready to go. She nodded her agreement and they headed to the assigned lounge where they were to change into clothes waiting for them.

As Mac and Alexis removed their wedding finery, they stared at each other with open ardor.

"This is really tough keeping my hands off you," he admitted sheepishly.

"I know, darling, but we have to show some decorum. After all, it wouldn't do to be caught buck naked `doing it' in this room," she teased.

"I know you're right but I'm in pain because of it," he joked.

Alexis had slipped on her lovely pale yellow frock that flowed in layers of chiffon down to mid thighs. She strolled over to Mac and requested, "Zip me up, Mac."

Mac's fingers practically burned her skin as they caressed the zipper upward. "Alexis…" he started huskily.

Alexis walked over to a wrapped elongated package laying on a table and returned to Mac, handing it to him.

"What's this?" he inquired.

"Open it. It's your gift."

Mac fumbled awkwardly with the bow and wrapping paper. He opened the jewelry box and found a plastic 5 inch tube that had a blue window on it. He stared puzzled at the gift, then at Alexis.

"What…?" He gulped not quite believing what he was seeing. Was this a pregnancy test tube that all his friends talked and joked about? "Is this…"

Mac couldn't seem to get the words out so Alexis stepped up close and replied, "Yes, darling. It is. I'm pregnant. Apparently I have been for awhile and that very light period I had was just some spotting."

Mac threw back his head and shouted with delight. He pulled her into his arms and kissed her soundly then took one hand and covered her lower abdomen. "We're really pregnant?"

Yes, Mac, we are. Are you all right with this?" Alexis was only slightly concerned about his reply.

"I'm absolutely thrilled, ecstatic, elated, overjoyed...all of the above and more." Mac lingered on her lips again. "I'm proud to be the father of your child and all of the others to come."

"You do know I expect you to keep that promise. I've always wanted a large family." Alexis grinned impishly.

"I'll do my best, darlin'. Now let's get out of here so I can practice some more." Mac finished dressing and pulled Alexis out the door to say their goodbyes.